beneath the
SECRETS

TALL, DARK
AND
DEADLY SERIES

NEW YORK TIMES BESTSELLING AUTHOR
LISA RENEE JONES

Beneath the Secrets
by Lisa Renee Jones

Copyright © 2012

Book 3 of the New York Times bestselling
TALL, DARK, AND DEADLY series

The Tall, Dark, and Deadly series includes:
Book 1: Hot Secrets
Book 2: Dangerous Secrets
Book 3: Beneath the Secrets

Also by Lisa Renee Jones

The Inside Out Series
If I Were You
Being Me
Revealing Us
His Secrets*
Rebecca's Lost Journals
The Master Undone*
My Hunger*
No In Between
My Control*
I Belong to You
All of Me*

The Secret Life of Amy Bensen
Escaping Reality
Infinite Possibilities
Forsaken
Unbroken*

Careless Whispers
Denial
Demand (May 2016)
Surrender (December 2016)

Dirty Money
Hard Rules (August 2016)
More information coming soon…

*eBook only

The Walker Brothers...

Tall, dark, and deadly, these three brothers run Walker security. Each brother is unique in his methods and skills, but all share key similarities. They are passionate about those they love, relentless when fighting for a cause they believe in, and believe that no case is too hard, no danger too dark. Dedication is what they deliver, and results are their reward.

Prelude

One Dangerous Night

The first meeting...

H ot women, fast cars, and living on the edge pretty much summed up Blake Walker's life for the past two years. All of which were simply diversions, ways to distract himself until he had the ultimate prize he sought…revenge. Though at the moment, the leggy brunette who'd just sashayed into Denver's 'The Rooftop Lounge' inside the ritzy hotel his client had booked for him, her hair pinned up, and her sexy curves tucked beneath a prim cream colored skirt and blouse, had his eye.

Blake draped his arm on the back of the booth he was lounging in, devouring her with his eyes, while he nursed a beer he didn't want. He'd seen enough booze and drugs in his days at the ATF to last a lifetime, enough death along with those things, to last a lifetime. No. Not enough. It would never be enough until the murdering son-of-a-bitch cartel leader, Alvarez, was ten feet under. Then there would be enough death and not a second sooner, and since that attitude didn't set well with his higher-ups, he'd decided working with his brothers at Walker Security sounded pretty damn good. Of course, his brothers Royce and Luke weren't keen on murder either but based on how they felt about their new spouses, he'd bet his weight in gold they'd change their mind if it had been their fiancée killed in cold blood.

The woman scanned the dimly lit modern room, taking in the carved out circular booths like the one he was in and the mini-round tables with candles flickering on top, until her eyes found him, and he sensed a hint of trepidation in her. He almost snorted. She was working for a guy named 'Richter', a high-up in one of the many corporate shells Alvarez used for money laundering, and she actually seemed to size up his long dark hair and leather jacket with disdain. He knew her type, the ones who justified their work in the world they were living by hiding it beneath righteousness or naivety. In her case, she came with a dose of prickly and prim, no doubt, for effect. Oh yeah, he knew her type all right, and didn't like them, but as her eyes met his a jolt of awareness rocked him. There was something about this woman. The idea of tearing away the mockery of her properness and forcing her to admit what she was appealed to him in a big way. After all, he needed intel, and what better way to get it than halfway to orgasm with the promise of going all the way. Get fucked or do the fucking. He wasn't getting fucked anywhere but the bedroom, and by choice, ever again.

She tore her gaze from his and his lips quirked as she scanned the bar yet again. Despite her rather successful attempt to look uneasy, he had the distinct impression she was counting heads, like he had. He did the inventory in his head again with her. A couple in the far right booth. Another in the far left. A middle aged drunk telling his troubles to the bartender and two girlfriends chatting it up at a center table. She wasn't naive, this one. She knew what she was doing. Finally, her attention slid back to him, her only prospect for the meeting her boss had arranged.

He arched a challenging brow at her. She straightened her spine and marched towards him. He watched her walk and didn't hide his admiration. He wanted her uncomfortable. He wanted her to slip up and tell him things she wasn't supposed to tell him.

"Mr. Wright?"

Blake gave a nod. "That's right," he joked, playing on words. "But call me Blake." He used an alias for his last name but found sticking to his real first name was safer than not. It made little slips of tongue less likely. "And you must be-"

"Tiffany Snow," she said, but there was something awkward about the way she said her name that made him question it being real. Of course, the fact that it sounded like a porn star didn't help him keep his mind off undressing her.

"I thought Rachel Merit was coming."

"She was suddenly tied up so you got me." She motioned to the seat. "May I?"

"Be my guest." He lifted his beer. "Drink?"

"No," she said, slipping her briefcase and purse from her shoulder. "I don't drink."

He barked out laughter.

Her brows dipped. "What's funny about that?"

"More ironic than funny considering who your boss is."

"I wouldn't know what that means. I'm new to Newport Industries."

"How new?"

"One month."

"And you were sent to meet with me? You must have

exceptional skills."

"I'm efficient."

"How efficient?"

Her eyes, a milk chocolate brown a shade lighter than his own, held his. "I guess you'll have to decide that when we complete out business."

Whoa Mama. There was an invitation if he ever heard one. So Alvarez had sent him a present to fill his fancy hotel room with. Wasn't that something? "I guess I will."

Her teeth scraped her coral painted kissable mouth. He could think of a lot of places he'd like that mouth. "I understand you have a file for me?" she inquired.

The file being dirt on a certain businessman her boss wanted to blackmail, a test to see if Blake was worthy of bigger and better things. Blake would have felt guilty about just how thorough his file was if said business man wasn't a lowlife thief. "And you have money for me?"

"If you're owed money, I assure you it's in the package. I'll just need the file first."

"It's in my room."

Those lush lips parted. "Your room," she repeated.

He leaned in closer. "Some things are better done in private. Wouldn't you agree?"

Seconds ticked by, and the air thickened, charged. There was more to this woman than met the eye, and he found himself wanting to discover every inch of that more, and then some. "My boss did stress discretion," she finally said, her voice just a bit breathless.

"Well then," he drawled. "Let's be sure and give it to him." He tossed money on the table and pushed to his feet, before offering her his hand to help her up.

She stared at his hand a moment, playing the cat and mouse game, oh so well. She wasn't a mouse though, this one. More like a wildcat, he was willing to bet, and looking forward to finding out.

She retrieved her things before standing up, ignoring his offer of help. "Lead the way, Mr. Wright."

Oh, he intended to. If she was willing to sell her body and soul to a murdering monster for a paycheck, he wasn't going to feel guilty about using her for everything she might have to offer.

The Exchange...

They stepped onto the elevator alone, and his little would-be good-girl secretary that wasn't, turned her back to the right wall to face him. Blake punched in the floor of their destination and leaned casually against the wall. She was wearing a thin dress and it was winter in Denver, Colorado. Where was her coat?

A couple pushed into the car just before the doors shut, separating the two of them, then backing against the wall so that they could still make eye contact. He sized up the couple – middle aged, corporate types – both wearing wedding rings he didn't think they gave each other. He dismissed them as no threat almost immediately, refocusing on Tiffany – if that was really her name.

They might not be alone but the awareness was there between them nevertheless, that charge he'd already felt in the air intensifying with each passing second in a way he hadn't experienced with a woman in far too long. Why it was this one he didn't know, but he figured it was simply the high of how close he was to Alvarez. Finally, he'd found his mockery of a corporate shell, and he was inches from locating him.

Two floors passed and the elevator doors opened. Blake motioned to the newfound informant, who didn't know that's what she was about to be, silently letting her know this was their floor. She pushed off the wall and headed into the hallway. He joined her, resisting the urge to touch her. Not yet. Soon. Very soon.

"I'm at the end of the hall," he commented.

"Of course," she said quietly.

He cut her a sideways look. "Of course?"

"I've never known anyone to be at the door by the elevator," she supplied. "Have you?"

He shrugged. "I never gave it much thought." But he had. The location of the elevator for fast escape was always a consideration, as was the long walk to what was likely a one night stand, in which you question how smart your actions were. Only he wasn't questioning any such thing. She was, though. Where she'd been cool and confident before, he sensed barely contained nerves that didn't quite match the persona beneath the exterior he'd assumed. What was it about this woman that didn't quite compute as right? And why the hell did he suddenly want to comfort her? He resisted the urge to scrub his jaw, aware of her beside him, of the feminine, alluring way she moved. Of the soft scent of some sort of flower – jasmine or honeysuckle – or some sweet something he'd never liked until now.

At the end of the hall, they stopped at his door to a room he'd intentionally had changed in case the original one had been bugged. Not that he couldn't debug or defunct anything electronic he chose to, but safe was always better than sorry.

Impatience wasn't a trait he favored, but his blood ran hot

for this woman and his hand moved quickly to swipe the key. On some level, he recognized this was an invitation for trouble. He shoved the idea away as ridiculous as he opened the hotel door and motioned her forward. She didn't hesitate. In fact, she rushed forward, seeming eager to get out of the hallway.

Blake shut the door behind him, sauntering into the room to find her tossing her purse and briefcase on the typical luxury room high back chair by the window. He shrugged out of his leather jacket and tossed it on the king sized bed separating them. "You have my money?"

"I'll need to review the file."

He crossed the room, stopping at the desk and pulled the chair out, putting them within a few steps of each other. Blake opened the drawer and removed the file, setting it on top of the desk. He tapped the top of it. "Now you show me yours. Full exposure at the same time."

Her lashes lowered, and he could almost hear her thinking about her next move, before her brown eyes met his and for just an instant he saw trepidation in her eyes. She blinked and it was gone, but he'd seen it, recognized it for the hesitation and fear that it was, and silently cursed. Holy hell. He was her first gig like this. She wasn't even sure this was where she belonged but something made her desperate enough to do this. Fuck me. He was going to try and save her.

"All right," she said, and she reached for her briefcase but instead of removing the file, she carried it with her towards him. She stopped at the chair and set it down, but didn't reach for the file. Instead, she stepped around the chair, close to him.

Blake didn't wait for her to act. He pulled her to him, and maneuvered her against the wall. "Why are you here?"

"I thought we were pretty clear on that point?"

"I'm not." He pressed one hand to the wall beside her, his body framing hers but not touching it. He wanted this woman, but if he could scare her the hell out of this room without touching her, it would be in her best interest. "Spell it out."

"I have something you want. You have something I want."

His body responded to that tease, his cock thickening against his jeans. "And yet you're in my room, alone with me. You have to know that's asking for more than a simple exchange."

"It's as simple as it gets. You brought my boss a file. If I like what's inside it, I'm to make sure you're rewarded. So I suggest you show me your file, Mr. Wright. Otherwise, you won't be getting anything."

She delivered the seductive promise with such Grande that he almost – almost – believed he'd been wrong about her, but not quite. "You don't have to do this, you know?"

"You're right," she said. "I don't. I can walk out of here with my envelope and leave you with yours. I just choose not to."

"What is it he's promised you to make you willing to sell your soul and your body for him?"

Her hand slid to his chest. "I have a choice." She leaned into him and pressed her lips to his. She tasted like the same tangerine of her lipstick, sweet and tangy, tempting.

He didn't respond at first, thinking through what came next, what he should do. She was inside Alvarez's operation. He had no reason to trust her, or help her, and he wanted her more than he remembered wanting anyone in a very long time. So, why was he hesitating to take what she offered?

With a low growl, he slid his hand to her back and called her bluff. If he was right about her, he'd scare the shit out of her and have one hell of a cold shower afterwards. His mouth slanted over hers, tongue delving past her teeth, hand settling on her back, molding her soft curves to his hard body.

She melted against him, a soft moan sliding from her throat, her arms wrapping around his neck. Holy hell, he thought again. He could make love to this woman. Make her feel soft, sexy, and pleasured, and enjoy every damn second of it, seduce her into helping him. They had chemistry and attraction that would make this easy to blow off as a hot night that wasn't as dangerous as it was for her future. But that wouldn't save her, and she needed to be saved. He didn't know why he knew this, but he did. The only way to help her was to scare the living shit out of her. To take her places she wouldn't want to go and force her to see that this wasn't where she belonged. That meant this was going someplace down and dirty, and hard and gritty.

His hand caressed over her side and upward, until he palmed her full, high breast, his fingers finding the already stiff peak of her nipple under the soft silk of her dress and, surprisingly, barely there bra. She arched into his touch rather than pulling away and he knew this was where he set the stakes higher. Where he pushed her.

He set her back from him, his eyes meeting hers, searching her face, searching her lovely, passion filled face, and damn it, he wanted her to stay all soft and wanting, just like she was now. But in all good conscience, and he hated he still had one, he couldn't let that happen.

Blake backed away and sat on the edge of the bed, and damn she looked sexy with her hair down. "Take off your clothes."

She blinked at him, and her creamy ivory skin paled even further, but she recovered quickly, drawing in a breath and reaching for the zipper running up the front of her dress. His blood thundered in his ears like he was some kind of randy teenager who hadn't seen plenty of hot woman, and hot flesh, before. What the hell was it about this woman that set off a firestorm inside him? But he knew. His gut twisted with just how well he knew. She was gorgeous, out of her element, and she needed to be saved. Like someone else he'd failed to save. And damn it to hell, he thought he had enough distance from this to be calculated and cold, to finish this once and for all.

The dress shimmered down his new temptation's hips and fell to the ground, leaving her wearing a cream-colored bra and panties set with little diamond sparkles, thigh-highs and heels. He drew in a heavy breath, reeling in the desire he knew he had to control. There was so much more on the line than sex, mostly for her.

She reached for her bra and he moved quickly, surprising her, and shackling her wrist. She was flat on the mattress, and beneath him in an instant, one of his legs between hers, because both would have been too much to bear. As it was, that scent of hers, all sweet and flowery, was like fire licking at his limbs. And his cock, which was against her hip, throbbed with the promise of how close he was to the also sweet V of her legs.

"You don't have to do this," he told her.

"I thought we already covered this?"

"Not well enough. You aren't too far gone to turn back."

"This coming from a man who has me almost naked in a hotel bed with him?"

"Almost, sweetheart. I didn't think you'd have the courage to really strip for me. Whatever it is you think working for this guy will fix, it won't. What do you need? Money? I'll give you money if you promise to walk away from this and never look back."

"So I'll work for you instead of him?"

"No strings. You never have to see me again."

"Are you seriously trying to save me?" she asked.

"Yes. I am."

She studied him a long moment before her fingers curled on his cheek, the simple, delicate touch, sending a rippling sensation through his body. "You know what they say about those who try too hard to save other people?" She didn't wait for a reply. "They say they need saving themselves."

His hand slid to hers. "I'm way beyond saving, sweetheart."

"So am I," she whispered.

"I don't believe that."

"Then you're looking too hard for something that's not there."

"I don't think so."

"If I can be saved then so can you."

His lips twisted cynically. "We aren't even in the same universe. Believe me. I'm lost. You can still be found."

"You sound so sure." She reached up and stroked his hair from where it already began to fall from the back at his neck, his fingers tugging it forward. Every time she touched him, his entire body burned. She had no idea how much willpower it required for him not to slide between her thighs and settle in for a long, hot night. "I wonder," she contemplated, studying him with big, gorgeous eyes, he could get lost in forever, "if maybe we should both try to save each other and then in the morning, pretend we didn't?"

Or maybe, Blake thought, in the morning he'd fly her off to some tropical paradise, away from this wicked winter hell of

Alvarez's world, and convince her she never has to come back.

The Negotiation...

Blake's mouth came down on hers, and this time he didn't hold back. He wanted to save her. She wanted to save him. She didn't have a chance where he was concerned, but the wicked heat of her kiss, the delicate play of her tongue against his, sure as hell would go a long way in helping him forget why that wasn't possible, at least, for tonight.

His hand slid down her neck, over the soft silk of her shoulder and he tugged her bra strap down with him. Her skin was cool and he was hot. He wanted her hot in a nearly consuming way. It was illogical but he really didn't care. His mouth traveled the delicate line of her shoulder blade and downward. Her fingers played in his hair, her touch affecting him far too easily, but then there wasn't a lot of softness he let in his life. Normally, he'd snatch her hand, and hold it over her head. He'd do the touching, not her, so why wasn't he doing that now? Why wasn't he stopping her? Why the hell was he lingering at the sweet spot at the base of her throat when he could be ripping away her panties and burying himself inside her?

After all, he'd been on the edge before he'd ever met her, ready to finally get what he wanted, what he'd craved for two years. Knowing he was still too far away. His need for an escape, for something hard, fast, and furious, should be driving him. Instead an inescapable, dangerously distracting, need to save this woman, to please her, consumed him.

His fingers traced the clip in the center of her bra and unsnapped it, closer to having her completely bared to him. He wanted her bared to him. He wanted her naked, panting, and screaming his name. Blake caressed away the silk of her bra and framed her high, full breasts with his hands. She arched into him, and moaned when his mouth closed down on the rosy peek of one nipple. He took his time, teasing her, licking her, enjoying her, rather than ravishing her, slowly kissing his way downward, until he peeled her panties down her hips.

Something dark and needy expanded inside him at the sight of the dark, well-groomed triangle of hair between her thighs. He slid off of the bed, and took the panties all the way down her legs, at the same time he went to his knees, pulling her towards him.

She rose up on her elbows, her big brown eyes wide with emotion, without arousal, and yes—there it was again – just a hint of trepidation. No matter how hard she tried to hide the truth, a night with a stranger wasn't the norm for her. Not even close.

His gaze raked over her lush breasts, his cock thick and pulsing, and he tugged his shirt over his head and got rid of it. He tossed one of her high-heels and then the other. "No shoes, keeps you from running away."

"Then maybe you better take yours off," she commented.

"I never run."

"Neither do I," she said. "But even the score. Shoes off."

His lips quirked at her challenge and he gladly complied. "Satisfied now?" he asked settling her feet back on his thighs.

"Not yet," she said. "But I have high hopes I will be."

He laughed at that bold statement. She was a contradiction of fearless and fearful that intrigued him. "You will be," he promised, and one by one, he rolled the lace-topped silk slices down her legs, skimming a path down her long, shapely legs.

The woman had a killer body that would have had any man begging to be right here, opening her legs to him. And open she did as he settled one delicate instep on each of his shoulders.

He stroked a finger down her core and her legs quivered. "Slick and hot," he approved. "You sure feel like you want to be saved."

"I'm not sure saved is the word-"

Blake buried his face between her thighs, and suckled her nub. She gasped in surprise and he watched her fall back onto the mattress, her pink painted nails digging into the comforter. He smiled with satisfaction, lapping at her, delicately teasing and licking, even as his finger slid inside her, stroking her. And she unraveled for him, oh yeah she did. Soft moans and sweet nectar that were so sexy and perfect he could have licked her all night, but she wasn't having it. She shattered for him, her body shaking, arching deliciously against his mouth and hand.

And then she rolled to her side, hiding her face, again with a contradiction. The bold beauty who'd challenged him to please her and now the shy beauty who'd just been pleased. Blake wasn't having any part of her hiding from him. If he was going to influence her, and clearly sex had become his weapon of doing so, he needed to get to her; he needed to connect beyond an orgasm.

Blake tossed his jacket that was still on the bed and slid in front of her, lacing his hand into her hair and forcing her to look at him. "What are you hiding from?" he asked, and he wasn't just talking about sex. "Me or something else?"

Her eyes went wide, sparking with emotion. "Nothing. I'm not hiding from anything." She slid close to him, pressing her soft, perfect body against his. "What are you hiding from? And why aren't you inside me already?"

The challenge ripped through him with the intended effect. He was instantly hotter and harder and that was a pretty sizable order considering how hot and hard he'd already been. Blake's mouth closed down over hers, and this time, he did devour her. This time, he took all she had to give, and give she did. She met each stroke of his tongue with fervor, drinking him, taking when he thought he'd be the one doing the taking.

She shoved him to his back and climbed on top of him. "I can't save you when you have your clothes on." She reached for his jeans and stroked the thick ridge of his erection. "And you really feel like you want to be saved."

He would have laughed at her using his line on him, but she distracted him by sliding down his zipper, her breasts eye-candy as she did. She tugged at his jeans and he gladly helped her walk them and his boxers down his legs.

"Your condom or mine?" she asked. "I assume you have one."

This time he leaned up on his elbows. "Back pocket. Where's yours?"

"My purse."

"You came prepared."

She retrieved the wrapper of two condoms. "I told you I'm efficient." She climbed onto the bed and between his legs, right in front of his shaft, her soft hand wrapping his width.

"It appears you are," he commented, only to find turn around was fair play as she bent down and sucked the head of him into her mouth.

"Sweet mother of Jesus," he murmured, but unlike her, he didn't lay back. He watched her lick him, suck him, for as long as he dared, before he reached for her. "Either put the condom on me or give it to me to do it."

She wet her lips, making his cock jerk. "I want to finish."

"Finish on me, baby. That's where I want you." He found the wrapper where she'd dropped it on the bed and tore it open, rolling it down his length, while she watched with so much admiration, he wasn't sure he or his cock could bear much more.

He scooted back against the headboard and pulled her across his lap. Her delicate fingers dug into his shoulders and he lifted her, fitting his cock to the silky opening of her body, and pressing inside. His breath lodged in his throat at the tight, wet heat surrounding him, and only when she'd taken him all did he feel it trickle past his lips, did his eyes open and met hers.

The connection took him off guard, the crackle of awareness that he felt both in his body and yes, beyond. Emotion expanded in his chest, and it made no sense. He didn't even know this woman. Tiffany. She'd said she was Tiffany. The name felt wrong, but she felt right. What the fuck was she doing to him and why was he letting her.

Suddenly, Blake needed that old high of intense pleasure, of driving himself over the edge of bliss where he felt nothing but a rush. He laced his fingers into her hair and buried his tongue in her mouth, devouring her, and pressing her down against his cock. Moving inside her, urging her into a rocking motion, and then pressing her backwards until her hands were on his thighs, her breasts thrust into the air.

"Ride me," he ordered, caressing her breast, kissing her nipple. "Ride, baby."

Her head dropped backwards, all that silky hair behind her, the creamy silk of her neck as sexy as the rest of her, moving against him, pumping his cock. He could feel her urgency growing, her need, and he had to taste it.

He pulled her to him, molding her close and dragging her mouth to his. His tongue stroked against hers and she gasped into his mouth. Suddenly, her body spasmed around him, grabbing his cock and milking his release. They clung to each other, shaking with the intensity of what had just happened between them.

When finally they stilled, he rolled her to face him, back the way they started, sliding one leg over hers, certain she was going to try to escape. She wasn't looking at him, and he tilted her chin up. "Is this where we exchange files?" she asked, before he could say anything.

"Not even close," he promised, brushing his lips over hers. "You haven't even told me your real name yet?"

"Tiffany. My name is Tiffany."

He stroked her cheek. "Tell me I'm the first you've ever done this with."

She laughed nervously. "Did it seem like the first?"

"Yes," he said. "The first time like this, for him."

She scraped her bottom lip. "I didn't do this for him. I wouldn't have done this for him. I did it for me."

The passion behind those words, the vehement force, spoke volumes. She'd made choices, just as she'd said she had, but she resented where they'd led her, where she felt she couldn't escape.

He rolled her to her back, keeping one leg around hers, framing her body with his elbows. "Did what?"

Her eyes glowed with challenge. "Fucked you but now we need to exchange files."

He saw the words as the wall they were. She was afraid he

was seeing beyond what she thought he should. "We have all night and I'm far from done with you." Blake slanted his mouth over hers and showed her just how not done he was with her.

The Escape...

Blake blinked awake as the maid walked into the room and screamed in embarrassment. He tried to sit up and felt the wave of nausea hit him like a head-on collision. Drugged. He knew the feeling. He'd lived it once before, on an assignment in Mexico City gone bad. The maid ran out of the room and the door slammed shut and thank God, because he was naked and headed to the toilet. He barely made it to the seat before he threw up. And threw up some more. He'd been screwed over by a beautiful woman. He would have laughed if he wasn't so fucking sick. He wasn't a fool. Not by a long shot, yet, he'd acted like one.

And six hours later, when he'd finally dressed and confirmed the file was gone, he was finally capable of trying to figure out what had happened. He sat in the hotel room and dialed the offices where Tiffany Snow should work and asked for her. And just as he expected, she didn't exist. Rachel, the woman who was supposed to meet him, wasn't in.

Fifteen minutes later, Blake found where Kyle, one of the Walker tech experts, and a close friend keeping his pursuit of Alvarez off his brother's radar, had parked a rental car in front of the hotel at a meter to wait on him.

Blake climbed into the passenger seat and slammed the door, snatching Kyle's sunglasses and putting them on. "Tell me you got an address on Rachel."

"Of course," Kyle said, giving him a sideways look from his too knowing green eyes. "You look like shit."

"Yeah. Thanks. You look like a smart-ass."

"Really?" he asked, pulling into traffic. "I had no idea smart-asses looked like blonde blue eyed Adonis."

"You don't have blue eyes."

"And you must be sick as shit because by default you just agreed I'm an Adonis."

Blake slid down into the seat and didn't bother answering. The movement of the car was pissing him and his stomach off. "Drive faster."

Thirty-minutes of hell Denver traffic later, Blake and Kyle entered the back of a small house owned by Rachel. When she wouldn't answer her door, they entered and found her tied to a chair and gagged. "Who are you?" she screamed the instant Blake pulled the tape off. "And where is the bitch who tied me up? I'll pay good money to kill her before my boss kills me for letting her do this to me."

Blake knelt down beside her. He'd failed to prove himself to the boss beneath Alvarez and he had to find a way to fix that and fix it now. "I'm the guy who is going to save your ass so your boss doesn't kill you." He'd give her the list and arrange to get her out of the country a few weeks later, before she decided to spill his identity. It didn't take long to convince Rachel of his plan.

There was just one lose end. Tiffany Snow. What had she wanted with that list? He didn't like unknowns. He didn't like being a victim. And he didn't like letting himself do what he swore he wouldn't do again. Get fucked. People got killed when you were that sloppy.

He was going to find Tiffany Snow. She could count on it. He was...

CHAPTER

ONE

One week later...

D on't get on that elevator."

Blake Walker ignored the warning spoken into his cell phone headset by fellow Walker Security pal Kyle Suther, and stepped onto said San Francisco elevator. He punched the button for floor twenty-five. "Too late," he replied, watching the doors close. "I'm already inside." And headed straight to a 4:30 meeting with Milo Mendez, the CEO of Newport Industries; a massive holding company that looked legit but laundered money for the Alvarez Cartel.

"Damn it," Kyle cursed, "I know how badly you want Alvarez, but this meeting is trouble. Get off now."

"Why?"

"Get off and then we'll talk."

"Translation," Blake drawled cautiously, certain he was being monitored. "You don't think I'll approve of your explanation."

"Because you never listen to reason."

"Try me."

Kyle made a frustrated sound and caved. "I just tapped into the company security feed. Tiffany Snow is sitting at the desk outside Mendez's office."

Tension shot through Blake's body at the name of the dark-haired beauty who, only a week before in Denver, had fucked him, drugged him, and stolen a file that was supposed to prove he was trustworthy to the cartel. "Tiffany Snow is here? In San Francisco?"

"That's right. You only thought you covered up the mess she created. She set you up and you're headed to your own funeral."

Blake's mind raced with the real possibility Kyle was right, but he quickly discarded it for logic. If Tiffany Snow was working for Mendez after stealing documents meant for the cartel, then she'd double-crossed them in Denver. That meant she had as much to lose by exposing what had happened in Denver as he did. That didn't mean she wasn't dangerous, or working for one of the cartel's competitors, but she wasn't working for Mendez or Alvarez either.

"I can handle this," Blake finally replied. "I'm staying the course."

"Whatever you're thinking about this woman, think again. It's too big a coincidence that you were just put on a plane to San Francisco from Denver with no notice, and she's there waiting on you."

"I'm doing this."

The elevator dinged and Kyle cursed, clearly having heard it. "Damn it, Blake, stay alive. If your brothers find out I helped you go after Alvarez and let you get killed, we'll both be dead."

"Thanks for the concern," Blake said dryly, "but don't worry. I'm not going anywhere but to my meeting." The doors slid open and Blake ended the call before stepping onto the shiny white and gray tile of the sleek triangle-shaped lobby.

"Nice to see you've arrived safely, Mr. Wright." the pretty twenty-something blonde behind the massive oval-shaped desk greeted him, using his alias. He'd never met her but he was clearly expected by her and, no doubt, Ms. Tiffany Snow. The woman waved him to his left. "Straight down the hallway. It leads directly to Mr. Mendez's private offices."

The fictional character he'd carefully crafted as Blake Wright, down to a birth certificate, and a name close enough to his own to make any slip-up seem an accident, was arrogant, an egomaniac who would expect to be escorted to his destination.

Appropriate to that character, Blake shot her an annoyed look and headed the direction she'd indicated. No doubt Mendez was trying to downplay Blake's importance, to shoot down his confidence despite a fictional track record of being good enough at neutralized threats of a lawful affiliation to those who lived unlawfully, to make him worth pursuing. What Mendez didn't know, but soon would, was that the only thing Blake planned to neutralize was him and his Kingpin boss, and no one, not even pretty little Tiffany Snow, was going to get in the way of making that happen.

***

He was tall, dark, and deadly if she'd ever seen a man who fit the description. Impossible to forget. Impossible to avoid apparently, too, since he was here in San Francisco where she was, and not in Denver where he was supposed to be.

Kara Tatum (AKA Tiffany Snow and Kara Michaels) watched Blake Wright saunter towards her desk in a loose-legged swagger, his jeans and a leather jacket and all that thick raven hair tied at his nape, giving him a rough, tough, edgy look that was sinfully hot. And somehow, some way, she managed to remain cool and composed on the outside when she was a volcanic eruption of fire and ice on the inside. It didn't seem to matter that she'd found out about his arrival an hour before and had time to strategize his impending visit; she was far from ready for another dose of this man.

This man. No. This monster. He was one of *them*, part of the cartel, and yet a week before, he'd managed to stir something inside her he shouldn't have. Made her want him when she should do nothing but hate him. Made her hesitate to drug him when she should want to kill him. And that was far more dangerous than the knowledge he possessed that could destroy her and people she loved, because it made him a weakness she couldn't afford.

Kara pushed to her feet to greet him, putting the persona of a cold-hearted woman that she wished she could be into place. Then maybe the torment she'd seen in this man's eyes when they'd been stripped naked wouldn't have made him feel human.

"You look surprised," Kara commented as he stopped in front of her desk, giving him a cool-as-cucumber lift of her lips. "I do love surprising people."

He towered over her petite five foot three height by close to a foot, his rich brown eyes fixing intensely on her. He was big and broad, and she wished she didn't know just how deliciously carved to muscular perfection he was beneath his clothes.

Long seconds ticked by without him speaking, his hot stare sliding over her pale pink silk blouse to the top of her black fitted skirt, then lifting, the look in his eyes telling her he remembered all too well what was beneath her clothing. Heat spread over her shoulders and down her arms, and her mouth went dry.

One of his dark brows arched and he finally broke the silence. "Surprise? Is that what you call this impromptu meeting?"

"Were you expecting me?" she challenged.

He studied her for a second, maybe two, that felt like another eternity. "Were you expecting me? That's the real question now, isn't it?"

"I have you on the schedule, Mr. Wright."

"Mr. Wright? Aren't we a little beyond formality?"

"No," she said tightly. "We aren't. We were business."

"Business?"

"Richter, the head of the Denver division used to work here," she explained. "He wanted to know you could stumble and cover your tracks before he recommended you to my boss."

"And he asked you to help?"

"He was certain you'd recognize his staff."

"And Mendez knows about this?"

She shook her head. "It's our secret."

His eyes glinted, narrowed, and he moved suddenly, leaning forward, his hands on her desk. He was close, so close she could smell the spicy, wonderful scent of him. "Why would you, or Richter, keep this our secret?"

"I don't know. I just know he told me to keep it a secret."

"For leverage over me."

"I don't know."

"And what did you get out of this?"

"A bonus."

Anger crackled off of him. "So he told you to fuck me, then

fuck me over, and you did it." He paused. "For money."

Kara had been confronted, she'd been in awkward positions, but not since her rookie days had she felt rattled like she did now. "I did my job."

"Which included fucking me."

Kara flinched, and not just because it was part of the character she'd created. She'd never meant to sleep with him. She just...had.

"Did it include fucking me?" he demanded softly, and the tightness in his voice was more an order than any shout would have been.

"I made my own choices," Kara rasped out, and though she needed him to believe her, to see her like a victim as he had the night they'd met, she wanted him to believe her as well. The idea of this man hating her answer, and her, bothered her. Lord help her, he was the enemy and she cared what he thought. She was in big trouble.

"And you decided to ensure you got your big payday any way necessary, even if it meant getting naked." It wasn't a question.

"No," she whispered urgently before she could stop herself. "That's not how it happened. I didn't intend for it to happen. It just...it felt...necessary."

"Fucking me was necessary," he repeated flatly.

"Yes." Her mouth was dry all over again, and good lord, she was dizzy remembering all the delicious things his mouth had done to her. "Necessary."

"I didn't realize you and Mr. Wright knew each other, Kara."

Kara jerked backward at the sound of Mendez's voice, but

not before she saw the slight narrowing of Blake's eyes. And damn it, she'd let him see her cards. Blake knew just how nervous she was at the idea of Mendez discovering what she'd done in Denver. He'd assume it was because Mendez was a monster, but he'd still have that leverage over her when she'd tried to make this secret leverage for her use instead.

"We were just getting properly acquainted," Blake drawled lazily, holding her stare a beat before his attention slid to Mendez.

Kara's stomach knotted at the way Blake had left the door open to tell Mendez he'd met her in Denver. "I was just about to let you know he'd arrived," she added, cutting her gaze to Mendez and the amused twist on his brutal mouth. Beneath the man's mid-thirties dark good looks and perfectly fitted designer suit was a tyrant who'd kill you at the snap of his fingers.

"I'm sure you were," he replied, and flicked Blake a look. "Join me, Mr. Wright. We have much to discuss."

Unlike everyone else around Mendez, Blake didn't immediately jump at his command. For several beats his eyes lingered on her face before he finally stepped away from her desk. A slow trickle of air slid from Kara's lips, tension easing from her body, at her escape from his too-knowing, too-compelling, attention. Compelling. Yes. He was compelling in all possible ways. Wickedly, intensely, hotly compelling. He demanded her attention, his presence resonating with the woman in her in a way no other man ever had. This was what every woman wanted to feel for a man, but thought she never would. And if she got lucky enough to have it happen to her, she wanted him to be the right man, a good man. In Kara's case, this man she was responding to was without a doubt the wrong man.

After an eternity seemed to pass, when it was merely seconds, the door behind her opened and shut. Kara cast a glance over her shoulder, ensuring she was alone. Then, and only then, did she slump over her desk, letting her long, dark hair cover her face, thankful no one could see her reaction to the man who'd just taken her by storm all over again. Blake not only put her on edge, he set her on fire and left her breathless. He was dangerous to her agenda, her big picture. Her reason for everything she'd done the past six months. Everything she'd given up. Everything she'd left that mattered. He was a weakness she couldn't afford and a problem she had to deal with quickly and efficiently before he destroyed everything she'd been working for.

CHAPTER
TWO

Blake followed Mendez into his office, the lingering scent of Tiffany Snow, or Kara, or whatever the hell her name was, spiraling through his nostrils and heating his limbs. The woman had drugged him and almost destroyed his reputation with the cartel, and still she had him hot and bothered and more than a little distracted. Not so much, though, that he hadn't seen the fear in her eyes when Mendez had assumed they'd known each other. Because she'd helped Richter for cash and her boss would see that as disloyal? Or because she was one big secret she didn't want revealed?

Pausing midway inside the office, Blake watched Milo Mendez round his massive cherry wood desk, a picture of greed and arrogance in the way he moved, the way he wore his fine silk grey suit. And most definitely in the glint in his dark eyes as he settled into a leather chair and claimed the position of power in the room.

Not about to give him that power, Blake feigned interest in his surroundings, not the man, inspecting the wall of windows to his left and the leather couch and chair to his right with exaggerated interest. "Nice office."

"Sit," Mendez ordered, indicating a visitor's chair, his tone etched with irritation.

Out of the blue, as they often came, a flashback of his Whitney lying in a pool of blood ripped through Blake, and carved out his insides. Mendez might not have pulled the trigger, but he was deep inside the wallet of the man who had. It was all Blake could do not to rip him from behind his desk and beat him senseless. His fingers flexed, curling into his palms, and the twitchy feeling that he used fast cars and fast woman to escape crackled along his nerve endings like raw electricity.

Silently Blake reminded himself that pleasure was always sweeter after being denied, and his revenge over Whitney's death was the only pleasure that had mattered for over two years. Mendez's beating was coming and Blake was damn sure going to enjoy the hell out of it.

Blake ambled toward the visitor's chair and dropped into the leather seat, schooling his features into a bored mask of indifference.

"Thank you for joining me on such short notice," Mendez offered cordially, like he had a truly cordial bone in his low-life body.

"Money talks and you made it worth my while," Blake replied, referencing the wad of cash he'd been handed before he'd agreed to take this trip.

"And as long as you're worth my while, I always will. As for why you are here. Unfortunately, my head of security has failed to address a critical problem I'd asked him to handle. He's now made an untimely departure, leaving me with the need to hire someone competent to address my problem."

Blake read between the lines. He was dead. "If he failed you, then I'd say the departure wasn't untimely at all."

Mendez gave him a quick incline of his head, approval glinting in his eyes. "Indeed. Nevertheless, I still have my problem and I still need it fixed."

"I'm contract only. I'm not looking for a staff job."

"Good, because I'm offering you money for solving a problem, not a full-time job." He didn't wait for a reply. "As I'm sure you're aware, Newport operates several national restaurant chains. One of those chains runs what I'll call a special inventory distribution and it's come to my attention that some of those orders have been shorted. I need you to find out who's behind it and make them go away."

In other words, someone was skimming drugs and selling them on the side and Mendez wanted Blake to put a stop to it. Worked for him. In fact, it had a limited downside. He simply took down one drug dealer to get to another. "How many locations are involved?"

"The restaurant has two hundred nationally, but the supply chain starts right here in California."

Blake read between the lines. "And you don't know if that's where the problem originates."

Mendez's expression tightened. "Our dearly departed head of security couldn't seem to find a problem anywhere, despite my knowledge otherwise."

"So I'm starting from scratch with a national chain of employees as suspects." Blake whistled. "That's a big project."

"I thought you were the best at what you do?" Mendez challenged.

"I am," Blake assured him, "which is exactly why I'm committed to a high-paying client in Europe next week. There's no way I can take this on for you right now. When I get back—"

"I need this handled now," Mendez snapped, his anger palpable. He didn't expect to be turned down, and that was the idea. Blake wanted Mendez chasing him, desperate to hire him.

Blake slid lazily down further into his chair, draping an arm on the back. "Which is why I'm not your man."

Mendez's eyes hardened, his expression all sharp lines and tension. He steepled his fingers together, fixing Blake in a stare meant to intimidate. He was pissed. It was all Blake could do not to smile.

"I was told you were eager to earn our business," Mendez ground out tightly.

"I have been," Blake assured him, "but while your organization had me jumping through hoops to prove I'm worthy, the guy in Europe was writing me a check."

"So it's all about money to you?"

Blake arched a brow. "What else is there?"

"Power."

"Money is power in my book."

Mendez's jaw clenched and unclenched before he abruptly grabbed a piece of paper, scribbled a number on it, and flipped it around for Blake to see it. "Is that enough power for you?"

Lazily, Blake pushed off the back of the chair and leaned forward to study the six-figure number. "It's a start."

Mendez's eyes glinted like black ice. "How much will it take?"

"Add another 100k to that number and California is my new European vacation."

"If you let me down—"

"I won't."

Mendez considered Blake a moment. "Half the money now

and half on the resolution of my problem, which I expect to include body bags."

Blake held up his hands. "I'll identify your problems. Disposal is on you."

"That's a hefty price you demanded for limited services."

"I'm guessing it's small compared to how much you're losing in stolen product."

A muscle flexed and contracted in Mendez's jaw. "How do you want this played? I can introduce you as head of security so you have full access to the staff."

"That works only if you understand up front that I'll play the bad guy ripping you off. It's the only way I can find out who's willing to join me."

"Understood."

"And I'll have a laundry list of data I'll need as well as full access to the relevant computer databases. I'll also need a vehicle. A 4Runner is my preference in case I need to transport anything or anyone. And, of course, money before I get started."

"I'll need a bank account."

"Cash," Blake countered.

He studied Blake a moment, his expression inscrutable. "It'll be delivered to your hotel by end of day. How do you want to start?"

"I'll visit the restaurants here locally. How many are there?"

"Three in San Francisco, but, of course, in Los Angeles and San Diego we have extensive operations. More than fifty restaurants."

"You said you knew there was a problem your head of security couldn't identify. Why are you so certain you were right and he was wrong?"

"Discrepancies in reports." Mendez punched his intercom before Blake could ask for clarification. "Come to my office, Kara."

The door opened almost instantly. "Yes, Mr. Mendez?"

Blake tensed at the soft, musical note of Kara's voice from behind him that too easily stirred memories of her naked in his arms, and of the soft little purrs of pleasure sliding from her lips. Damn it, what was it about this woman that got to him? He'd spent two years living in the fast lane, in and out of women like they were a drive-thru, living for short-term highs and quick escapes. None of them did this to him. Not one. Just her.

Mendez motioned her forward. "Join us, Kara."

Blake heard the swish of her skirt behind him a moment before she appeared at the side of the desk. His gaze lifted, skimming her petite but curvy hips hugged by the snug black skirt she wore, and he remembered in far too vivid detail how well she fit pressed against him. His dick pressed thickly against his zipper, his body betraying him, uncaring about what a lying, conniving bitch she'd turned out to be. And she was. He couldn't afford to believe anything else.

"Kara's intimately aware of our situation," Mendez announced, "which is why I'm loaning her to you for the duration of your stay."

Intimately. The word ground through every nerve ending Blake owned and he wondered exactly how affectionate she'd been with Mendez. "How intimately?"

Her brown eyes shot to his, and to his surprise he found a hint of indignation, as if she read his thoughts and wasn't pleased. And damn it, there was a genuineness to her emotion, a wounded animal look deep in the depths of her stare, that twisted him in knots. For some ridiculous reason, he clung to the belief that Mendez, or maybe even Alvarez himself, held something over her, or she wouldn't be here. But a victim wouldn't have had the skills to pull off Denver any more than a simple secretary would.

"I'm the one who discovered the discrepancies in reports that told us there was an inventory problem," she explained of her involvement.

He arched a brow. "Were you now?"

"Yes." Her eyes held his. "I was."

Blake stared at her, and damn it, he didn't like how easily he could keep staring at her. He cut his gaze to Mendez. "How long has Kara been with you?"

"I've been with the company for six months," she answered herself, drawing his attention back to her.

"And already making a name for yourself," he commented dryly, and watched her delicate little hands, hands that he knew to be soft and incredibly talented, curl around a pad of paper with a white-knuckle grip that confirmed just how nervous he was making her. Good. She should be nervous. He wondered how many men she'd slept with to get to this level of trust this quickly.

"Mr. Wright will have level 5 security access," Mendez instructed Kara. "He'll be taking on the role of new head of security as of tomorrow morning. See to it he's well taken care of. Whatever he needs or wants, I expect you to ensure he gets."

To her credit, Kara appeared cool, collected, and unfazed by the command that put her in the hands of a man she'd both fucked and fucked over, because she had to know he wasn't going to just let it go.

"Of course," she agreed coolly, her gaze flicking to her bosses. "Is there an office I should assign Mr. Wright?"

Blake pushed to his feet. "Whatever office you assign me I won't be occupying. I'll, or rather we'll, be working incognito, which means we'll be using my hotel room. Unless, of course, you have a problem with that?"

There was a subtle shift in her posture, a stiffening of her spine. "No. No problem at all. Whatever you need, Mr. Wright—"

"Blake," he corrected. "As far as I'm concerned, sharing a hotel room wipes out formality. Don't you agree?"

Her chest rose and fell before she dodged a direct reply and simply said, "Blake."

"Arrange a 4Runner for Mr. Wright's use," Mendez directed, clearly keeping up his end of formality, "and buzz us when it's ready."

"Yes, sir," Kara said. "I'll get right on it." She flicked a look at Blake. "Anything else you need immediately?"

"Plenty," he commented, "but we'll take it one thing at a time."

A muscle in her creamy white throat rippled. "Then I'll get the vehicle handled." She flicked Mendez a look. "Is there anything else?"

"No," he said. "You're free to go."

She headed for the door and Blake was eager to follow, his blood pumping at the promise of the nice long chat the two of them were going to have, where clothing was most definitely optional. In fact, clothing wasn't optional at all. He was going to strip her naked so she had no place to hide another dose of whatever she'd drugged him with last week.

It was a satisfying thought until he turned to find Mendez looking like a cat who just ate a canary. Mendez could see Blake's interest in Kara, and he would use her against him if given the chance. And any time someone became a tool in a weapons chest, their life was on the line. No one was going to end up dead because of Blake—no one he wasn't damn certain deserved to be dead.

"Nice piece of ass," Blake said, making sure he was as crass as possible. This was about making Kara a body, not a person. "Sure you want her alone in a hotel room with me?"

"I'm no one's guardian angel," Mendez replied dryly, and the message was clear. She was part of his payment. Blake wondered how many men she'd pleased to satisfy her boss and disgust burned in his belly.

His teeth clenched. "If she loses her usefulness, I'm giving her back."

"I'd like to think you'll solve my problem before that happens."

"I'll need more than a night to solve your problem. I'm not promising I'll need more than that with her."

But that was a lie. He'd had a night with her and still he needed another. No matter how much Blake told himself that Kara, like everyone else the past two years, was simply a tool to get what he wanted, blood in exchange for blood, there was something about her messing with his head. Something that had taken hold of him and wouldn't let go. And that made her a distraction he couldn't afford, dangerous beyond a loaded gun with her finger on the trigger.

He had to get focused, put her in perspective as what she was…an enemy who could get him dead before he'd gotten the payback he was after.

CHAPTER
THREE

Kara buzzed her boss to tell him Blake's truck had arrived, and then pressed her hands to her desk and willed her nerves to calm. She was shaking inside and out, trying to gather her composure and her things before she had to face Blake again, all too aware that he knew she was lying about Denver. She'd seen it in those keen, deep, dark brown eyes of his. If he didn't kill her for drugging him, Mendez would if he found out she wasn't what she seemed to be. Her only cold comfort in her situation was that Blake would look bad—incompetent, even—if he told Mendez he'd been undone by a woman, and he wasn't likely to let that happen. She just had to stick to her story and she'd be fine. Right. Fine. She was headed to a hotel room with a man that thought she was better off silent and six feet underground.

The sound of the door opening behind her had Kara jerking backwards and smoothing her skirt, putting on the game face that was wearing on her. She hated Mendez Mendez more today than ever before. He'd handed her over to Blake like a wrapped package, and, ironically considering her choices last week, all but telling her to strip down and pleasure him. She wasn't his whore or Blake's, but yet, somehow, she'd become that and more. But it didn't matter. She'd do what she had to do. She had a purpose. She had a reason for being here and doing this job—that mattered more than anything else.

Kara turned, expecting to face both Blake and Mendez, but found only Blake present. Their eyes locked and held and Kara felt the connection like a hard punch in the chest, the sizzling attraction between them impossible to escape. His expression darkened instantly, and she could almost taste his anger, as if he didn't want to feel this spark between them any more than she did. She wasn't comforted by his desire, by how it might give her influence over him. Men in this world would slit your neck for making them feel something they didn't want to, and she'd already given him a reason to kill her by way of Denver.

Delicately, she cleared her throat, afraid of not finding her voice. "The 4Runner is waiting on you in the garage. You're at the Tuscan off the pier, so you'll have a parking garage for easy access to the vehicle. It's also right by the pier Newport uses for critical product distribution, which I thought you might find convenient. What time should I be at the hotel in the morning?"

He barked out laughter and sauntered toward her, the dark rumble of sound expanding the broad, stellar chest his leather jacket did nothing to hide. He stopped toe to toe with her, an inch separating his boots and her high heels.

His gaze slid over her face, down to her mouth, lingering, and lifting. "You don't seriously think I'm going to let you out of my sight tonight, now do you?"

His nearness rushed over her, sending waves of tingling sensations through her body. This time it was her gaze that went to his mouth before she could stop it, and she could almost taste him on her lips, taste her on his lips. "I'm not going anywhere if that's what you think," she finally managed.

"Not going anywhere without me," he corrected and leaned in close, his lips near her ear, his breath hot on her neck. "We have trust issues, you and I, sweetheart. You're staying by my side."

Oh yes, they did have trust issues, which had to be why her heart was racing a hundred miles an hour. Didn't it? "I was doing my job."

"We'll be talking about how you define your job. You can count on it." He took a step backwards and motioned her forward.

She didn't know what was more striking in that moment—how much she wanted him close again, or how much she knew getting away from him was absolutely necessary. She reached inside her drawer to grab her oversized black Coach purse, and a pang of discomfort tightened her chest. It had been a gift for her twenty-seventh birthday, a year ago in a week, from someone very special. Someone she wished was here now.

Kara drew a deep breath and shoved aside the thought, all too aware that it was going to clutter her mind with emotion, and emotion wouldn't achieve her mission. She shouldered the purse and shut the drawer to find Blake's keen stare on her face.

Eager to escape his inspection, she snatched her long canvas jacket and put it on, then retrieved her briefcase. She didn't look at him; afraid he'd see too much, afraid she'd feel that funny punch in the chest that one of his deep stares created.

Kara walked past him, toward the elevator. He fell into step beside her. Still she stared ahead and tried not to be aware of how big and tall, and deliciously, dangerously male he was beside her. Damn the man for getting to her and seeing beneath her carefully crafted alias. And he did. She knew he did. Damn herself for allowing there to be anything to see. She was trained better than this, but then, she wasn't supposed to be the one handling a job this personal.

Together, too in unison for Kara's comfort, they stepped into the elevator and Blake stayed by her side, only inches separating their arms. Kara punched the button for the garage level. Blake turned to face her, resting a shoulder on the wall, watching her.

Kara turned to face him, taking in his hooded gaze, his long, dark lashes concealing the thoughts she desperately wanted to read. "Are you just going to stand there watching me?"

"That's the plan."

His tone was lazy, but she caught a hint of amusement etched in its depths. She didn't like it. Not at all. "Because you're trying to make me nervous."

"Because I'm trying to figure you out. If that makes you nervous, you must have something to hide."

The doors opened and a man and a woman entered, saving her from a reply. Thankfully, Blake pushed off the wall and faced forward, giving her a small reprieve from his intent inspection. Another stop and a group of people shoved inside. Suddenly, Blake was pressed to her side, from hip to shoulder, and she could barely breathe. Memories of him touching her, of him naked and on top of her, inside her, beneath her, assailed her. The car moved ridiculously slow, leaving too much time for the vivid replaying of hot, erotic shared moments with an enemy she should never have slept with. Yet he still tempted her. She felt selfish and weak, shallow even for allowing lust and attraction to dictate her desires, when there was so much on the line.

Finally, the doors opened and several people exited. Blake had room to move, but he didn't. Kara's gaze lifted to his, challenging him to step away. His lips twitched, his hot stare filled with refusal. He wasn't going anywhere and neither was she.

By the time they reached the garage level and the rest of the crowd had piled out before them, Kara was on fire, tingling from head to foot. She was also ready to face the facts. She'd made sure she kept her life simple, free of bonds that could be broken, bonds that were painful when ripped away. Therefore, she'd radiated toward men she knew felt the same way. In theory, Blake fit her profile perfectly, except for two very distinct reasons, most importantly that he stood for everything she despised. Which made the second difference all the more baffling. Unlike other men before him, she was completely, utterly affected by Blake, even fully dressed and trying not to be.

They exited the stairwell with several other people nearby and she motioned to the silver 4Runner sitting in the space by the door. "That will be you, and the keys are in the ignition. The bag you brought was transferred from the car that picked you up from the airport." She dug her keys out of her purse.

His hand slid over hers, twining with her fingers, and around them. "You won't be needing those."

Heat darted up her arm and over her shoulder to her chest and her gaze rocketed to his. The instant awareness between them shook her to the core. "I have to be able to get home tonight."

"No, actually, you don't." He dislodged the keys from her hand and motioned her forward. "Your ride awaits."

Several staff members walked by and Kara could feel their eyes on the two of them. "I'm not staying the night with you."

"Mendez said to do whatever I want and don't you do whatever he wants?"

"I do my job."

"Which included fuck—"

"Stop saying that over and over and assuming you have the answers. You know nothing about me or my motivations."

"I have a good idea."

Why did her gut tighten at the accusation in his voice? Why did she care what he thought? "No," she ground out. "No you don't." She let the emotions she felt about her real situation bleed into her words, or maybe there was no "let" about it. She'd been operating in a zone for months, trying not to feel anything, to stay focused. Only two times had she failed, and both times were with this man.

His lips twisted sardonically. "I have to admit, you play the victim well, but you won't play me again. We both know you're weaving lies to everyone around you. No victim does that. I'm getting answers and I'm getting them tonight."

Those dangerous emotions she was feeling jabbed her in the chest, made her vulnerable, made her need to get away. "I'm taking my car or I'm not leaving." His hand was still over hers, holding her and her keys, making her hot and confused when everything had been so clear until he'd shown up in the picture. "Let go. Unless you think you can't keep up with my ten-year-old Ford Focus."

His eyes narrowed sharply, but the handsome planes and angles of his face remained unreadable. "Where are you parked?"

"The space beside you."

A second passed, then another and he released her hand and motioned her forward. Kara didn't hesitate to seize her victory. Her chin lifted and she started walking. Blake pursued instantly, behind her, stalking her, the short walk to his passenger door and her driver's door. This man made her feel exposed, out of control. Bad things with lives on the line, and not her own. She wasn't worried about herself. She'd learned years ago that to do what she did, you had to wake up ready to die, but she was never, ever; ready to let someone else die.

She clicked her keychain so that her locks opened and reached for the handle. Blake reached around her, the front of his thigh pressing down the length of hers starting at her hip, the feel of him stealing her breath. "Don't even think about running," he warned.

Heat washed through her and over her at his touch, and she was shaken by the depth of need she felt for him. She didn't look at him for fear he'd see her reaction. "I have nothing to run from," she said, and silently added, because I have everything to lose if I do.

Silence greeted her declaration, the seconds ticking by again, and she held her breath, waiting for his reaction. Finally he stepped back, and instead of relief, ice slid over her where heat had been moments before. She didn't understand the sensation any more than she understood anything this man made her feel.

Kara yanked open her door and he walked to the 4Runner. She slid into the car and tried to tell herself everything was fine. But it wasn't fine. Blake saw too much. "You have a good story," she reminded herself, needing to hear it out loud. She'd covered her bases, created her identity without flaw. Except for Denver, she thought. It had been a last-minute decision and she knew better than to make unplanned moves. Her stomach knotted with the realization she'd screwed up. If Blake mentioned Denver to Richter, he'd discover she wasn't working for Richter, Newport, or the cartel that night she'd stolen his files. She'd be dead for sure, which meant she had to do what she'd come here for and get out of here. She was out of time.

CHAPTER

FOUR

Why the fuck couldn't he stop thinking about getting her naked again? And why was he still feeling this ridiculous urge to save her when she'd thrown him under a bus in Denver?

Blake pulled the 4Runner out of the garage behind Kara's car, cursing her for distracting him, and fighting a flashback of blood and loss and...more blood. Damn it to hell, the acid burn of the past never faded and, no matter what he did, no matter what the momentary rush of pleasure or adrenaline rush he created, it always came back. Even trying to make it go away felt wrong, like he was trying to wash away Whitney, when he'd have traded himself for her in a heartbeat. Finally, he had the chance to do the only thing he had left...avenge her. He wasn't going to let anything, or anyone, stand in his way.

His cell phone rang and a glance told him it was Kyle. Blake answered to hear, "Were you going to call and tell me Denver didn't get you killed, or just drive the new 4Runner around town and break it in?"

"You knew I made it out of the building alive the same time I did, or we wouldn't be talking. Someone is skimming product and selling it on the side. Mendez slid me inside by naming me as his head of security."

"What happened to the prior head of security?"

"He failed to solve this problem."

"He's dead."

"I'm sure."

"Good opening for you, but I'm scratching my head. I thought for sure when we saw your Denver playmate waiting on you, you were about to be ten feet under."

"According to Kara, the head of the Denver division was testing me to see if I could stumble and recover before recommending me to Mendez."

"That doesn't seem like a test. It sounds like a setup for blackmail, a way to control someone he gets inside Mendez's operation."

"My thoughts exactly," Blake agreed dryly, pausing at a stoplight behind Kara.

"And Mendez's secretary is helping to undermine him. It pulls this together for me. It makes sense."

"Yeah." Blake let out a breath, not sure why that logical answer to why Kara had been in Denver didn't feel right to him.

"You don't think so," Kyle observed, having spent enough years working with Blake to know him better than even his brothers did.

"Something doesn't add up," Blake admitted. "What do you know about her?"

"On paper, she looks like a perfect candidate to be motivated by money. She's caring for a mother with Alzheimer's disease who has no insurance."

"But?"

"But she's too squeaky clean. No other family, no ties. Her identity reads like something I'd create to go undercover."

The light turned green and Kara started moving again, and Blake followed her. "Find out when she went to Denver, if she was alone, and who paid her expenses."

"I'm on it, but I'm guessing it was all cash no matter who is involved."

So was Blake. Kara turned right and he followed, bringing the pier and the hotel sign into view.

"We have to consider the possibility she could be working for an agency. Royce could call in a favor and run her through the FBI database—"

"Forget it. I'm not having my brother, who has a pregnant wife at home, involved in this."

"He doesn't have to know it's for you."

Blake grimaced. "This is Royce we're talking about. He'll figure it out." And he'd lecture Blake about having a death wish and try to intervene. "Start with finding out about her Denver travel. And see if you can track any calls between her and the head of the Denver division." Kara pulled into a parking garage. "I need to go. I'll call you when I can talk." He ended the connection, pulled into a spot beside Kara, and watched her kill her lights as he did the same.

Blake waited on Kara to exit her car before grabbing his duffle and exiting his own, the timing meant to ensure she didn't have the chance to drive away while he was outside his vehicle. Once she walking toward her trunk, he joined her and took her briefcase.

Surprise flashed in her eyes, like she didn't expect him to be a gentleman, and he had reason not to be with her, without question, but manners were inbred by his military father. "So you can't hit me with it," Blake explained, his hand brushing hers, the connection sending a jolt of pure lust rocketing through his blood.

She shivered and hugged herself, and he knew she wasn't reacting to the cool evening air floating off the nearby ocean, but to the instant heat simmering between them. "I'd have thought you'd be more likely to hit me with it."

"Never hit a woman," Blake assured her, his nostrils flaring with the soft, familiar feminine scent of her he'd been dreaming of for a week now. "Spanked a few, but—"

"Way too much information," she said, holding up her hands and looking appalled.

"I'm pretty sure you have a creative enough imagination to figure it out on your own anyway." But the truth was, despite the hot night they'd spent together, there was an innocent quality about her that defied how sizzling she'd been in bed with him. Not innocent, but…something. He doubted seriously she'd gone to any of the many places he had in the past two years. He motioned her toward the elevator. "Let's go have that chat we need to have."

"You know everything there is to know," she insisted, falling into step with him.

"I doubt that," he commented dryly.

Her brow crinkled. "You doubt and assume too much."

He almost choked on the irony of that statement. "Only when I have reasons and you've given me more reasons in a week than most do in a lifetime."

She punched the elevator button. "Or you're so cynical that you see things that aren't there."

He stared down at her, thinking how petite she was, how delicate and easily hurt she appeared. How in need of protection.

That's what made woman such weapons. They made a man forget they could pull a trigger just as easily as he could. "We're both working for Mendez and you think I'm too cynical?"

She bit her bottom lip. He wanted to bite that bottom lip. He wanted to lick it and her. He was going to lick it and her. "I suppose you do have a point there," she conceded.

They stepped into the elevator and she hit the lobby floor, which was the only option. She leaned on the wall and faced him. He leaned on the wall and faced her. Neither of them spoke as the elevator creaked upward, but the sexual tension between them blistered the walls. She sucked in a breath as if the heat was too much to handle and cut her gaze. Whatever her motivations for sleeping with him in Denver, whatever his for that matter, they'd wanted each other and they still did.

The doors opened and she glanced back at him, pausing as if she knew they were headed to bedroom bliss, and there was no return once they were alone. She was right. She exited with him at her heels and into the typical upscale hotel lobby, including random seating and lots of tile and chandeliers. At the check-in desk, Blake gave his name and waited until the attendant slid a key toward him.

Blake slid it back. "Change my room."

The fifty-something male frowned and Blake could feel Kara staring at him. "Is there something wrong with the room?" the man asked. "Or...you haven't seen the room."

Blake looked at the number on the envelope. "Superstitious. I hate the number 260 and the entire second floor. I need another floor and room."

A few minutes later they headed to the final bank of elevators and the seventh floor, where a family of four joined them. They exited at the seventh floor and she motioned to the right. "Lucky 711 is this way."

He smirked and fell into step with her down the hallway. "I prefer to ensure my privacy."

"He didn't have the room bugged," she commented. "I made the reservation and he never asked me the details."

They stopped at the door and he swiped the card. "Since I know you don't want this conversation overheard any more than I do, I believe you." He shoved open the door and grabbed her purse.

"What are you doing?" she demanded, holding onto it.

"This isn't déjà vu, sweetheart. I won't be having any toxic surprises tonight."

She glared at him. "I don't—"

"I'll be finding out for myself."

She wet those lips he was thinking about licking, His cock jerked, blood running hot. She was killing him, and not softly.

"I guess I would feel the same way," she admitted finally.

"I guess you would." He glanced down at her hand still holding the purse.

She hesitated a moment but let it go before entering the room. His blood ran hot. Kara, alone in a hotel room. He wasn't complaining. It wasn't déjà vu. It was "take two" and one hundred percent on his terms.

FIVE

K ara trembled as she walked into the room and all the way to the ceiling-to-floor windows, aware of the bed to her right like she'd never been aware of a bed in her life. Feeling like a deer being stalked by a leopard, her chest was tight with a rush of adrenaline and emotion—fear, she realized. She didn't often feel fear. Not until recently. Not until she'd realized how close she was to losing the only thing she had left in this world. But it wasn't Blake that scared her tonight when it should be. It was how much she wanted him, how much she wanted him to be something other than she knew him to be. And it was that kind of thinking that tangled women up with men like him and got them killed.

The sound of the door closing behind her set her heart racing and she turned to find Blake flipping the lock. They were alone. She was locked in here with him. In Denver, she'd thought she'd never see him again when she'd decided to sleep with him. Everything had changed now.

He dropped his bag, and her briefcase, on the floor by the door, but held onto her purse. He paused by the bed to his right and unzipped it. "You do know a girl's purse is sacred."

"So are the next few hours of my life. I don't intend to spend them hunched over a toilet from one of your cocktails." He dumped the contents of her bag on the bed and Kara held her breath, waiting for what he would reveal. Her Glock .22 bounced onto the bed.

He arched a brow. "Anger issues?"

"I won't apologize for carrying protection."

He dug through the rest of the items in her purse and stuffed it all back inside. "I won't ask you to apologize for the gun," he finally surprised her by saying, and stuck the Glock back in her purse. "In fact, I'd be disappointed if you were foolish enough not to protect yourself, considering who you work for. That doesn't mean I want to make it easy for you to use it on me." He back-stepped to his bag and squatted down, punching in a combination on a lock connected to the zipper and then opened it. He snatched up her slim briefcase and didn't bother to look through it before placing it inside his duffle along with her purse.

"If you want me to go over the restaurant operation, I need that," she commented.

"I don't. Not tonight. We have other things to deal with first."

Okay then. They had other things to deal with. She did wonder why he'd bothered looking through her purse and not her briefcase, but it didn't matter. The bottom line was the same. Her gun, her purse, and her car keys were now out of her reach, under his control. She was under his control. Trapped. At his mercy. Heat pooled low in her belly. Why, why, why was this man being in complete control so damn thrilling? She tried to tell herself it was a survival instinct, a way to get past being his captive, but it wasn't. It so wasn't. It was him. It was something he ignited in her she'd never felt before.

He straightened, big and broad, deliciously male, and shrugged out of his leather coat, tossing it on top of his bag. "Your turn," he said, his voice a soft command. "Take off your jacket."

In her mind, she knew she should decline, set the stage early that she wasn't his willing slave. She should set ground rules for what was going to be more than this one night. But it was just a jacket and she was fully clothed underneath it. To decline seemed the wrong battle to fight.

Kara reached for the tie at her waist and pulled it loose. Blake leaned a shoulder on the wall to his left, watching her, those dark eyes hooded, impossible to read. But she didn't have to. The heat simmering between them prickled at her skin, teasing her senses.

Slowly she slid the garment off her shoulders and set it on top of the chair in the corner to her right. Blake's gaze raked down her body and back up again. Kara crossed her arms in front of her chest. "I assume you have questions. I've already given you answers."

"Get undressed."

Kara gaped at the unexpected demand, her arms dropping. "What?"

"You heard me. Get undressed."

"No," she said, exasperated, angry. "I'm not getting undressed."

"For all I know you have drugs you intend to use on me, or worse, stashed in your clothes. Fool me once, sweetheart, but never again. So either you get rid of your clothes or I get rid of them for you."

"I'm not getting undressed."

53

He pushed off the wall and took a step toward her. Kara's heart jackhammered and she held up a hand. "Don't even think about it."

"You do it or I'll do it."

"Forget it, Blake," she said firmly. "You want to talk, then talk."

"I talk better with you naked."

"I don't."

"Too bad."

They glared at one another, the air crackling with the tension between them, the distrust, the anger, and the desire. Kara swallowed hard. They were going to end up naked. She knew it. He knew it. Her mind raced. She wasn't going to play a victim. That wasn't who she'd created with this identity, nor was it who she'd been with him before now. It wasn't even who she was as a person. No matter who he was or what he was, she couldn't escape this moment in time with him, nor did she truly want to. Living in the moment was part of what she'd been trained to do. She wasn't going to get emotionally attached, and letting herself enjoy this man physically might even save her life. It might be bad logic she'd question as sane later, but it worked for her now.

Her chin lifted. "You want me to get undressed, then you get undressed."

His eyes darkened, narrowed, and something unreadable, dangerously hot and edgy, flickered in their depths. He stepped forward, taking a long stride toward her. Then another. Kara stood her ground, expecting him to stop in front of her, to touch her. Please yes. Now that she'd decided to do this, she was all about him touching her. But he didn't stop right in front of her and he didn't touch her.

He stepped to her side, his shoulder parallel to hers. "You don't make the rules this time, Kara. I do." He moved behind her, framing her body with his, but still he didn't touch her. Anticipation burned through her. She *wanted* him to touch her.

His breath rasped along her neck and ear, a warm tease that slid along every nerve ending she owned with electric results. "So when I say get undressed, I mean get undressed."

"And if I don't?"

"You will."

Kara tried to turn. His hands went to her hips, fingers pressing deliciously, possessive into her body. "Stay facing forward," he ordered. "This way there's no chance you can pull any slick moves like you did in Denver. I can see...everything."

Everything. He made her want that and more. "And here I thought you weren't the kind of man who was afraid of a woman. I guess I was wrong."

"Don't taunt the lion while you're in his den, Kara. You might not like how he responds."

Her sex clenched at the warning and she silently replied, *or maybe I would like how he responds.* Yes. Yes she thought she might like it quite a lot.

"Undress," he ordered again.

"Make me," she challenged, ready to hear his proverbial roar.

CHAPTER
SIX

T he next thing Kara knew she was facing the wall, her palms against the hard surface, and Blake's powerful legs were framing hers. His big hands skimmed up her waist, over her breasts, and his mouth settled near her ear. "Is this what you wanted? A reaction?" He unzipped her skirt. "Because you got one, baby."

Kara swallowed against the dryness in her throat. "Yes. I wanted a reaction." It was the truth. Knowing he wanted her, that he couldn't resist, affected her, made her ache low in her belly.

"Why?" he demanded, sliding her skirt down her hips until it pooled at her feet, leaving her in her panties and thigh-highs. "Because you thought you'd make me let down my guard again?"

"Did it work?" Kara asked, swallowing hard as his finger traced the silk strand of her thong between her now bare cheeks.

"Like I said, fool me once, baby. Never again." His hands went to her hips, his thick erection nuzzled to her backside.

"Who exactly are you trying to convince?" she challenged, sounding breathless. "Me? Or you?"

He made a low, rough sound and then his hand reached

around her and caught the top of her blouse, ripping away all the buttons. "How's that for convincing us both?"

Kara gasped and her nipples puckered into tight knots of need. "I have to wear that out of here." Her voice was raspy, a barely there rough whisper she didn't even recognize as her own. God. What was this man doing to her?

"You should have undressed on your own, then." He pulled her blouse down her shoulders, and when she expected him to remove it, he used it to hold her wrists behind her back. "I told you," he warned, his hot breath fanning her neck near her ear, "don't taunt the lion in his own den."

"It's a hotel," she reminded him defiantly. "It's not your den."

"You really do like to live dangerously, don't you?" His voice was dark, edgy, and he twisted her shirt into some sort of knot that bound her wrists, binding her and putting her fully at his mercy. She should have objected, feeling fear or panic. Instead, heat flooded her body in a rush of adrenaline and desire. She'd never been tied up by a man, never allowed one that kind of control, and this was not the man to start giving it to. But her body defied her, her skin tingling, her sex tight and aching.

"Don't you?" he prodded.

"Did you ask a question?" Was she supposed to remember what he said when she was naked with his hands all over her?

He laughed, low and husky and her sex clenched with the sound. Everything about this man made her crazy hot and out of control, clouding her mind and logic, and leaving nothing but desire and need. "I asked if you liked living dangerously. Do you like the adrenaline rush? The danger?"

"I guess it depends on how you define danger," she managed

hoarsely. He was danger, and pleasure, and all things sinfully tempting, and impossible to resist.

"I'm beginning to get the idea your definition needs work," he accused roughly, shoving away the silk of her bra and working her nipples with short little pulls that sent ripples of sensation through Kara's body.

She tried not to pant. She tried to act cool and in control when she was melting into a big puddle of need and desire. "Considering I came here alone with you of my own free will, I think you might be right." The very fact that her hands were bound should set off all kinds of alarms for her, not the arousing erotic pleasure it was becoming.

His tugged her backwards, cradling her body against his hard, warm chest. "Or maybe," he murmured, accusation lancing the otherwise gently spoken words, "you have a hidden weapon that's giving confidence, like the drugs you used on me last time." His teeth scraped her lobe. "That would make me very unhappy."

A shiver raced down her spine and Kara knew Blake felt her tremble even before he challenged. "Scared? Or did I just hit a nerve?"

He was hitting all kinds of nerves. She was wet and hot and…"I'm naked and it's cold, and where would I hide anything at this point?"

"Only one more place I can think of." Suddenly he was on his knee at her side, tugging down her thong and all but lifting her to rid her ankles of the entanglement of clothing there. Almost instantly, his mouth was at her hip, lips teasing the curve between it and her waist. A shiver ran down her spine, her body sensitive to every touch of his hand, every movement he made.

He splayed a hand on her belly, and more anticipation swelled inside her as he lazily caressed her there, his fingers going lower each time, but still not low enough. She could barely breathe for the desire to push his hand where she wanted it, where he knew she wanted him. And when his lips pressed to her hipbone, she was so ultra sensitized that it was as if they scorched her skin, burning her like hot coal would a cold night.

"Perhaps here," he suggested, his fingers finally sliding between her thighs, into the silky wet heat of her aroused body.

"Yes," Kara whispered, unsure what she was answering, besides 'here' being exactly right in every way. There was nothing but the desire she felt for this man, and the way his thumb flickered over her swollen nub. The way his lips, tongue, and teeth, were trailing the length of her waist to hip. She wanted that mouth to go lower, to replace his hand, to lick her and taste her and…he slipped two fingers inside her.

Panting, she wished her hands free from her blouse around her wrists behind her, wished she could whisk fingers into his hair to steady herself. Blake's free hand palmed her inner thigh, widening her stance, making her feel even more unsteady. She swayed and his palm curved on her leg, holding her. All the while, his fingers were doing delicious things, stroking her, caressing her. Kara moaned, tingling all over, unable to hold back the sound of pleasure.

"At least I know you enjoy your work," he said with a low voice that was downright burning with acid.

The insult jolted Kara back to realty, and she stiffened, her hot blood going icy. What was wrong with her? How had she let herself get lost in this man? He was the enemy. She was just another whore to pleasure him before he did who knew what to her to make her pay for Denver. Suddenly being bound and at his mercy wasn't erotic at all. It was dangerous. He was dangerous. She, well she was just a fool.

Adrenaline exploded from Kara and she acted without thought, seeking escape. Swiftly, she twisted around, managing to take him off guard, and he wasn't able to stop her. She wobbled without her hands free though, and he was already on his feet, wrapping her in his embrace, and melding their bodies together.

"Easy now, sweetheart," he warned, his long hair falling loose from the clasp at his neck, and damn it, it made him look sexy. Like a sexy asshole who was probably a murderer just like Mendez.

"I'm not your whore or Mendez's," she hissed.

"You fucked me for a bonus in Denver." His voice was hard, his eyes even harder.

"I told you that wasn't part of the job any more than tonight is."

"That's not what Mendez said."

Kara's stomach knotted with this news despite already assuming as much. Suddenly, she was intensely aware, and resentful, of her nipples pressing into his chest, of her being naked and him fully dressed. "You both have the wrong girl, then."

His hand went to her hair, twining almost roughly around a section. "So it's okay to drug me but not fuck me for money?"

There it was. A verbal slap. How had she expected less? "You're here. You got the job. Isn't that what matters?"

"If the results what you want, then the means to which you get it with doesn't matter. Is that how you sell things to yourself?"

"I never intended to sleep with you," she blurted, unsure why it was so important he believe her, unsure why her voice trembled when she never lost her composure. "It just happened."

"I thought it was necessary?"

"I could have drugged you without staying."

His eyes narrowed. "I doubt that, sweetheart."

"Do you even remember how I drugged you?"

His expression darkened. "Why don't you tell me."

"How I did it isn't important." She drew a breath and let it out, softening her voice. "What's important is that I didn't have to get naked to do it. I didn't. I promise you. I stayed by choice."

"By choice," he said, his voice tight, gravely.

"Yes," she whispered. "By choice."

He stared at her long and hard, and the air thickened around them. She felt his muscles coil beneath her touch, sensed the anger in him begin to shift, change. His gaze darkened, heated, flickering with something she couldn't read, something intense, that quickly turned scorching hot. Desire radiated off of him, consuming her in the process. Suddenly she felt him everywhere, inside and out. His fingers flexed in her hair and it was as if a band had been pulled tight and snapped between them. They moved at the same time, leaning into each other, reaching for more, whatever more might be.

His mouth slanted over hers, his tongue pressing past her teeth, stroking deep, tasting her, claiming her. Passion overcame her, washing over her in a wicked flush of tingling skin and the tremble of her legs. But there was more than passion and desire. There was so much more. *Too much* more. There were emotions she didn't understand, emotions that were dangerous with a man who could destroy her. And there was relief, crazy ridiculous relief, that he knew the truth now. That he knew that she hadn't slept with him for anyone but herself. She cared what he believed of her when she shouldn't care at all. It was insanity. He made her crazy, opened her up inside and exposed something raw and vulnerable that she didn't want exposed. She shouldn't even want him to touch her, but *oh yes*, she did, and to the point of barely being able to breath for her need for him.

His hands stroked over her waist, caressing her breasts, and she arched into him, panting into his mouth. He reached behind her, surprising her by tugging away the blouse, and releasing her hands. He lifted her and before her arms and legs fully circled his body, he'd set her on the desk on the opposite side of the room. Kara had barely steadied herself with her hands behind her when Blake settled into the chair in front of her, and lifted her legs over his shoulders.

Kara sucked in a breath at the intimate, vulnerable position she was in, wearing nothing but thigh-highs and heels, spread wide open for him. A sense of that vulnerability mixed with extreme arousal overcame her, scared her. Suddenly, desperately, she needed some form of control, some ability to impact what came next when she had none now. "Blake, I—"

"We'll talk later," he said, and with a hot flick of his gaze over her breasts, he leaned down and licked her clit. And then licked it again, and again, until he suckled her nub with a gentle, perfect pressure that had her lashes lowering, her body quivering. So much for control. She needed a plan, a defense. Right. Defense. That's what she needed. He slipped two fingers inside her sex, stroking her, pleasing her. She moaned and decided the plan could wait until later.

CHAPTER
SEVEN

S he shattered for him, the sweet honey of her release teasing his tongue and thickening his ridiculously hard cock. The already insane and intense ache to be inside Kara deepened, became nearly unbearable, but it was the kind of ache he knew how to satisfy, the kind that he often sought as an escape from the torment of the past two years. Finally he was with this woman in the place he belonged, in a place where only one thing mattered. Hot, sweaty, forget-everything-else sex. It was the only place the enemy belonged, the only place he could afford to let her, or anyone else for that matter, perhaps, ever again. This was a place, a feeling, he could deal with. This, Blake could embrace.

Just thinking about being naked with Kara again had his blood roaring in his ears, pumping through his body like liquid fire. Blake licked her clit one last time, feeling her tremble and soften into the aftermath of release. He eased her legs off his shoulders, then lifted her from the desk. Her legs wrapped his waist, arms wrapped his neck, and she buried her face in his neck, tangled her fingers in his hair. There was something about her gentle fingers on his scalp, the way she held him, the way her soft curves pressed into his, and her silky hair tickled his cheek, that broke through the fog of desire and allowed an uncomfortable pinching sensation in the center of his chest. Emotion. It was emotion. He hated flipping emotions. Emotions led to attachment, and attachment led to trouble…to loss and pain, and…more trouble. He wanted none of those things ever again, most especially not with the woman formerly known as Tiffany Snow.

He simply wanted to give the one woman he'd ever loved the only send-off he could by way of the slow, painful death of the man responsible. He didn't give a damn who thought that was wrong. He could bet Whitney didn't either considering she was dead and in the ground. Damn it to hell, why was he thinking when he could be fucking? It was past time to get naked and deep inside Kara.

Blake lifted Kara and carried her toward the bed, settling her onto the mattress. He tried to pull away from her, intending to make quick work of undressing, but she wrapped herself around him, and somehow their eyes locked. And Holy shit, the impact of that connection all but knocked him over. His breath lodged in his lungs, and his damn heart raced as if he were running a marathon. He had no idea what it was about this woman, but she reached inside him and twisted him in knots. His gaze dropped to her mouth, her lush, tempting mouth that he wanted to kiss way too damn much for comfort. His teeth ground together, the muscles in his body tightening. It was time to shove Kara into a "fuck only" box, and make damn sure she knew that's where she belonged.

With a low growl, Blake slanted his mouth over hers, devouring her, hungry for that dark place he knew would allow him to escape, to get lost in pleasure. His tongue suckled Kara's, and then delved deeply for a long, seductive lick.

She moaned at his invasion, a delicate, sweet sound when he knew she was anything and everything but sweet. But she sounded sweet now and tasted it, too. Sweet and delicious and addictive. Too addictive. He couldn't stop kissing her. Damn, he needed her wrapped around him, all tight and wet, the way he remembered her feeling in Denver.

With a low growl, Blake tore his mouth from hers, intending to push away and undress, but the creamy expanse of Kara's throat called to him, demanding attention. His lips trailed over it, downward, while his hands caressed her breasts, his mouth finally settled on her quivering belly. He believed her when she'd said Denver had felt "necessary". She was too responsive, too completely his when he touched her, for it to be a lie. His ability to affect her drove him wild, made him even crazier with desire for her. But it was still just sex and he planned to make sure she knew it, too.

He pushed away from her, tugging his shirt over his head. She sat up, her breasts high, her nipples puckered, and kicked away her shoes, lounging in front of him, watching him with a languid quality that reminded him of a regal feline, ready to be served, pleasured. Her gaze followed his jeans and briefs to the ground, her dark lashes lowering over her chocolate-brown eyes, and lingering on the thick jut of his erection. Holy fuck, she was killing him, and the flick of her tongue over her bottom lip that made his cock jerk, told him she knew it, too. She was everything and anything but sweet, and he'd be smart to remember that.

Blake snatched a condom from his jeans before tossing them aside. She scooted to the edge of the bed and held out her hand, her legs opened just wide enough to tease him with a glimpse of what was between. "Can I?" she asked softly.

Damn, she did the "innocent temptress who wasn't innocent at all" role to perfection. And that temptress called to his need for control, a need that had become bigger, more powerful, more demanding, every day since he'd left behind the ATF, every hour he didn't have his revenge.

"Since you asked," he murmured, stepping closer to her.

Her fingers closed around the package he held, her gaze lifting. "You aren't very good at asking."

"I have my moments."

"Just not with me." She ripped open the condom.

"No," he agreed. "Not with you." But he had a soft spot for her. And soft spots were like poison kisses, easily lethal. It angered him. *She* angered him. If only that was all she did to him.

She reached for his cock and he grabbed the condom and pulled her off the bed and against him. "I don't like games."

"I wasn't aware we were playing one." Her gaze cut to his chest, a sign she didn't believe the words.

"Yes. You were and we are, but know this, Kara. Whatever the outcome of this game, I'm going to win." His mouth slanted over hers, crushing her lips to his, his tongue stroking against hers with rough, angry thrusts meant to claim her, claim everything about her, and them, and this night. She moaned and leaned into him and that punch in his gut she so easily created happened all over again. Damn it to hell, he thought again.

Blake flipped her around, pressing her knees into the mattress, and holding one hand on her lower back. "Don't move." He felt the tension in her spine, her desire to resist, and he held her there, waiting for her spine to soften into submission, before he lifted his hand and rolled the condom over himself.

He came back to her, widening her legs and ignoring her anxious look over her shoulder. Blake fit his cock into the slick V of her body and ignored his instinct to ready her, wasted no time with a prelude. He drove into her, hard and deep, and she arched her back, pushing her hips into him. His fingers curled into her hips, and he thrust against her, pulled back, thrust again. Trying his damnedest to send her a message of who was in control and to fuck her out of his system, to fuck himself into the kind of bliss that tore away the memories, the pain, the need, he could never fill. This is what he did. He rode the ride, the woman, the adrenaline, until there was nothing but pleasure. Nothing but release. And then there was just nothing. At least for a while, until next time.

Too soon, the blood pounded deep in his groin, tugging at his balls, at his body, forcing the moment of release, forcing him to let go of the escapism of the moments before he came, and the adrenaline slid away into the muddled darkness of the aftermath of the sex.

Sweat gathered on his brow, his muscles bunched beneath his skin. Blake groaned with the tug of his release, trying to hold back, unable to succeed. He lunged hard into Kara and shook with the intensity of his shaft hitting the deep center of her body, of her muscles clenching around him and pulling his release from him. Time faded into shadows, sensations, pleasure, until he collapsed on top of Kara, and she flattened onto her stomach. The sounds of their breathing filled the room, the sense of reality returning slowly seeping into Blake's mind. The sense of Kara beneath him, of him liking her there, of her feeling right there, with it. The scent of her teasing his nostrils, sweet and feminine, and soft.

Blake started to roll to his side and take Kara with him, but he caught himself a second before he did. What the hell was he doing? Cuddling? Flipping cuddling? He was losing his f-ing mind. Blake rolled off of her and shoved off the bed, standing up and giving her his back, before stalking toward the bathroom, ridding himself of the condom and tossing it into the trash. He glowered at himself in the mirror a moment, but didn't dare leave Kara alone. He had no idea how she'd pulled off drugging him before. He wasn't leaving her an opening to do it again.

He stalked back to the main room and found Kara sitting up, her knees curled to her chest. "Why after you insisted I come here do I feel like you now want me to leave?" she demanded.

Blake snatched up his jeans and started to tug them on. "I don't fucking want you to leave."

"You aren't very convincing," she snapped back. "And you say 'fuck' and 'fucking' a lot."

Blake's hands settled on his hips. "You have a problem with the word 'fuck'?"

"You use it in every other sentence."

"So I've been told." By his brother Royce's wife, Lauren, who was one of the only women he knew who came off sweet and still fought like a tigress. Until Kara. And he liked it. He liked it a little too much. His cock thickened. Apparently, it did too.

"But you don't care enough to stop," Kara commented.

"It's not that I don't care." Blake ran a rough hand through his hair, and he forced his shoulders to relax on a breath. "It's a habit. I picked it up from a client I worked for." He sauntered to the desk chair and sat down, trying not to think about Kara spread wide on the desk. He failed and adjusted his jeans. "Someone would say 'Good morning' and he'd reply with something like 'Good morning and fuck you.' Now where is product I ordered?'" Kara's eyes went wide and Blake grinned. "Or there was this time he took a bite of his food in a restaurant and dropped his fork in distaste and grumbled 'fuck', then glared at the people walking in the door and told them to 'run for their fucking lives'."

Kara laughed, a soft, feminine note that did funny things to his insides. "He sounds both horrible and entertaining."

"He was a jerk but a damn entertaining and efficient one, too. He did his job."

"Which was what?"

"Security."

"Sounds like he might need some protection of his own."

Their eyes locked and held and the air thickened instantly. His muscles bunched, tension rippling through him. If anyone needed protection, it was him from this woman. For now, he'd settle for a distraction. He reached for the phone. "You hungry? I'm ordering pizza. You can go over the restaurant staff with me while we eat."

"Yes," she said softly. "I'm hungry."

The air crackled and damn if he wasn't ready to say "fuck the pizza" and go with her instead. He arched a brow. "For pizza?"

"Pizza. Yes. Cheese." His lips hinted at a smile that said she knew what he was thinking.

"Cheese. Somehow I thought you'd be more complicated than that."

"Sometimes the answers are simple."

Blake snorted. "Rarely."

"I didn't say easy. I said simple. There's a difference."

"Touché," he murmured, releasing a heavy breath on the word. After all, what he wanted was pretty cut and dry, pretty damn simple. Find the enemy. Kill the enemy. And damn it, to save Kara, which should *not* be on the list. And save her from what anyway? Mendez? Richter? Herself?

Blake scrubbed his jaw and turned away from her, reaching for the phone, and hesitating. Kyle was right. She could be undercover with an agency and he could get her killed if he wasn't careful. Considering the last woman he'd tried to save had ended up dead, maybe he needed to just get the hell away from her. But he knew that wasn't going to happen.

Fuckfuckfuck and add about a thousand more "fucks", because not only was he entangled with this woman, and on dangerous ground, he knew he was going to try to stop saying "fuck" because she wanted him to. He cared what bothered her. He hadn't let himself give a damn what anyone thought in a long while and he didn't want to give a damn now. But he did.

Oh yeah. He was fucked up where this woman was concerned. He might as well order the pizza and stop wasting time trying to convince himself he wasn't.

Then he'd "fuck" her again and hope she didn't do him "Denver style" afterwards.

CHAPTER

EIGHT

When Kara heard Blake order four pizzas, her blood ran cold at what seemed the certainty that guests were coming. She wasn't waiting around to be dessert for a bunch of Blake's crew, who surely he'd called to San Francisco. What had she been thinking to come here alone? And why did she keep thinking that sleeping with a monster was anything but sleeping with a monster? He was one of them. She hated them.

Kara waited until Blake turned his head to try to locate the address for the delivery order and she scrambled across the bed and snatched up his shirt (since he'd destroyed the buttons on hers, damn him) and tugged it over her head. Next, she darted for her skirt halfway across the room. She silently cursed when she heard him hang up the phone and adrenaline raced through her with the urgency to dress. A second before she'd been about to claim her garment, his hand shackled her wrist.

"What do you think you're doing?" he demanded as they both straightened.

"I'm not your crew's chew toy, Blake. I know you think I'm some sort of whore, but I'm not. I'm—"

"What? What in the hell are you talking about, Kara? Chew toy? My crew?"

71

"You heard me. I'm not a toy for you and your crew to pass around. I don't care what Mendez told you. I'm not. Let me get dressed and either treat me with respect and let me help you do your job or I'm leaving."

"Wait." He shook his head, looking truly baffled. "You think I have people coming here and I plan to let them use you however they please?" He glanced at the phone and back at her. "How did me ordering pizza turn into this?"

"Don't play naive. It doesn't suit you."

"Sweetheart, I wasn't even naive the day my mama popped me out and the doc slapped my ass. But apparently I do need the just-born-yesterday version of where this assumption came from because not only is no one else coming over. I'm not big on sharing."

Kara drew back to study him closer, taking in the strong lines of his masculine face, the openness of his normally shielded dark eyes. He really seemed sincere in his claim. "But you ordered four pizzas."

"Well, yeah. Of course I did. There are two of us."

"I won't eat two pizzas."

"One for you and two for me. Then an extra for breakfast."

Her brows dipped. "You can eat that much pizza?"

"I like pizza." Amusement danced in his dark eyes. "So…you assumed I was bringing in 'the crew' because of the pizza I ordered?"

She blinked. "Well, I—"

"Overreacted," he finished, pulling her close, his strong arms wrapping around her and his long dark hair tickling her cheek, and her senses right along with it.

"If you're telling the truth," Kara bargained, trying to ignore the slow spread of heat through her limbs, "prove it and let me get dressed."

"I like you better naked."

She ground her teeth and tried to push away from him. He held her easily. "No one is coming but you aren't getting dress. You drugged me, Kara. I'm not giving you a chance to do it again."

"I can't be naked every time we're together, Blake."

"Every time we're alone suits me just fine."

She ignored the erotically charged reply that only made her more aware of his broad, well-muscled, bare chest. "How are we going to work together if you don't trust me?"

"And you trust me?" he challenged.

"No, I don't trust you. Why would I?"

"Exactly. No one trusts each other in this world." He surprised her, sliding his hand under her hair and pulling her mouth to his. She surprised herself by not even trying to shove away. The feel of his hard body next to hers, his powerful arms holding her, was just too overwhelmingly right, even when it should be wrong.

His lips brushed hers, tongue teasing hers in a feather-light touch that left her trembling with need. "Taste that?" he murmured, his breath a soft, hot whisper teasing her lips with the promise of another kiss she desperately wanted. "Taste how much we want each other?"

"Yes," she whispered before she could stop herself, but then it wasn't like he didn't know she'd just melted into him, that he possessed the power to easily seduce her.

"And how easily," he continued, "we escape the distrust between us when we're touching each other?" The words lingered in the air, the crackle of desire between them nearly combustible. He was right. At this moment, she could forget everything but him. She could get lost and…and just like that, he released her, stepped back from her, denying her his touch.

"Our hot encounters, Kara, are the closest thing to trust you'll get in this life, and with someone else, they might get you killed. They make you drop your guard like you did to me in Denver. Get out while you can, Kara. My offer still stands to help you do it. Mendez will never know. I can make you disappear and whatever problem you are trying to deal with by working for him."

An offer to be his kept woman shouldn't make her stomach flip-flop, but it did. In some demented and odd way it called forward her long-dead schoolgirl Prince Charming fantasies. Only in those fantasies, Prince Charming hadn't been a criminal. It was a sobering thought that snapped her back to reality. "No," she whispered. "That's just another way of being on someone's payroll. I'm not interested."

"I'm offering to get you out, not keep you in with me. Cash, living comfortably, and anything else you need, for as long as you need it."

Baffled, she stared at him. "Why would you want to help me? You barely even know me. And I didn't think…"—she stopped herself from saying "men like you"—"…just why?"

Shadows danced deep in his brown eyes, the same tormented kind she'd seen that night in Denver. "You aren't lost yet." His voice was a rasp of sandpaper. "Not like me."

Her mind replayed something she'd said to him back in Denver. If I can be saved, then so can you. He'd replied *We aren't even in the same universe. Believe me. I'm lost. You can still be found.* Emotion welled in her chest with the certainty of some deep pain haunting this man. She was right. There was more to Blake than met the eye.

But could she be saved? It depended on how this mission ended. It depended on what it forced her to do. And she'd do anything, absolutely anything to get what she'd come for. "You don't know me well enough to know that."

"I know. I know because I still see hope in your eyes."

It was all she could do to not press her fist to the ache in her belly his words created. She did have hope. It was small but it was real, and she was desperate to discover it was for good reason. But that hope had everything to do with why she couldn't walk away.

"I'll make you a deal," she said, fighting the tightness in her throat. "I'll let you save me the day you let me save you."

"I told you, Kara, I can't be saved. I've made my choices. I have my reasons for staying my course. I'm headed to hell and I've accepted that."

And to make this "hope" reality she knew that she was headed the same place. "Then I guess I'll see you there."

His eyes narrowed, sharpened. "I find it hard to believe that a woman who's working in a dangerous environment to take care of a sick mother would welcome a trip to hell."

"How do you know about my mother?"

"I had someone inside the company files before I ever walked into the building." And, thanks to the contract he and his brothers had with a large number of airports, he'd been able to charter Kyle to San Fran the minute he'd known his destination. "I know what your HR file, DMV, and any other public record in existence says about you. I know Richter and Mendez believe you're doing this to pay for your mother's medical." He closed the distance between them, towering over her again, the heat of his body radiating into hers. "I believe that's what you set them up to believe; otherwise you'd jump at my offer to get out."

"How does being in debt to someone else inside this life get me out, Blake? At the pay Mendez gives me, I only have to work here a year to leave on my own, on my terms."

"No one leaves Mendez on their terms. Why do you think I contract only for my clients? So they don't own me, Kara."

"Mendez doesn't own me."

"He does. You just don't know it yet. Or else you know something I don't know, and I'm leaning in that direction." A knock sounded on the door and Kara almost jumped. "That would be our pizza," Blake said. "Not my 'crew'." He reached up and gently slid her hair behind her ear, then leaned in close, his lips brushing her earlobe. "I'm not buying your life story and, one way or the other, be it you telling me, or me finding out on my own, I'm going to discover the truth." He stepped away from her and walked toward the door.

Kara stared after him, barely able to breathe, frozen in place. Time stood still and her mind raced. She was in so much trouble with Blake, it would take a shovel and ten men she didn't have to dig her out.

"Kara, can you grab the drinks?" Blake called from the door.

Grab the drinks? That snapped her back to reality. She was in a t-shirt and nothing else. Kara scurried to peek around the corner to find the door angled so that Blake's body blocked her from view.

"I'm here," she said, and he handed her two liters of soda. Kara rushed away from the view of the door as he called out,

"Order some ice, will you?"

Ice. Right. Kara set the drinks on the nightstand and headed to the desk. By the time she called downstairs, Blake was placing the pizza boxes on the bed, inspecting the contents of each. It was an odd moment to Kara, as if they were some normal couple sharing a hotel snack. And she was going along with it, as if she didn't know he was going to discover who she was, and then she'd be dead.

***

He'd slept with the enemy and now he was eating pizza with the enemy. On a bed. With her leaned against the headboard, her long, sexy legs stretched out beside his, hers crossed at the ankle. And she was wearing only his shirt. Which he liked her in a little too much.

This wasn't the first time Blake had slept with an enemy, or shared a meal with one for that matter. It wasn't the first time he couldn't keep his eyes off the enemy either. Only this time it wasn't out of concern he might be stabbed in the back if he looked away. It was because Kara, with her long dark hair and creamy white skin, seemed to seduce him simply by being there. There was only one other woman who'd ever compelled him as she did. That he didn't know if she was the true enemy was a problem he had to fix yesterday.

"Cat got your tongue?" he asked, reaching for his third slice.

"You have a lot of pizza to eat. I figured I better let you get to it but..."

He finished off a bite and arched a brow at her hesitation. "But?"

"I have ideas on who's stealing from Mendez." She placed a slice of pizza on a napkin. "I brought the data to show you. I really want to show you but it's in my briefcase."

"What ideas?" He filled his glass with soda and offered her more with a lift of the bottle. "And have you told Mendez?"

Kara held out her glass. "This person cheating him is a family member of Mendez's. I'm not sure how he'll take it."

"So you'd rather I deliver the bad news?" he asked, setting the bottle back on the nightstand.

"Seems a smart choice to me."

He inclined his head in agreement. "As smart as packing a weapon which I assume you know how to use?"

"Yes."

"How'd you learn to shoot?"

"My father," she said without hesitation but her voice soft, barely there.

"The fisherman."

She rotated to her knees to face him. "Don't."

"Don't what, Kara?"

"Don't try to figure me out."

"Why?"

"Because it's wasted energy when I can give you what you want."

Her. He wanted her. His fingers curled on into his fist. No, damn it. He wanted Alvarez and he wanted him dead. "Which is what, Kara? What do you think I want?"

"To impress Mendez."

She wasn't wrong. Mendez was his ticket to Alvarez. "Go on."

"It's his nephew. He runs the shipping operation."

"Did you tell the former head of security?"

"He was in on this entire theft ring."

"You seem certain."

"If you let me have my briefcase, I'll show you why you should be, too."

Blake considered her a moment and pushed off the mattress, grabbing the pizza boxes and setting them on the desk before returning to the side of the bed. With his hands on his hips, he studied her. "You want your briefcase; tell me how you drugged me."

She hesitated, her lips thinning, but she agreed. "Fine. Yes. I'll tell you. It wasn't hard. The drug I used makes you pass out within ten minutes of contact with the skin."

Holy hell. Blake didn't even want to think about how dangerous that could be in the wrong hands. His simple mission to kill Alvarez had just gotten as complicated as reading a map after a bottle of bourbon. "What drug?" he demanded tightly. "I need a name."

"I don't know the name."

"I don't believe you."

"Right. We have trust issues. You've told me."

His jaw tightened. "Start with how and when you used it on me."

"It comes in thin white strips. You can rub them on any surface of an object or directly on the skin. Once a person touches it, the drug absorbs into the blood stream. So…you see. I was telling the truth before. I didn't have to stay with you that night in Denver. I could have placed the drug on the folder and left right after I got to your room."

Their eyes locked and held, the air crackling with electricity.

Blake let this fears over this new drug slide away, his need to know where she was going with this suddenly all that mattered. "And yet you didn't leave."

"No," she said softly. "I stayed."

"Why, Kara? Why did you choose to stay with me?"

NINE

Why? Blake's question hung in the air and Kara didn't know the answer. Why hadn't she left that Denver hotel room without sleeping with him? She'd contemplated that question over and over in the past week, unable to stop thinking about him. She didn't have an answer besides that she'd been feeling alone, as if the world was on her shoulders. She was alone. No one was helping her. Whatever she made happen, she made happen. And in his eyes, she'd seen pain and torment so like what she felt, that she had actually believed, if only for one night, they might just save each other. And they had, or he had her. He'd taken her away, made her feel whole again in a way no stranger should be able to. She'd needed it and him.

"Kara," Blake prodded.

Her gaze snapped back to his, from the floor where it had settled. "I stayed with you and I didn't have to. It's the only answer I have. I just...I don't want you thinking I slept with you to get that file. And I didn't want to drug you. I struggled to go through with it."

"But you did," he observed again, but his eyes were softer now, his voice gentler.

"I had to. You have to know that." And she had. Just not for the reasons he thought and damn if her stomach didn't knot with the half-lie. How could she feel guilty for lying to a man who'd kill her if he knew the truth? Or at least hand her over to someone who would?

"Yes," he said after an eternal silence. "You had to."

Relief washed over her that she told herself was about gaining his trust, avoiding danger, but it was more than that. When she'd looked in his eyes in Denver, she'd felt a connection she couldn't seem to shake.

"You shouldn't have been there at all," Blake continued. "You helped Richter gain leverage over both of us. He'll wait for the right time and blackmail us both because he knows what we both know. Mendez won't be happy about you helping Richter or me letting myself get drugged."

But she hadn't been working for Richter at all, and Blake was too smart not to figure that out if she didn't distract him and fast. "Then we have to stop these theft issues. That has to help us with Mendez."

"Don't kid yourself. No matter what good you do for him, if Mendez finds out you undermined him, it won't matter. We need a plan if he tries. I'll have my team work on something we can use as leverage on him but if he contacts you, I have to know right away."

"I'll get your briefcase," Blake said, heading to the hallway where he'd left his bag.

Kara pressed her hand to her knotted stomach, feeling like she was swimming in the quicksand of her lies and she had this wild, ridiculous urge to tell him everything. She barely contained a nearly hysterical laugh at how deadly a mistake that would be.

Blake returned and set her case on the bed between them. "Show me what you've found."

Seizing the chance to shift the topic from Richter, she quickly removed her MacBook Air and powered it up. "When I first told Mendez about the discrepancies," she explained, settling against the headboard, her legs stretched out in front of her, "I hadn't put two and two together. The data showed random places where the restaurant data and the pier 'special product' shipment numbers didn't match. But since then, I've found four more cities with those kinds of discrepancies, and…" She clicked on a collage of photos, showing two men exchanging envelopes and turned the screen for him to see more clearly. Blake moved to sit next to her, their bodies aligned from hip to foot. She swallowed against the dryness in her throat, and continued. "That's Ignacio, the nephew," she said, pointing out the man on the left with a scar down his cheek and long black hair. "The one on the right is Alex Gomez. He's the regional manager for the restaurants here locally."

Blake stared at the photo and then glared at Kara. "You took these shots?"

"Yes."

He rotated to stare at her. "Are you flipping nuts, Kara? If you would have been caught—"

"I used a long-range zoom lens. I wasn't even close to them. The fact that was able to, though, tells you how poorly they're running the operation." Kara pulled up another picture, this one of a small boat floating next to a larger one, and men loading it with boxes. "It looks like they skim the product right here on the pier. Once it leaves though, I'm clueless. I don't know where it's going or who might be involved. I just know Ignacio is where it starts."

He cut her a sideways look. "You're just a secretary, my ass."

She bristled. "I'm offended by that statement for every secretary that saves her boss's ass about ten times a day."

His lips twisted wryly. "When's the next shipment out?"

"Midnight tonight." She glanced at the clock. It was already ten. "In two hours."

"Then I think tonight is the night Ignacio meets the new head of security."

Kara shut her computer. "I want to go."

"No."

"I can point out things you wouldn't see right away."

"I'm not putting you in danger."

Kara felt like she was in the Twilight Zone. A few hours ago, she was worried he'd want to kill her. Now, she was convincing him she didn't need to be protected. This was just…odd. "I thought you weren't letting me out of your sight? I could still run."

"You won't."

"Are you 100% sure?"

His lips thinned. "Fine, you can ride along, but you're staying in the truck."

"Fine, but that won't keep me from running. You'll need me by your side."

"I'll cuff you to the wheel."

Her eyes went wide. "You wouldn't."

"Try me." He didn't give her time to ask if he even had a set of cuffs, before he ordered, "Get dressed. We have a stop before we go to the pier."

"What stop?"

"Your place."

Kara blanched. "My place?"

"That's right. I'm moving in. That way you are in my sights all the time."

"No. You can't." He couldn't. This was bad.

"I am." He rounded the corner to the hallway, disappearing out of her view, and she could hear him doing something with his bag.

Kara's mind raced for a way out of this, but she was coming up blank. Blake had already seen beneath her story and while she was smart enough to have nothing damaging lying around her place—she was too well trained for that—it didn't matter. Blake would see the facade of a real life in her fluffy decor and use it to unwrap the truth. He'd confirm what he suspected, that her life as she'd put it on paper was fiction.

"Hop to it," he said, reappearing and tugging a shirt the rest of the way down his chest, and over his rippling, spectacular abs. "Let's get out of here."

"I live in a tiny studio. You won't like it."

His eyes danced with mischief and heat. "All the better to get to know you in."

"What if I don't want you to stay with me?"

"Sorry, darlin'." He scooped up his socks. "This time if you drug me and I pass out it's going to be in your bed."

***

Blake pulled up to a parking meter behind Kara's car as she parked, and glanced at her apartment directly to his left, which was more a wooden house broken into small units and framed by two more just like it. Kara killed her lights and he quickly dialed Kyle for the second time since leaving the hotel ten minutes before.

The instant Kyle answered, he said, "You had to park in front and under a streetlight? Thanks for making it impossible for me not to be seen."

"If your job was easy," Blake said, unzipping his bag to remove the plastic bag holding a glass Kara had used in the hotel, "you wouldn't like it."

Kyle started to grumble and Kara got out of her car. Blake hung up on him, setting the bag with the glass on the seat and hoping they'd get a match on her identity. He snatched up his duffle and the pizza boxes, then climbed out of the truck, feeling tension coil in his gut. Not only did he have Kara to figure out—and yes, protect because he couldn't fight the feeling he needed to—he was damn worried about this drug. A substance like that could be a terrorist weapon, and Blake couldn't pretend it didn't exist just to achieve his own agenda. He had to find the source of that drug and destroy it. If he couldn't, no matter how much he didn't want to get his old club involved, he was going to have to bring in the ATF.

He met Kara at the hood of his truck and he didn't miss the nervous look on her face, but she shivered against the year-round chilly San Francisco night air and quickly headed toward the door. "Home sweet mansion," she said when she'd unlocked the apartment and flipped a light on the inner wall.

Blake stepped inside the warm entryway, and glanced up a flight of stairs that seemed to lead directly to a dimly lit living area. Kara flipped the lock into place and he followed her to the next level.

At the top, Blake found himself standing inside a small studio with light hardwood floors, a living area with one red leather couch and a chair, and to its right, a canopy bed. Kara's canopy bed, where he would be sleeping with her. The wild, wicked things he could do to her in that bed heated his blood, as it would most men, but for reasons unknown to him, his chest tightened with emotion right along with his groin.

Kara delicately cleared her throat. "Let me take that pizza. You'll be glad you brought it. I don't have much in the fridge."

"I'll fix that tomorrow."

Kara wet her lips, reminding him of how soft they were pressed to his, and looking nervous in the process. He didn't think she got nervous often. "Right," she said. "Of course." She rushed off to the small kitchen opposite the living area and he let his bag drop to the ground, taking in the room. There were pictures of San Francisco and little trinkets on a table and bookshelf, but not one personal item. It looked like one of the places they would set up as part of a cover.

Kara returned and motioned to a partitioned wall near the bed. "I'll change so we can get out of here."

Blake watched her disappear around the makeshift wall, her shadow reflecting from behind it, a teasing silhouette of her undressing. He ground his teeth against the tightening of his groin. Kara wasn't what she seemed, but she awakened something inside him, something he'd thought died with Whitney, something more than passion. The raw, seeping wound inside him, dark with emotion, was still there, but there was more now. There was...hope.

Grimacing, he ran a rough hand through his hair and turned away from the screen. If he fell for this woman and she burned him, he wasn't sure he had it in him to get back up again. He wasn't going to fall for her. He'd protect her. That was it.

Blake drew a deep breath and turned right back around again, proving to himself this woman did not have him by the throat, just the balls and he could pry her hand off those. His gaze went to her silhouette, the shadows outlining her naked body as she reached for a pair of pants. Blake's cock went instantly rock hard and his control, the control he'd claimed to own so fully, threatened to snap. After a moment of fighting it, he decided to embrace what he was feeling and make sure she did, too. He stalked across the room and around the panel, the sweet, feminine scent of Kara slamming into him almost as fiercely as her creamy-white naked body.

She gasped as he drew her into an embrace, his mouth closing down on hers, commanding her to give herself to him, his tongue seducing hers into a response. Her body softened almost instantly, and it turned him on, and then pissed him off. She was good at turning him on. Too good.

He pressed her against the wall, twined his fingers into the dark silk of her hair, and forced her gaze to his. "It would be better for you to tell me who you are now, on your own."

"I'm Kara," she panted. "I've always been Kara."

"End the game here and now," he growled. "Don't make me do it for you."

"You think this is a game to me? This has never been anything further from a game to me."

"What do you call secrets and lies? A game. A dangerous game. You have nothing personal here, not even a picture of your mother."

"If I have her picture that makes her important to me. There are people, like Ignacio, that might decide that means she's worth hurting."

"And yet you told Mendez and Richter."

"I did what I had to and a public announcement isn't required."

He glared at her, probed her eyes. "You have an answer for everything, don't you?"

She sucked in a breath, a tormented look flashing in her eyes. "No. If I did, I wouldn't be here."

More of the game, but beneath it was real pain and it spoke to him. He knew it, understood it, and owned it with far more gusto than he wished to claim. And he wanted to own her. It was a barbaric thought, but he owned it for that, and for where it came from. If he owned her, he'd take her someplace far away from here, and keep her safe. He was damn near desperate to keep her safe and he knew why, he knew the past was messing with him, he knew he couldn't escape it, or the guilt over Whitney's death that ate him alive.

Bitterness ripped through him and acid burned in that open wound that was a cavern inside him. His mouth came down on Kara's again, rough with anger, at his loss, at Kara for making him care enough to be here right now, ready to bury himself in her, not some nameless woman who didn't give a shit about him. Who wouldn't be around to worry over the next day.

His tongue delved deep into the warm, sweet recesses of Kara's mouth, his hands sliding over her breasts, thumbs teasing her nipples. A haze of lust and desire overcame him, fed into her, and she responded, touching him. He lost himself in the rush of heat over his skin, the silk of her floral-scented hair on his face. He didn't remember how his pants got down or how the condom ended up over his shaft. There was only the sizzle, the touches, the taste of her on his tongue, and the moment he lifted her leg and watched the lines and shadows of desire on her beautiful face as he pressed deep inside her.

Blake framed her face, staring down at her. "Fuck me here and now, and like this, a million times over. But don't fuck me outside of this."

"Blake—"

He kissed her, hard, punishing, because he knew he wasn't looking for a promise she wouldn't keep, but he had one to give her, one he would keep. He tore his mouth from hers, and stared down at her. "You're in over your head and I'm going to keep you safe. The only person who is ever going to kill you is me, and I plan to do it with pleasure." He drove into her and went to work, keeping his vow.

CHAPTER
TEN

Kara was a whirlwind of emotions as Blake parked the truck in the hotel garage they'd left earlier, to be near the pier. There was something happening between them, something she wasn't going to want to walk away from. She kept telling herself it was her using him to hide from the heartache she feared her mission was going to bring to her. But if that were true, it was only true because deep in her soul, she connected with Blake. She felt his pain, too. To believe he was one of them tore her apart. Yet she had every reason to believe he was, and nothing but what he made her feel to believe otherwise.

Blake reached under his leather jacket and gave her gun back. Her gaze lifted to his at the sign of trust that reached so much further than her purse he'd already returned. "You stay in the truck and lock the door," Blake ordered. "But use that if you need to."

"Why not let me introduce you to Ignacio?"

"I don't want you attached to this. I can introduce myself."

"Blake—"

He leaned in and kissed her. "You might be playing with your life, Kara, but I'm not."

She grabbed his arm. "Don't get killed. I'm not done with

you yet."

His lips lifted. "Sweetheart, I'm not done with you either and I don't die easily. You'll figure that out soon enough."

He was out of the truck before she could stop him and knocking on the window to tell her to lock up. She did as he wanted and sat there, watching him saunter away, relieved he'd had someone drop weapons at her door. He'd armed himself to the hilt. Oh, how a day changed things. She went from him being a threat to her worried about the threat to him.

"He's still a threat, Kara," she whispered, warning herself not to forget something so important.

She spent the next twenty minutes reminding herself of that fact, and that twenty minutes turned to forty. She was nervous. What if something had happened to Blake because of her information?

Kara ran her hands down her black jeans, trying to contain her nervous energy. She'd had enough of the sitting-duck routine. She grabbed her purse, and slid the gun inside. She found a piece of paper in her purse and left Blake her cell number. Next she snatched the truck key and put it in her black leather jacket, for easy access if she needed to get out of here quickly.

Once she was out of the truck, she headed toward a building she'd found that offered good coverage for photos just across the street. Five minutes later, she'd squatted behind a wall and removed her binoculars to check out the pier and hopefully locate Blake.

Scanning, she found the pier and her blood ran cold to see it empty. Something was not right. Something was—

"Hola, Kara," came a familiar male voice that made her

blood run cold.

Kara glanced up to find Ignacio standing above her with a gun in his hand. Blake might not be able to keep that promise he'd made earlier. Ignacio wouldn't hesitate to kill her, and there would be no pleasure involved.

CHAPTER
ELEVEN

S he's with me and if you don't drop the gun, I'll take you to visit my pops."

Relief washed over Kara at the sound of Blake's voice and the sight of him holding a gun on Ignacio, though she had no idea what the heck he meant by visiting his "pops". Maybe it was some sort of slang term Ignacio understood but, truly, she didn't care. Only seconds before she'd thought she was dead, about to be shot to death in a dark corner, squatting behind a brick wall. Turned out the retail strip she'd thought a perfect spot to spy on the pier, where the Alvarez Cartel shipped off insane amounts of illicit drugs under Ignacio's supervision wasn't so perfect at all.

"Your pops?" Ignacio snapped. "What the hell does that mean?"

Okay, so apparently Ignacio didn't understand Blake's slang either, but it was distracting him from firing the gun so it worked for her. Kara used the opportunity to ease her hand inside her purse, and close it around the base of her Glock.

"Pops," Blake said with a snort. "My father. The man who donated sperm to birth me so I could hold this gun I'm pointing at your head. Comprende?"

Ignacio chuckled, but it sounded strained. He wasn't amused

at Blake's arrogant, nonchalant smart-ass remarks. Kara was, or she would be if Ignacio wasn't still pointing the damn gun at her. "So our new head of security needs his father to do his dirty work?" Ignacio asked.

Blake shrugged. "What can I say? My pops gets pretty lonely. I hear being dead does that to a guy, though. Would you like to find out for yourself?"

Despite her obviously dire situation, Kara had to choke back laughter that would surely get her a bullet in the head. Oh my God, Blake was crazy and she loved it.

"Do you know who I am?" Ignacio challenged indignantly. He was all about being the boss man's nephew, but didn't seem to mind stealing from the drug shipments behind his uncle's back. Of course, he didn't know they knew that yet.

"Yep," Blake confirmed. "I know who you are. Now ask me if I care."

Kara's lips twitched. Oh yes. Blake was a piece of work all right. It was almost like he was daring Ignacio to shoot him. Oh God. Her stomach knotted with realization. Blake *did* want Ignacio to try and shoot him. He was taunting Ignacio into turning the gun on him. Blake was risking his own life for her; a man she was sure would kill her if he knew the truth of who she was and what she was after. Could she get any more confused or conflicted over this man than she was now? Because damn it, she knew he was aligned with the cartel and was easily someone who would kill her if he knew her secret, but still, she couldn't bear the idea of him dying to protect her.

The cold steel of her weapon comforted her only slightly, considering she couldn't see Ignacio's face through the drape of his long, dark hair to gauge his reaction. The barely lit corridor of the building they were in front of didn't help either, nor did the late hour, but she didn't miss the way his shoulders bunched and his spine stiffened before he added, "My uncle—"

"Won't care if I kill you," Blake assured him. "Not if I give him a good reason for doing it. And I'm real damn good at justifying why I kill people. Put the gun away, or I'll prove just how good. Of course, you won't be around to be impressed, but I'm sure your replacement will be."

"Not until you explain how our meeting ended twenty minutes ago and you're still here."

"The devil is in the details, man," Blake replied, "and I intend to know them all. Consider me the devil in your uncle's pocket. I want to know everything you do and not just what you say you do."

"Mendez is my uncle," Ignacio all but growled. "Check up on someone else."

"He wants me to check up on everyone. You included."

Ignacio stared at Blake. Blake stared at Ignacio. Tension laced the air, thick like quicksand about to swallow them whole. Kara was pretty sure she could feel herself sinking now. Her fingers flexed on her gun, her body tense and ready for action, all too aware that all Ignacio had to do was move his finger and she was dead. Her only comfort was the knowledge that Ignacio knew Blake could kill him just as easily.

Finally, Ignacio moved, holstering his weapon under his leather coat. "You want to see my operation, you ask."

"Why would I do that?" Blake challenged, letting his gun drop to his side and reaching for Kara's hand to pull her to her feet by his side. Protective. Possessive. It was getting harder and harder to remember he was the enemy.

"Because I said," Ignacio growled.

"You got something to hide?" Blake asked.

Kara discreetly stuffed the binoculars she was holding inside her purse; afraid the sight of them would only bring attention to her spying and ignite more trouble.

Ignacio glared at Blake. "Most of my men won't ask questions before they shoot."

Blake arched a brow and holstered his gun under his jacket as Ignacio had done. "Sounds like a good way to draw unnecessary attention to the operation. I'm not sure that's what your uncle has in mind."

"You're good at justifying why you kill someone," Ignacio said. "I'm good at making bodies disappear."

"Interesting," Blake said dryly.

Ignacio scowled. "What does that mean?"

Blake shrugged. "Just taking in the details, man. Finding out who is who in this operation."

Ignacio bristled, clearly not liking that response, and without warning, his gaze snapped to Kara. "Why are you here?"

Kara opened her mouth to reply, but Blake beat her to the punch. "She's here because I want her to be." He wrapped his arm around her shoulders and pulled her under his arm, sending heat darting through her body.

"And how does my uncle feel about you *wanting* his secretary?"

Secretary. Kara liked that word. It downplayed her many skills outside the office. Exactly why she kept her mouth shut. Good little secretaries didn't tell nasty drug-smuggling cartel members to go fuck themselves. Good girls in general didn't tell people to go fuck themselves, but she'd left the good girl behind several months ago.

"Your uncle is pleased to give me whatever resources I need to ensure his operation is without problems," Blake assured him.

"So he loaned you his secretary?"

"I wanted her," Blake stated flatly. "I generally get what I want."

Kara tried to hide the tension coiling in her spine at the obvious declaration that she was now Blake's woman and his property, but she knew his motivation. The men in this world didn't kill each other's women. It was like some unwritten code of honor, when they had so little anywhere else. Blake was trying to protect her, but that didn't make it easier to play the role of his bedroom bunny.

Ignacio's gaze raked over Kara, hot and sticky like a summer day you wanted to escape but couldn't, before he cut Blake a look. "I hope she's as eager to please as my uncle is to punish those who cross him."

"Punishment is underrated," Blake said dryly. "I guess that's why your uncle hired me. I get what he wants. And, on that note, I'll be getting back to work." He drew Kara's hand into his and started to walk away, pulling her with him.

"Wait," Ignacio called, halting them in their footsteps.

Blake turned back to him, casting him an expectant look.

"We've gotten off on the wrong foot," Ignacio said. "Why don't I buy you a drink?"

Blake turned back to him and Kara did the same. "It's a little late for a drink, don't you think?"

"Welcome to my world, where we sleep in the daylight and make the most of the night."

Blake's lips compressed. "Are the restaurants open late?"

"Twenty-four hours," he said. "It keeps the activity looking honest."

"All right then," Blake said. "A drink at one of the restaurants works for me. I'd like to see how they operate."

Ignacio's gaze flicked back to Kara and she saw the suspicion in his stare, the hate. "Will she be joining us?" he asked, as if she wasn't even there when he was looking right at her.

"Yes," Blake said. "She will."

"Excellent," he commented. "Always happy to buy a pretty lady a drink."

Oh yes, Kara thought. He was ready to buy her a drink all right, and then find a creative way to drown her in it. He'd decided she was a problem and he'd stay away from her for now, but later, if he had the chance, he'd smash her like a fly. But he wouldn't get the chance, she reminded herself. She'd smash Ignacio long before he smashed her, if Blake didn't beat her to the punch. She had a feeling he just might.

"Pine Street's the closest location," Kara said tightly, seeing this as an opportunity to get inside the restaurant she'd been scouting for some time, and perhaps inside the back warehouses the cameras kept her away from.

"Pine Street it is," Blake said, lacing his fingers between Kara's. "We'll meet you there." He didn't give Ignacio a chance to reply. He pulled Kara with him and started walking toward the parking garage. His pace was steady and calculated, but she could feel the urgency building inside him, the fire about to combust. It was as if the instant they stepped away from Ignacio, something inside him snapped. Had something just happened or had he been containing this back there with Ignacio? And if he was, my God, how?

"What's wrong?" she asked the instant she felt they were safely out of earshot.

"Not now. Wait."

His tone was sharp, his grip on her hand tight. "Blake—"

"Not," he ground out, "now."

Tension crawled inside Kara and took root, and her hand went to her purse to once again grasp her weapon. She could only assume someone must be following them, close enough that he feared they would be heard if they spoke, or worse. That they were about to be attacked and he was trying to hear a perp's approach. Ignacio was as low as they came. It would be nothing for him to kill them right here and now. And, as he'd said, he was good at getting rid of bodies. She knew that for a fact. Knew it in an intimate way she wished she didn't.

The entrance to the parking garage came into view and Blake seemed to speed up, not slow down at the dimly lit tunnel it resembled. Kara relaxed marginally, seeing that as a sign he felt they were leaving the trouble behind.

Once the truck was in sight, Blake clicked the automatic locks and she rushed to her door and climbed inside, pulling the door shut. She turned to Blake as he did the same, intending to ask questions when he slammed his hands down on the steering wheel. Kara flinched.

"Fuck, fuck, fuck!" he exclaimed, raking fingers through his hair, long, dark strands falling from the tie at his nape and hanging around his face. His grip closed into a vice around the wheel and Kara could see his muscles quivering as he grappled with whatever had him in knots.

She held her breath, waiting expectantly, long seconds ticking by, while Blake clearly stood on the edge of a proverbial cliff about to jump. Kara could feel his tension and she actually felt herself tremble, her stomach knotting with the pain and torment that radiated off of him. Whatever the darkness was that she'd sensed in him the first time she met him had been triggered. Something had reached in deep and dragged it to his surface. It was crazy, but on some unexplainable level, she knew this man, and understood him, knew he was motivated by some deep hurt that carved him inside out. The idea that she could understand an enemy and make him human rather than a monster was a terrifying thought. She wanted to reject the idea. But she couldn't. Not with Blake.

She didn't give herself time to think. She reached for him. The instant she was about to touch him, it was as if he knew. His hand snaked out, fingers wrapping her wrist, and the next thing she knew she was flat on her back with him on top of her.

CHAPTER
TWELVE

She was soft beneath him, and Blake's mouth came down on hers, his tongue caressing hers with desperate, hungry strokes, drinking her in, drowning the past in the present. He hated the past, hated the memories and the way they sideswiped him, controlled him. The past was controlling him now, and in a big way.

One minute he'd been with Ignacio, the next walking away, reliving Whitney bloody and dead in his arms. He'd made it to the truck without being overcome with the acid burn of hate and hurt that memory produced, but it hadn't been easy. And when Kara had touched him and that image of Whitney had transformed, becoming her instead, it had been like a premonition that he was going to get her killed, too. Like she was going to matter to him and he was going to fail her, as he had Whitney. And damn it to hell, he didn't want her to matter. He didn't want to care about Kara or anyone else ever again. He *wouldn't let it happen.* Kara was a tool for revenge, to get to Alvarez, and hot sex along the way. Which was exactly why he was going to fuck her right here in the truck, in the garage.

Blake curved his hand under her hips, shifting his hips to fit into the V of her body, nestling his cock against her. She moaned and arched into him, so freaking soft on the outside, curvy beneath him, the floral scent of her delicate, and yet she was hard, tough, war-ready in a way he'd never suspected the first night in Denver.

Blake licked into her mouth, drank in the sweet honey flavor of her passion, of his passion mixed with hers, feeling the burn of insane need for a woman he barely knew driving him wild. He needed her, and he needed this right now. This was an escape from the rage going on inside him, the certainty he'd gotten Whitney killed, and that he was on the verge of getting Kara killed when he was only trying to save her. An image of Kara lying in his arms as Whitney had flashed in his head again. Damn it to hell, why was he thinking about this again? Why was he thinking at all?

He tried to deepen the kiss, to forget again, but it was too late. He was back into the acid burn of the past, the fear it would become the present. He didn't trust Kara, but he trusted himself even less. Damn it, he was pissed. At himself. At her. At his inability to control what he was feeling and thinking.

Blake tore his mouth from Kara's, staring down at her, their eyes connecting, the cabin of the truck a sauna of desire and lust, and for a moment he could once again think of nothing but how good it would feel to be inside her. She was making him crazy. "Who the *fuck* are you?" he growled through clenched teeth.

Her chin lifted. "I could ask the same of you, because we both know you're more than you seem."

She was smart. Too smart. Too tempting. Too everything. "I'm the bastard who just aligned you with me, life or death, sweetheart."

"Why?" she demanded. "Why save me? You don't even trust

me."

"I might need you." The words, meant to be flippant, hit him hard. *He* might need her, and not just for the job. Damn it to hell, she was twisting him in knots, claiming *him*, not the other way around. He would not let this woman mess with his head and distract him. "I might need you to get what I want," he repeated to prove to himself he could say it again and not have it affect him as it had the first time. It didn't work, and that pissed him off all over again. This was sex damn it. Just sex. "And I damn sure want to fuck you." His mouth closed down on hers again, one hand sliding under her backside, shifting her, and settling his thick erection in the V of her body. His other hand slid over her waist, back up and around her breast.

She moaned and sunk deeper into the kiss, teasing him with wicked little licks that had his cock doing all of his thinking, and, for the moment, that's what he wanted. Finally, yes. He could forget. Ignacio would wait on their arrival. The bleeding ulcer of memories in his mind wouldn't. If he didn't shred them and fast, they'd shred him.

Time disappeared into in a whirlwind of his mouth on her mouth, on her neck, on the swell of her breast above her bra. He shoved her shirt and bra up and suckled her sweet little nipple, and damn, when her fingers sliced into his hair, he felt a shiver of pure pleasure down his spine. Good, too good when he didn't know who she was, what her agenda might be.

Blake pressed her hands over her head, nipped her lip. Damn, he loved her mouth, full and soft, and wickedly feminine. "I should cuff you to the steering wheel and keep you here until you tell me what I want to know." His free hand raked over her naked breast, tweaking the nipple.

"No time," she panted, arching her back. "Ignacio's waiting."

"He's waiting because I want him to wait. If I see him in my current state of mind I might kill him before I get the proof I need to justify it."

"Is that what you're looking for with me? Proof I'm some sort of traitor so you can kill me, too?"

"I don't want to kill you." He lowered his mouth to her ear. "But make no mistake. If you give me a reason to, I will and so will they. Get out while you can. Go and never look back."

"I can't," she whispered, no hesitation. Two simple words etched with a world of pain and desperation.

He pulled back to look at her, trying to read her expression through the shadows in the dimly lit garage. "Why? What does the cartel have on you?"

She turned away, giving him her profile. Still holding her hands over her head, he reached up and framed her face with his free hand, pulling her eyes back to his. "What does he have on you?"

"Nothing. He has nothing."

She was lying. He heard it in the quiver of her voice and he suddenly didn't want to know the truth. He didn't want her to be the enemy. He released her and sat up, sliding behind the wheel and running a rough hand through his hair, his nerves so on edge his skin was twitching. He cut her a sideways look. "No matter how good you think you are at keeping a secret, I'm ten times better at uncovering them. I'm going to find out what you're hiding. You can count on it."

***

Kara slid into a booth at Shivers, a Chili's-style restaurant that drew big crowds, while Ignacio claimed the seat directly in front of her. Blake eased in beside her, settling his leg intimately against hers, and she tried not to think about his confident promise to unveil her secrets. She had to stay focused on the here and now, and hope they might get a tour of the back warehouses she'd been unable to find a reason to get inside. If she could locate the cameras, and the various entrances, then she could enter again without being seen and get a closer look.

"What can I get you to drink?" a waiter asked, stopping at their table with supreme speed.

Ignacio started speaking to the man in Spanish and Kara's gaze shifted beyond his shoulder, to a corner booth where a young, twenty-something blond female in a waitress outfit huddled with the restaurant manager, Eduardo, a bit too intimately to be his employee. Kara's nerves prickled and her fingers curled into her palms. Women had a way of disappearing after coming to work at this location, and it was all she could do not to go yank the girl up and send her home before she got into trouble, or worse, dead. Mysteriously, their HR files were deleted after they went MIA from their jobs, as if they never existed. And the HR person actually claimed they never existed. Kara couldn't push without raising suspicions, but she'd taken to copying every file for the employees as they were made. No one else was going to just disappear without her having proof they'd existed.

"Kara?" Blake's voice snapped her back to the table, and when her eyes met his, she felt that familiar flutter of awareness he so easily created in her.

"Yes?" she answered, barely finding her voice as the memory of being beneath him in the truck swept over her.

"What do you want to drink?" he asked softly, a warm quality to his brown eyes saying he hadn't shaken off their intimate encounter anymore than she had.

"Drink. Right. Yes." Kara cast the waiter an apologetic look, her senses reeling as Blake's hand settled on her leg, heat pooling low in her belly. "Sorry. Coffee, please."

The waiter departed and Ignacio's gaze settled on Kara, his lips twisting snidely. "I thought I was buying you a drink?"

"I prefer a clear head," she replied tightly. *And a steady hand on my gun.*

"Talk to me about the staff here at the restaurant," Blake said, pulling Ignacio's attention to him, and Kara had the distinct impression it was intentional. He didn't like Ignacio focusing on her. That made two of them.

Ignacio stared at her several more seconds that felt like an eternity before shifting his attention to Blake. "What do you want to know?"

"Who's in the know about the true nature of the operation?"

"The restaurant runs like any other with a staff who know no differently. Eduardo, the manager, and the entire warehouse staff are, as you say, '*in the know*.'"

"How many does that make?"

"Thirty, mostly non-English-speaking illegals who do our handling."

"What time do the daily shipments go out?"

Kara watched Ignacio's jaw flex, a subtle sign he didn't like to be questioned. But then, no one had questioned him in a long time. "Ten. That allows us the coverage of restaurant traffic."

"And who's in charge of overseeing the product making it to the pier?" Blake asked.

"Eduardo signs it out and I personally sign it in."

"Every day?" Blake pressed. "Seven days a week?"

"Monday and Thursday only," Ignacio corrected. "The Coast Guard has a bigger presence on the weekends. We still run the boats, but without product."

Kara's gaze flicked back to Eduardo and the girl as they got up and headed toward the back. A powerful urge to follow, to know the girl was okay, if only for now, overcame her. "Excuse me," Kara said. "I need to go to the ladies' room." She snatched up her purse and didn't look at Blake or Ignacio, but Kara could feel Blake's eyes on her, hot and heavy, and she knew she wouldn't have long before he'd come after her.

Quickly, Kara cut behind the bar, following Eduardo and the girl into the hallway that led to the bathroom and a series of offices that she'd tried to get into once before but found locked. The hallway was empty but one of the office doors was cracked open.

Kara eased her way to the wall by the opening, flattening against the wall, and she could just barely make out Eduardo's voice. "I need the blonde," he said. "Now. Tonight."

"I can't get her here until tomorrow night. She said she has to—"

"The boat leaves at 4am. Tomorrow night is too late."

"Eduardo—" The female yelped. "Ouch. You're pulling my hair. It hurts."

"I said I need her here tonight. If she isn't on that boat that goes out you'll be on it instead, which means you'll be everyone's fuck buddy on the island."

"I'll find a girl."

"That girl. It has to be her. We've cleared her records

already."

Kara's stomach rolled. She'd been right. They were running some sort of sex operation with the women they made disappear. She didn't want to think about what that meant for her personal agenda. She couldn't. Not now, or she might lose it and go in that office and shoot Eduardo. That wouldn't get her the answers she so desperately needed.

"Go get her," he ordered, and Kara whirled to escape and smacked into a hard body. *His body.* Her nostrils flared with the spicy, familiar male scent of him and she knew even before her gaze lifted that Blake was standing there.

His hands closed gently around her upper arms, those dark brown eyes of his searching hers. "What are you up to, Kara?" he murmured softly.

A second later, a woman yelped behind her. Kara cringed. This wasn't going well. Not at all.

"What's going on here?" she heard Eduardo say, clearly having joined the girl.

"Looking for the bathroom," Kara blurted, whirling around to face Eduardo and the girl only to have Blake's hands settle on her shoulders, his big body pulling hers against his.

"Yes," he said. "Can you tell her where the bathroom is?"

Eduardo, a tall man with short, spiky black hair, narrowed his eyes on Kara and then let them lift to Blake. "Behind you."

"Right," Kara said. "Thank you." She turned away and darted for the women's restroom, while Blake introduced himself to Eduardo.

Kara cleared the doorway to the restroom and leaned on the sink, thankful the two stalls beside her appeared to be empty. Her heart hammered in her chest, and not just because that was too close a call. Because she'd confirmed what she feared was happening to the women that had gone missing. Because Blake's hands on her shoulders, the protective, possessive thing he kept doing, felt too good and too right. And because he was going to ask questions she didn't want to answer. Now he was going to push her harder. The only real comfort she had in all of this was that the missing women, one in particular, were likely alive. She just had to figure out where they were.

The door to the bathroom opened and she whirled around to find Blake stepping inside. "What are you doing?" she demanded, only to find herself against the door with Blake's legs framing hers, his hands curving around her waist. Heat shot through her body, fogging her brain. Damn it, no man affected her like this until now. Why why why did it have to be him?

"What are you doing is more the question," he said. "And don't tell me looking for the bathroom."

Lying in this case would get her nowhere. And she hated lying to him anyway. "I saw the open door and heard voices. I thought I might hear something useful."

"You had a gun at your head once tonight. You really do like to live dangerously, don't you?"

Her throat went dry. She had. He was right. And he'd tried to save her. "You tried to get Ignacio to point that gun at you instead of me. Why?"

Surprise flickered in his eyes. "Why?"

"Why?"

"I told you," he said softly. "I might need you." His lips quirked. "Besides, it's what us macho men do, baby."

It was one of his flippant remarks that he did so well but it was flat without the cocky attitude he'd mastered like no one she'd ever known. There was more to this man than met the eye, and she wanted him to surprise her. She wanted him to be someone he wasn't. But isn't that what all women who got mixed up with a man like him wanted? What they convinced themselves was possible to justify being with a man destined to destroy them?

And still, with that logic playing in her mind, she found herself gently touching his face, letting her fingers trail over the dull stubble of a new beard, her chest tight with emotion. "Thank you."

He reached up and covered her hand with his. "For what?"

"For saving my life." She wet her lips. "I owe you."

"You don't owe me anything."

It was another unexpected answer. A man like him would be expected to hold people captive, use everything against them. But he wasn't.

"I take that back," he said. "You owe me—"

The door moved behind them and Blake held it shut. Kara wanted to scream with the interruption that kept her from knowing what he'd been about to say. Before she could find out if he would prove himself like the others in the cartel, holding her for ransom.

"Quickly," Blake pressed, "what did you overhear from Eduardo?"

"Nothing." She cut her gaze to his chest before she could stop herself, a sure sign of a lie to a trained eye. "I didn't have time to catch anything. They were already leaving the office." She tried to push away from him. He held onto her and damn it, her gaze lifted to his.

He stared down at her, his eyes keen, too keen, and suddenly his fingers were under her hair, wrapping her neck. He pulled her hard against him, his mouth slanting over hers, his tongue stroking hers in a short, intense kiss that she dared to let herself revel in. Too soon, though, the door jerked behind them again and he tore his mouth from hers, his eyes capturing hers. "You do know we're going to talk when we get back to your apartment, right?"

"Talk?" she asked innocently.

"That's right," he assured her. "And, depending on how cooperative you are, handcuffs may or may not be involved."

Kara swallowed hard, feeling heat radiate down her spine. He meant it. He'd cuff her and torment her, tease her, drive her to the edge of orgasm and pull her back until she was going insane. And she just might, because there was no way she could confess anything to him. There was too much to lose.

"And when do you talk, Blake?" she challenged.

"Talking isn't my specialty, as you'll find out tonight."

He pushed off the door and pulled her around to exit before she could say more, and she had the distinct impression he didn't like where this conversation was going. Even more so when he quickly pulled her into the hallway, where they found Ignacio and Eduardo waiting on them. Somehow, she doubted that was a good thing.

THIRTEEN

Y ou two need a private office or what?" Ignacio asked.

"Yeah," Blake said. "Yours up for grabs?" He glanced at Ignacio. "Or maybe yours?"

"Aren't you the funny man?" Eduardo asked sarcastically.

"Ha ha," Blake said. "Only I wasn't joking. I need an office to work out of. This seems like as good a location as any."

"The way he eats," Kara commented, "a restaurant might not be a bad idea."

"She has a point," Blake said approvingly. "Food at my disposal is always a plus."

"No space to spare here," Eduardo said. "I guess you'll have to try another location."

"Maybe in the warehouse," Blake countered. "Why don't you take me on a tour?"

Eduardo crossed his arms in front of his chest. "It's closed for business tonight, but hey, if you want to see a bunch of pallets, sure. We'll take you on a tour."

"We'll risk being bored," Blake assured him.

"Come back tomorrow night," Ignacio said. "The crew will be here. You can see everything."

Or nothing, Kara thought. Tonight was about women and

sex, not drugs, and damn it, she wanted to launch herself at both of these men and throttle them.

"That works," Blake said, surprising Kara. "What time tomorrow night?"

"Nine," Eduardo said. "That lets you see the entire process."

"Nine it is," Blake agreed.

It was all Kara could do not to gape and then object, but already Blake was ushering her away, his hand firmly wrapping her upper arm. In a blink, she was leaving behind a chance to see the warehouse and headed for the exit. She had a bad feeling she wouldn't be coming back with him tomorrow.

The instant they were out of the building, the cool San Francisco night air whipping around her, she challenged him. "Why would you leave without seeing what they might be hiding?"

Blake cut her a sideways look and clicked the lock of the truck on the key ring. "Ignacio would have called and told them we were coming. There's nothing to see they don't want us to see."

"Tomorrow there definitely won't be anything for us to see. We didn't give them much warning tonight, and what about getting an idea of the layout and trying to ensure a way back in when they don't expect us?"

He stopped at the tail of the truck and turned to look at her. "And all of this is the thought process of a secretary?"

She drew back slightly. "You think a secretary can't logically think through how to deal with a problem? We have a theft issue."

He scrubbed his jaw and laughed. "Well played, Kara. You're good. Fast-talking and sharp with your answers. Just not as good as me. I'm not buying your motivation."

She ignored the remark. What else could she do? "My gut says we need to tour tonight. We'll discover something we need to find."

His lips compressed. "Because you overheard something you didn't tell me about."

"No." Damn, her voice squeaked. She was so bad at lying to him for some unnerving reason. "Because, like I said, my gut says so."

"Give me more than that or we aren't going back in."

She inhaled and forced it out. "We need to go back in."

"Not a good enough answer."

"Damn it, Blake—"

His grip curled around her arm and he gently, but insistently, pulled her against him. "You're too on their radar and we're going to get you off." He kissed her, fast and hard. "End of story." He released her. "Now get in the truck."

She glowered at him, furious. She didn't like being ordered around. She didn't like him playing protector when she knew he was one of them, able and willing to slice her throat if he gave her reason. He'd all but said so in the truck earlier. And she was going to give him reason to do it when he discovered her identity. Time was everything for all kinds of reasons. What would he do if she headed back to the building besides follow?

"Don't do it," he said softly, telling her he'd read her mind. "You won't like how I respond."

Kara studied him, considering the threat, her breathing labored when it should be controlled, her anger barely contained. She wasn't afraid of him. No. That wasn't true. She was afraid of him, and how irrational he made her act. And she was afraid of dying before she did what she'd come here to do. "I don't need a bodyguard, and that's not what you were hired to be. Mendez hired you to solve the theft problem."

"Says the woman who had a gun pointed at her head tonight and needed a bodyguard."

Her fingers curled by her sides. "I was trying to find you. I was afraid something had happened to you." Her stomach knotted all over again with that confession. One minute she was thinking he was a killer, and the next trying to protect him. She was conflicted, screwed up beyond reason, over this man.

He arched a brow. "Were you now?"

"Yes. You were gone too long." She grimaced and played the same cards he had in the truck. "Nothing can happen to you. I might need you."

"You might need me?"

His eyes heated and damn it, so did her skin. "To get this theft issue under control."

"So you thought I needed a bodyguard?" His eyes twinkled with mischief. He was way too amused by the direction of this conversation.

Kara grimaced. She wasn't winning the battle to go back inside so she'd pick one she had a shot at. "That's it. This conversation is over. Let's go back to my place and see who can cuff who first. As angry you're making me, I'm betting I get the upper hand." She turned and headed to the truck.

His deep, sexy laughter followed. It rippled down her spine and settled in low and hot in her belly. The man got to her way too easily. Oh yeah. She'd be cuffing him all right and enjoying every second of it. Then she'd slip out and find the blond girl before she ended up on some drug cartel main menu.

***

Blake followed Kara up the stairs to her apartment, locking the door behind him, his blood pumping hot, adrenaline pulsing through him. He wanted this woman. Damn it to hell, he wanted her in a bad way. Bad enough that it was time for answers. Time he knew who he was climbing into bed with.

He watched her hips sway as she headed up the stairs and followed in hot pursuit, anticipation burning through him, his cock already thick with arousal. Her long dark hair lay like silky strands down her back and he imagined it draped over his stomach with her mouth on his shaft, caressing him into the sweet bliss of escape. The instant she stepped onto the top level landing of the apartment, he had every intention of scooping her up and taking her to bed. He never got the chance.

As if she'd plucked his fantasy from his head, she cleared the last step with him directly behind her and whirled on him, facing him, only to immediately sink to her knees at his feet. Holy shit, leave it to this woman to turn the tables on him. Her hands went to his thighs, climbing up his legs, and his dick responded, standing at attention, and pressing uncomfortably against his zipper.

"Still want to tie me up?" she asked, stroking the thick line of his erection.

While he'd certainly not complain about this woman's mouth on his cock, sucking him and licking him, he saw this as what it was. Her attempt to gain control. She clearly had no idea how much he enjoyed owning it himself and how certain it was that she had no chance of claiming it as her own.

Blake shackled her wrist and pulled her to her feet, hard

against his body, all her soft, sexy curves fitted against him. "I'm not playing this game and losing, sweetheart. You won't be needing your hands. Just mine." He stroked her back, molding her closer, feeling the warmth of her seep through their clothing like liquid heat consuming them. "Comprende?"

Her chin lifted defiantly. "No comprede".

Blake tilted his head and kissed her neck before his lips pressed to her ear and he promised, "You will when I'm done with you." He picked her up and headed to the bed, the possessive thunder of man claiming a woman rumbling within him.

"When you're done with me?" she challenged, clinging to him. "When *I'm* done with you is more like it."

His muscles tensed and heated with the erotic challenge. Blake realized right then what he'd been missing, what he needed. Just being in control wasn't enough. He liked the challenge, the sweetness of winning the battle to get Kara to submit to him. With everyone else, it had been easy to command them, practically mindless control. With Kara, nothing was easy, but it was good. Real damn good.

He set her down at the foot of her bed, his gaze flickering over the feminine blankets, his mind imagining her naked beneath them, naked beneath *him.* His hands settled on her shoulders and he pinned her in a stare. "If you thought you'd seduce me into foolishness like you did back in Denver, you underestimated me."

"I didn't seduce you," she objected. "I—"

He turned her to the bed, a sound of surprise sliding from her lips. Immediately, he shackled her legs with his and tugged her jacket down her arms, determined to get her in that naked state he was fantasizing about as quickly as possible. The instant her jacket was gone, she tried to turn. He didn't let her, lifting her shirt up and then quickly unhooking her bra.

Before she even knew what had happened, he'd tugged her back against him, his hands cupping her breasts, his mouth pressed to her ear. "Tonight, I own you," he murmured, and he couldn't believe how much he wanted that, how much he wanted her.

"Never," she declared, but the hoarseness of her voice told a different story. She was already sinking into the confines of desire and need, where he intended to immerse her. Where he intended to join her.

Blake plucked at her nipples, scraping his teeth over her earlobe. "We'll see, won't we?"

"Yes," she agreed breathlessly. "I guess we will."

"Get on the bed."

"No."

He smiled into the soft floral halo of her hair, the silky strands tickling his cheek, and pressed her forward until her hands hit the mattress, forcing her to crawl on top of it. She made a frustrated sound he saw as challenge. He wanted her moaning, begging for more. Telling him what she wanted and how she wanted it.

His hand slid over her jeans-clad backside and up her waist to unsnap her jeans. Her hand went to his, trying to stop him. He countered her action by flattening her onto the bed, framing her body with his, his cock settling against her lush backside. She rewarded him with one of those moans he craved, and her hips lifted against his.

"I love how you smell," he said, burying his face in her neck.

"Sweet talk won't get you anywhere."

His lips twitched. "No?" He slid his hands under her and cupped her breasts. "Where will this get me?"

She made another soft sound of pleasure before denial whispered from her lips. "Nowhere. It gets you nowhere."

"It doesn't feel like nowhere." His palms moved downward, exploring the delicate lines of her waist and back, before he pressed his hand between their bodies again, and found her zipper, stroking lower, into the sweet V of her body. "I want you naked."

"You always want me naked."

"And that's a problem why?"

"You plan to use sex as a weapon."

He unzipped her pants. "You might find telling me your secrets comes with reward, not punishment."

"Just because I don't fit some mold for a woman you have set in your mind doesn't make my life and story fake."

He nipped her earlobe. "Sweetheart, I told you. Fool me once, but never again. I know you aren't who you say you are." He tugged her waistband down and eased her jeans down her body, and all but groaned at the sight of her panty-less, pretty little backside.

Blake leaned away from her to free the jeans from her feet. As he expected, Kara scrambled up the bed, twisting around to face him, her high, full breasts swaying with the action. Damn, the woman had a hot little body. And yeah, he'd had his share of hot bodies, but there was just something about Kara that set him on fire.

Blake reached in his pocket and pulled out the rubber-band cuffs he'd stuffed there, climbing onto the bed. She backed away and hit the headboard. His lips curved. The sight of her there, her creamy white skin, her dark hair draped over her bare shoulders, was pure perfection. She was exactly where he wanted her to be.

Without a moment of hesitation, Blake straddled her, pressing his free hand to her face and twining his fingers in her hair. "You know I'm going to cuff you. It's inevitable."

CHAPTER
FOURTEEN

H e was going to cuff her. It was inevitable. Kara should have known it before. Why she'd fooled herself into believing she could get the upper hand, she didn't know. But fighting Blake wasn't the answer. It wasn't going to get her out of here to save that young girl Eduardo intended to turn into a sex slave of some sort. She had to succumb to him and hope he went to sleep sometime soon. It was her only hope. Drive him into that post-sex oblivion that was male slumber and pray she survived his demands for answers she couldn't give. His hand raked over her breast, and she swallowed hard against the wonderful tingling sensation that told her she was fooling herself. She wouldn't survive his demands. She wanted to trust him. She wanted to believe he was a good guy.

"I guess you're afraid to let *me* cuff *you?*" she challenged.

"Afraid?" he asked, laughing. "Hmmm. Maybe I am." His hand, still laced in her hair, forced her gaze to his, his eyes meeting hers. His voice softened. "In fact, Kara, you scare the shit out of me."

Her chest tightened with the raw quality to his words. "I don't know what that means."

"I think you do." He shackled her wrist and slid the cuff over it before she could stop him. "I think you completely understand."

"No," she whispered, tugging on her arm when he lifted it to the bar behind her and attached it. "Don't cuff me to the bed." Her free hand went to his shoulder, and she meant to push but she didn't. Damn it, why wasn't she pushing him away? "Don't, Blake." He cuffed her other hand and settled back to stare at her. She swallowed hard, feeling helpless and vulnerable with her hands over her head, her breasts thrust forward. "Is this where you torture me for information I don't have?"

"With pleasure, sweetheart. It'll hurt so good, I promise." He rose up and tugged his shirt over his head.

"You promise," she repeated, her words rasping in her dry throat as he tossed his shirt away and exposed his impressive, muscular chest. His hair fell from its clasp, in long, dark strands to brush his broad shoulders. "You promise until you decide to kill me."

He went completely still, his eyes steady on her face, never shifting to her naked, exposed body. "I've given you no reason to believe I'd kill you."

"You said you'd kill me if you had to."

"And with the way you handle a gun I'm pretty sure you'd kill me if you had to, too."

"With good reason."

"I'm no different than you, sweetheart."

"Ignacio would kill me for looking at him the wrong way. How do I know you aren't the same?"

"I didn't kill you for drugging me."

"You thought about it."

"No," he said solemnly. "I didn't. I just wanted to fuck you again. You seem to have that effect on me."

Her skin flushed with the bold statement she knew was meant to distract her from what was important. "You work for the cartel. Problems get solved by killing people."

"You work for the cartel. I'm a contractor with loyalty only to my paycheck. I'd turn around after this job and help destroy Mendez if the money was right. And feel free to tell Mendez as much. I'd say that to his face."

Her mind was reeling, and her emotions, too, none of which made any sense to her. He made no sense to her. "Then why are you pushing me so hard?"

"What are you so afraid of me finding out?" he asked instead of answering her question.

"I'm not afraid."

"You said you were."

"So did you." She tried to turn the tables. "Of me."

"I said you scared the shit out of me." His eyes flickered with shadows, and she saw the torment in their depths, heard it as he spoke. "And you do. And you know why? Because I have to know whatever it is you're hiding and I dread finding out what it is. I shouldn't feel that way. I shouldn't care."

"Because it'll make killing me harder," she whispered, taking only small comfort in his torment being a sign he didn't really want to, that he actually felt this connection to her that she felt to him.

He opened his mouth to reply and she shook her head, suddenly overwhelmed with unexplainable emotions. "Don't answer. Please. I don't want to know what you'll say. We all have secrets. Mine are personal. They don't affect you."

"I need to decide that."

"No." Her fingers curled into her palms. "No damn it, you don't." Frustration filtered into her voice. "Stop pushing me."

"You know I can't."

"You can. You say you aren't loyal to Mendez. I'm helping you do what you were hired to do. That's what matters. You know all you need to know."

He framed her face and the touch was like sweet bliss, a relief. She didn't understand why, but she'd needed him to touch her. "I don't know what I need to know," he said, "until I know everything." His thumb stroked her cheek, a soft caress that sent a shiver down her spine and tightened her nipples. "Everything, Kara. I have to know everything. I want everything."

The way he said the words, like he had to own her, like he did own her, shook her to the core. She'd never wanted to be owned. She never considered that any man could own her, but she feared this one could, and would, if she let him. "You can't have everything."

He answered by leaning in, his mouth slanting over hers, his tongue delving past her teeth, doing a sensual slide into her mouth that sent a wave of heat through her body. "What you tell me stays with me," he vowed. "Trust me, Kara."

Her chest tightened uncomfortably, emotion welling inside her. Trust him? Was he serious? And why why why did she want to? This was how people got killed in this world. They fell for this kind of man, these kinds of promises. "I barely know you."

He settled his cheek against hers, his lips against her ear. "You know me," he said. "I see it in your eyes when you look at me." He palmed her breasts and molded them together, teasing her nipples with his thumbs, and her thighs burned, the urge to clamp them around his hips impossible to suppress. "And I feel it in the way you respond to me."

His gaze raked her breasts, a hot stroke like his hand, before they lifted back to her face, and she felt the familiar punch of connection captivate her. He captivated her. He leaned in and kissed her again, a deep, sensual slide of his tongue against hers that seduced and drugged. And when his mouth moved to her breast, oh God, the hot suction of his mouth on her nipple was driving her crazy, driving her absolutely insane. She arched into him and his hand curved under her backside, shifting her weight, fitting the V of her body against his thick erection, the proof he wanted her as badly as she did him.

"You want me inside you?" he demanded against her mouth.

Yes. Please. "I want out of these cuffs," she panted instead. "I hate not being able to move."

"I like you in them," he countered. "I like me in you."

Yes, she thought again. Him inside her. He wouldn't be asking questions. He wouldn't be teasing her. "Then what are you waiting for?"

"Your secrets, baby." He moved then, dragging his palms down her sides in a seductive path over her ribs, to her hips, until he pressed his mouth to her stomach, his hair tickling her breasts, her skin. And when his chocolate brown eyes lifted to hers, he didn't push her, or torment her like she thought he was going to. He took his declaration someplace completely unexpected and erotic. "I want to discover them all, every sweet spot you own."

His fingers slid between her thighs, and she gasped as he delved into the wet, sensitive flesh, his shoulders pressing her thighs apart, his breath a hot tease, promising all kinds of pleasures to follow. And then his fingers were inside her, and his mouth closed down over her swollen, sensitive clit.

Her eyes fell shut, every nerve ending in her body alive with the feel of his mouth, his fingers, his tongue…oh God, his tongue…he was licking her now, driving her crazy. Licking and pumping his fingers. She jerked against the cuffs, trying to reach for him, frustrated when she couldn't. Her legs lifted, and she wrapped his shoulders, trying to hold him in place, trying to make sure he didn't stop too soon. She was close. So very close to release.

"Not yet," he said, and his mouth was gone from where she wanted him most, his fingers too, his lips trailing up her inner thigh.

She glowered at him, the ache between her thighs and in her nipples, too much to take. "You're killing me. You know you're killing me."

A wicked smile touched his lips and he licked her clit and then slid up her body and kissed her. "Killing you with pleasure. Remember that."

He pushed off the bed, reaching for his boots, and Kara quickly scooted away from him, sitting up and leaning against the bed, her knees to her chest. Protecting herself from another attack of pleasure turned to pain. But there was no protecting her from the impact of him sliding down his jeans and boxers, his erection jutting forward, thick with his desire and with the promise of the satisfaction he'd denied her.

He tugged a condom from his pocket but didn't put it on. She wanted him to put it on, she wanted him inside her, and yet, she wanted to escape before she did something foolish and trusted this man.

His knees hit the mattress and he crawled toward her, and she had the impression of a wild, wicked beast in pursuit of what was his. Right then, she wanted to be his. She wanted everything else not to matter, to just disappear. The hunger in him washed over her, the possessiveness, and her body responded, the slick heat of arousal glossing her thighs. His hands came down on her knees. He kissed one and then the other.

"Open for me, Kara." And his eyes met hers and she saw what was there, the demand she give him more than her body. The certainty she would if she wasn't careful, if she didn't do something to stop where this was going. She couldn't afford to be weak. She couldn't let herself give into the temptation to trust him.

"No," she whispered. "I can't."

"You can."

She wished she could touch him, that her hands were free. "You want too much."

"I want everything. I told you that."

"Everything is too much."

He reached for her legs, easing them down, and pulling her beneath him. And she let him. She didn't have it in her to fight what she felt for him, not like this, naked and pressed close to him. Not with his cock thick between her legs, and him hard everywhere she was soft, right where everything else felt wrong.

He stroked hair from her face, staring down at her, and she saw that raw vulnerability in him she'd first seen in Denver, that pain he lived with, that made her ache with him. That she somehow knew he let few people see, but he let her. He surprised her then, reaching up and releasing one cuff and then the next, then cupping her face. "Everything is *definitely* not too much."

The way he said those words reached inside her and grabbed hold. She was falling for this man and falling hard and in that moment she couldn't seem to care why that was so wrong. "Blake," she whispered; a plea for some invisible perfection only he could give her.

His name barely left her lips when his mouth came down on hers, his tongue stroking into her mouth, claiming her, tasting her. She moaned and passion exploded between them. Wicked, wonderful passion that made everything else fade. There was something happening between them, something she couldn't escape. She was lost in him, lost in everything that could be, if only they were two different people. If only things were different. But they weren't—and yet, they were. When they arched into each other, kissing, touching, hungering for one another, it wasn't fucking. It was making love, and that's what would make the moment harder when it was over. The moment they lay there, bodies sweaty and sated, wrapped in each other's arms. Because in that moment, she knew she still had to do what she had to do. She tried to comfort herself by telling herself he'd do the same to her, that he was probably planning to do just that. It didn't make it any easier though to face the facts.

She'd made love to him and now she had to fuck him over.

***

Blake's eyes snapped open from where he laid on the bed, on his stomach, playing as if he were asleep. The mattress had shifted and he could hear Kara dressing. He'd rolled off of her not long after they'd…fucked. Or whatever that had been. He refused to let it be more when she was clearly not done lying to him. What a damn fool he'd been to think he could break through her walls and get her to trust him. To hope she wasn't trouble, but someone in trouble. Hell, he still wanted to believe that and he dreaded what he knew was before him…the truth.

The sound of her tiptoeing away and then taking the stairs ground along his nerve endings and he didn't even wait for the door to open and shut before he sat up and reached for his phone to dial Kyle.

"I tagged the truck with a tracking device," Kyle answered.

"She took my truck?"

"Yep. Smart girl, that one. Left you without the means to follow."

Blake grimaced and ended the call, dressing and then making his way to the rental in front of the building where Kyle was waiting on him. He was done playing games with Kara. She was going to find that out fast.

CHAPTER
FIFTEEN

B lake stood in the shadows of the building where Tami Wright, the blond waitress who worked for Eduardo, lived, watching her load her car with suitcases, with Kara by her side. What the fuck was she up to? Was she involved in the drug theft along with this Tami chick, and trying to cover it up?

Once the bags were in the trunk, Kara handed Tami an envelope and then hugged her, stepping back and watching as the other woman climbed into her beat-up Volkswagen and drove away. Blake let Tami go, knowing Kyle would follow her and track her destination.

Kara eyed a small piece of paper in her hand and started to walk unknowingly toward him and the side of the building where she'd parked the truck, but she hesitated as she neared the dark enclave where he was waiting. Secretary, his ass, he thought for the millionth time. She was trained and trained well, her instincts on high alert. She cut to her left, away from him, and he stepped out from the darkness.

"Kara."

She stilled and turned back to him, her face washed of the shock he sensed in her, her body stiff with discomfort she didn't hide as well. "Blake."

"You didn't really think you could sneak out that easily, did you?"

"I can explain."

"I'm sure you can." He motioned the direction where she'd parked. "In my truck."

She shook her head. "No. That doesn't seem like a smart idea, because—"

"I'm not going to kill you," he said, grabbing her arm and pulling her with him, irritated he could read her thoughts and that's where her head was at. "And damn it, I wish you'd stop saying I am. It's starting to get on my nerves."

"I could scream," she threatened, all but making him drag her.

"And risk your identity being exposed by the police? I doubt it." He glared at her. "I told you. I'm not going to kill you. Turn you over my knee and spank your pretty little ass, most likely. That I'd enjoy."

She gaped. "You wouldn't."

"Wouldn't I?" They were at the truck, and he pressed her against the door, trapping her there, his hands by her head. "What are you doing with Eduardo's employee?"

"I plead the fifth."

He ground his teeth, studying her in the beam of the high moon above. "Why are you here, Kara? Because it looks bad. It looks like you're involved in the thefts."

Her eyes went wide. "No. I'm not. That's not it." She crossed her arms in front of her. "It's…it's something completely different."

"I'm listening."

"Tami was in trouble. I was helping her."

"What kind of trouble?" he pressed.

"I couldn't just stand by and let her be one of the girls they're selling to the highest bidder. I couldn't bear to let it happen." She inhaled and let it out. "I just couldn't." She raised her hands. "Whatever that means happens to me, then it happens."

"What the hell are you talking about? What girls being sold to the highest bidder? By who?"

She studied him, looking baffled. "You don't know?"

"Fuck no, I don't know. What girls being sold to whom, Kara?"

"I'm not completely sure. I just know there have been girls disappearing, and they work at that restaurant. I overheard Eduardo telling Tami that she was going to be sold off if she didn't deliver this other girl he wanted to him."

Blake scrubbed his jaw and cursed under his breath. "Why didn't you tell me?"

"You work for Mendez, Blake. I know you say you're a contractor, but—"

"I damn sure don't support selling off woman, Kara. That's some fucked-up shit." He lowered his voice. "When I told you that you could trust me, I meant it."

"I don't trust anyone involved with Mendez."

"And yet you're involved with Mendez."

"I told you. I have to be or I wouldn't be."

"For the money."

"No. Yes. For my family. We can't do this now. The other woman Eduardo wanted. She has no family and he's cleared her records in some way and intends to make her disappear. I have to get to her and get her out of town."

"You have her address?"

"Yes." She held up the piece of paper.

He took it from her and he glanced down at the address. "Give me my keys."

She fished them from her purse and he motioned her inside the truck. Once they were inside, he started the engine. "Where's Tami going?"

"The Omni in San Jose. I wanted her across the bridge and in something high end and secure where Eduardo couldn't get to her easily. It seemed the best option until I could get to her until I could make other arrangements for her."

"Other arrangements," he repeated.

"Yes."

"What arrangements?"

"I didn't think that far ahead."

Smart answer, but he wasn't buying it. She knew what she was doing. He called Kyle and gave him the rundown. "I'll get the other girl and take her with me to pick up Tami," Kyle said. "We're going to have to get them into protective custody, Blake. You know that. We have to talk about what that means."

In other words, if they let the feds know what was happening; Blake would get pulled out of the cartel and investigated. He scrubbed his jaw, considering the very real possibility he needed to get his brothers involved. They had a soft spot for women. No matter how much they worried about Blake and Alvarez, they wouldn't blow a chance to break up an operation selling woman off like shoes in a store. "Just keep the two women safe tonight," Blake said. "We'll deal with the rest tomorrow."

"There's something else you need to know," Kyle said, and

something in his voice had Blake stiffening.

A few seconds later, Blake had listened to the news Kyle had to share and his gut was one big knot. He ended the call and didn't look at Kara. He couldn't look at her now.

"Who is that you're talking to?" she asked. "What's happening?"

"That was a trusted friend. He'll make sure the women are safe." He put the truck in reverse and didn't say another word, his mind and emotions racing, that dark place he so often visited threatening to take control.

Kara must have sensed it because she didn't speak and barely made a sound, but as soon as they pulled up to her apartment, she was out of the truck, as if she couldn't escape fast enough. At her door, he pushed it open and she stared up at him, hesitating to go inside.

His eyes met hers, and he saw her trepidation. She might not know what he'd found out on that phone call, but she sensed something was up. And oh yeah—something was up, all right. "I'll pick you up and carry you in if I have to," he promised.

She inhaled, as if steeling herself for what came next, and headed inside. He pursued her and shut the door, shackling her arm and pressing her into the wall, his legs shackling hers. "I know who you are, Kara."

CHAPTER
SIXTEEN

I know who you are, Kara.

Kara's heart raced at Blake's declaration, his strong, powerful body trapping hers against the entry wall inside her apartment and preventing her escape, his hands pressed to the surface by either side of her head. He was caging her, trying to intimidate her. Trying to get her to admit what he couldn't know. Reassuring herself she'd covered her tracks well, she searched the hard lines of his handsome face, probing his rich brown eyes, and finding none of the passion and heat they'd held only hours before—just hard steel and anger.

Memories of what had passed between them before she'd left him sleeping in her bed, of hours of erotic lovemaking, of the connection they'd shared that defied him working for one of the most lethal cartels in the world, confused her and twisted her in knots. She hadn't wanted to want him. She hadn't wanted to leave him. "If this is about me sneaking out—"

"I know who you are, Kara," he repeated, and that same hard steel from his eyes was in his voice.

He couldn't know, she assured herself. It was impossible. "No matter how many times you insist otherwise, I'm still just me. I'm still Kara Tatum—"

"Wrong answer," he said, and there was no time for her rebuttal. In a flash, he'd grabbed her purse, with her gun nestled inside, and tossed it to the ground. Kara jerked to retrieve it at the same moment Blake lifted her and threw her over his shoulder.

"Blake, damn it," Kara hissed as he started up the stairs, her long, dark hair falling like a mask over her face. She was all too aware of how he played control games and manhandling her was one of them. She was even more aware of how much he, and them, turned her on, and what dangerous territory she was in with this man.

"Curse me all you want," he said, as if it was the exact reaction he wanted, his hand sliding to her backside, "but you're going to tell me what I want to know." His fingers splayed wide on one of her cheeks, stirring the memory of his threat less than an hour before. I'm not going to kill you. Turn you over my knee and spank your pretty little ass, most likely. That I'd enjoy.

"I know what you're doing," she accused, certain he was taunting her, trying to jumble her thoughts. "It won't work."

"We'll see," was all he said, reminding her that the threat of the spanking had been both erotic and frightening simply because he'd been furious when issuing it. Considering they were already at the top of the stairs, she needed a plan to make sure he didn't get to act on it. Already, though, Blake was pacing forward, and the living area to her left told her he was headed straight to the bed again. The bed where she'd once dared to think she could seduce and control him. That had been a joke. Convincing herself otherwise as she almost did would be a mistake, one too easily repeated.

Desperate to get him talking, and keep her clothes on, she

blurted, "I had to go help those girls. You have to know that."

"This has nothing to do with them," he half growled, "though you can bet we're going to talk about you sneaking out and stealing my truck." His fingers flexed on her backside and he gave it a hard smack.

Kara jerked in shock, heat racing from her backside through her body at what was a decidedly angry and erotic contact. "Damn you, Blake," she ground out again, only to find herself planted in a sitting position on the mattress with Blake towering over her. "Stop trying to intimidate me. I told you. It won't work. It's just pissing me off."

"No?" he challenged, staring down at her, looking every bit the renegade she'd found him to be, his eyes half-veiled, long strands of raven hair falling from the tie at his nape, framing his perfectly carved, handsome face. "Because I'm pretty sure I can find a way to be intimidating if I need to be. Maybe, considering the games you've been playing, you should be far more afraid than you appear to be."

"I'm not afraid of you, Blake. And I'm not afraid of your spanking me or handcuffing me for that matter."

"Maybe you like those things a little too much."

"Maybe you just want me to like them."

"Maybe," he said, his voice both a soft caress and a rasp of sandpaper, "I do."

Kara's nipples tightened and the air crackled with sexual tension. Was she seducing him or was he seducing her? Wait. Was she trying to seduce him? No. She wasn't. That was dangerous, and yet somehow her eyes went to his mouth, that seductive, punishing, pleasing mouth. Dangerous didn't seem to matter anymore. All she could think about was how much she wanted that mouth on her body, how good it would feel. How good he would feel. She was pretty sure she'd thought these things were all bad ideas a few minutes ago but she couldn't remember why.

"There's a whole lot more than me to fear, Kara."

Her gaze jerked to his and reality slammed back into her. If he only knew just how true those words were, and suddenly she was angry with him for his involvement in all of this and for making her actually want to believe he could be saved. "Maybe it's you who should be afraid of me."

His mouth curved in a sardonic smile before he grabbed her vanity chair from beside her changing panel, and sat it and then himself, directly in front of her. "Why don't you tell me why that would be, Kara? Enlighten me."

Her anger deflated instantly. Oh, crap. Something in his tone had her doing a double take. Did he know the truth about her? "Because," Kara said, driving forward with her intended point, albeit missing the bite of anger she'd been embracing previously, "I see too much. I know there's more to you than what you're doing for Mendez. Or maybe there was and there isn't any longer. How else can you work for a man like Mendez? He's selling women to the highest bidder and you're supporting that indirectly."

"I'm no more a part of the cartel than you are, sweetheart."

"Wrong answer," she bit out angrily, using his own words. "No one takes the money of these kinds of people without justifying what they're supporting."

"Well, then," he purred, with a kind of poisoned seductive quality to his voice, "let's talk about how looks can be deceiving and how you shouldn't judge a book by its cover. Ladies first, and I'll spare you the talking in circles. You say you're Kara Tatum, a secretary trying to make a living to help your poor, sick mom. I say you're Kara Michaels, an FBI agent on a vigilante mission."

His words blasted through her like a freight train, crushing her chest, and all but flattening her. It was all Kara could do not to flinch. There was no way he could know this unless he had someone inside the feds. "Ex," she lied in a last-ditch effort to save herself. "I'm ex-FBI."

He flattened his hands on the bed on either side of her, his big body crowding hers. "Stop lying to me, Kara. I know you think you have to, but it's really fucking pissing me off. I can deal with you being FBI. I already suspected it. The lies are another story."

"Is that your plea for trust? I'm fucking pissing you off?"

"I'm done with pleading." He grabbed her legs and tugged her forward, closing his legs around hers. "Consider this a demand. And just in case you think I don't know as much as I do... you're on leave of absence and you're not on any documented undercover operation."

"If you know so much why do I need to tell you anything?"

"What are you after?" he demanded, ignoring her question.

"I don't—"

"Don't fucking lie to me again, Kara."

"Stop with the fuck fuck fuck!" she exclaimed, grabbing handfuls of his t-shirt. "It's getting old, Blake, and now you're pissing me off."

A moment of surprise flashed on his too-handsome face that only made her glare harder at him. She didn't want to desire this man, yet over and over he made her. He glared right back at her.

Words were lost to the crackle of electricity between them. Seconds ticked by and with each one she became more aware of him, of how close her actions had brought their bodies, their mouths.

He cursed softly, and then his hand slid to the back of her head, fingers splaying wide into her hair before his mouth slanted over hers. Kara moaned as his tongue dipped into her mouth, for a fast, hot caress followed by his demand. "You're going to tell me what I need to know. You know that, right?"

"You can't fuck me into telling you," she replied, trying to sound tough despite the warm tease of his breath against her lips and she failed miserably. Instead, she sounded breathless, and as needy as she felt.

"I'll fuck you, sweetheart," he promised, "because I want to and you want me to. Foreplay is you telling me what you're after."

Heat pooled low in Kara's belly and rushed through her body, proving this man was dangerously in control of her in ways she should be, not him. He had torn down her mental shields, made her vulnerable in ways she swore she never would be with anyone. "I hate you right now," she whispered, only she didn't hate him at all. In fact, she felt more for this man, this dangerously wrong man for her, than she had any before him.

He laughed low in his throat, a sexy rumble that made her sex clench, a moment before he kissed her again, stroking his tongue against hers in several deep, luxurious caresses. "If that's how hate tastes," he murmured against her mouth, "I'm addicted."

"I bet you say that to all the FBI agents before you—"

"Don't say 'kill them' or I might seriously have to—"

"Spank me?" she challenged, before she could stop herself from her deep need to challenge this man. "You can try but you won't succeed."

CHAPTER
SEVENTEEN

K ara had barely issued her challenge when she was flat on her back with Blake on top of her and her hands pinned over her head. "Don't tempt me, Kara," Blake warned. "That would be a hell of a lot better than killing you, which is what every one of the cartel would do if they heard you were FBI. What the hell were you thinking coming in here alone?"

Alone was dangerous. Alone made her disappear too easily. "Who says I'm alone?"

"I know you're alone. Why, Kara?"

Kara squeezed her eyes shut and fought her urge to trust Blake, but the fight lasted all of two seconds. She was alone. She was alone and she needed his help. She forced her gaze to his. "I was desperate."

"Why would you be desperate?"

"It isn't just me on the line here, Blake. You have no idea how much trust I really am putting in you to tell you this."

"So you're not alone?"

"I am. I'm alone." More than she ever had been in her life. "It's...my sister disappeared two months ago. Officials came up clueless and while they promised they were still trying, it wasn't enough for me."

"And your investigation brought you here," he supplied.

She gave a nod. "She came here for a job as a merchandiser for a large retailer, but it was eliminated when she arrived. The last I heard from her, she was waitressing and trying to find something better. Then…she just went silent."

Understanding registered in his face and he released her hands, settling his weight on his elbows on either side of her. "And she was working for one of the cartel's restaurants."

"Yes." She hesitated and then let her hands settle on the warm wall of his chest and somehow the connection made her feel safer. "She worked at the one we were at tonight, but of course, the company files have no record she ever existed. And she'd started dating a man who fits Ignacio's description." Fear for her sister burned in her belly. "The landlord at her apartment said he'd never heard of her. I know where she was living. I talked to her every day until she disappeared."

"If the cartel is looking for women they can wipe off the map, her connection to you would rule her out. She doesn't fit the profile."

"She has no connection to me on record. My father was FBI. Years ago he penetrated a motorcycle club, and they came after him, and our family. The FBI split us up and created new identities for both me and my sister. We didn't find each other again until I used my resources to make it happen."

"Why did your father let them split you up in the first place?"

She glanced down. "He's dead." Bitterness twisted inside her and she forced her gaze to his. "Our parents didn't survive the attack." Rushing past her confession before he offered sympathy that never helped, she quickly added, "I know my sister got involved with Ignacio. I'm just praying she's still alive."

Several beats passed, his expression impossible to read—until, abruptly, he moved, sitting up and giving her his back. Kara pushed to a sitting position, unsure what to think, watching him scrub a hand over his face before he stood up and whirled on her with a challenge. "And you thought you'd just walk into the cartel and find your sister yourself?" he demanded, his hands settling on his hips. "Are you insane, Kara? We're talking about one of the largest, most dangerous cartels in the world."

She scooted to the end of the bed and curled her fingers into the mattress. "This is my sister, Blake. This isn't about the cartel. This is about her. She's all I have." Her voice cracked. She hated how weak it made her seem. "I don't know if you have siblings. I don't know how important they are, but—"

"Two brothers," he surprised her by sharing. "And yes. I'd die for either or both of them but that doesn't mean I'll let you die for yours. What was the purpose of drugging me in Denver?"

Kara blinked at the sudden turn of subject, but she rolled with the punches, too deep into this to turn back now. "I wanted the documentation you were handing over to the cartel."

"Why?"

"I never worked for the Denver operation. I knew about the meeting through Mendez and I knew high-level officials would be in the reports. I thought some of them might be tied to the missing women in some way. And I'm not stupid enough to think I could do this all on my own, by the way. That list had powerful names on it. If I can tie one of them to the sex-slave operation, even slip it to the press, then I can convince my superiors to take action."

He glared at her, fury pouring from his eyes. "I could have killed you, Kara. If I was anyone else, I would have killed you. You're over your head and headed to the bottom of the bay with concrete blocks on your feet. If you think I'm going to let that happen, think again."

She should have been comforted by his protectiveness. She wasn't. Not when she was confident he meant to interfere in all the wrong ways in her investigation. "I'm going to find my sister."

"I'm going to find your sister," he corrected. "But right now, I'm going outside to make a call. Don't even think about trying to leave. I'll be by the door." He pushed to his feet and headed across the room and down the stairs.

Kara was on her feet in two seconds flat, running for the kitchen and opening a cabinet, pulling a gun out of a box of cereal and then running for the window, hoping she could hear his call. Praying he wasn't going to call Ignacio or Mendez. Praying she'd been right to trust him.

Cracking the window open, she squatted down and listened, letting the heavy weight of her weapon be her security blanket. When Blake returned, she was going to be ready for him.

***

Kara had too much in common with Whitney, and Whitney was dead. He wasn't letting Kara end up that way too.

Fighting a bloody flashback of the night Whitney had died, Blake walked down the stairs of Kara's apartment with every nerve ending in his body jumping. That night, that damnable night, when Whitney had been undercover inside the cartel, lived deep in his soul, a rabid animal clawing away at him, slowing ripping him to pieces. And now Kara was inside the cartel, just as Whitney had been, too close to a man who would slit her throat and forget her before the blade ever left her skin. She was too close to dead, too easily stolen away. It shouldn't matter. He shouldn't care, but he did. This wasn't how things were supposed to happen. He wasn't supposed to give a damn about anything but killing Alvarez.

Shoving open the door, he exited into the cool San Francisco air, the breeze a welcome relief from the heat of his anger and, yes, his fear. He'd not felt fear in a long damn time, but he felt it now. Fear pissed him off. Fear gutted a person and destroyed them. Fear did not let him hunt Alvarez with all guns blazing, balls to the wall.

"Fuck!" he cursed, using the word Kara hated because she hated it, because he didn't want to feel this growing attachment to her. Pacing, he tried to burn off the adrenaline burning through his body. Kara was going to hate him when he was done with her tonight, and trying to convince himself that was for the best. It was what had to happen. He couldn't keep her close to him as he had Whitney. He couldn't risk getting her killed. Kara hating him might be good. Maybe then he could stop thinking about her, stop with this damnable distraction that was going to make him give a damn if he was killed. Giving a damn and fear—two things that would be his weaknesses to Alvarez, and both came down to one person. Kara. Kara was his true weakness.

Blake stopped pacing, scrubbing a hand over his face. Grinding his teeth, he snatched his phone from his pocket and glanced discreetly at the window above, finding the barely there crack he expected to see. Kara was listening to see who he called. There had never been a chance in hell this woman was a secretary, and if she thought Mendez was stupid enough to believe that himself, she was wrong. He'd figure her out sooner than later, if he hadn't already.

Dreading the call he was about to make, Blake punched the auto-dial for his brother Luke. "Where the hell are you?" Luke asked the instant he answered. "You damn sure aren't on the job you said you were on. I checked. I've left you three messages. Why aren't you answering your phone?"

"Why were you checking on me in the first place?"

"Where are you, Blake?"

Blake sat down on the step in front of the door and sighed, accepting the inevitable beating his brothers were going to give him when they heard the details. "In San Francisco."

"Tell me this isn't about Alvarez."

"Okay, I won't. I've stumbled onto a slave trade operation going on down here. Young and pretty girls are being kidnapped and forced into things I don't think either of us wants to imagine. I've got two I rescued who need a safe house. Kyle has them locked down in a hotel right now." He paused and glanced over his shoulder up at the window, before turning his back to it and lowering his voice. "Actually, make that three women who need protection. I have one with me."

Luke cursed. "And let me guess. Alvarez is running the operation."

"Yeah." Blake ran his fingers over his jaw. "Alvarez is running the operation."

"How deep are you into this?"

He rotated back around. "I'm working as head of security for one of his top men."

"Damn it, Blake—"

"I'm going to get enough shit from Royce over this, so save me yours," Blake snapped. "I have women who need help and a shot at bringing this asshole down once and for all. Are you in or out?"

"You know we're in. We'll charter a flight and get a team there tomorrow. I'll work on arranging a safe house."

"Kyle has his hands full taking care of two of the women. I need you to check on someone for me. I need to know everything you can find out about Anna Michaels. Her sister is Kara Michaels, an FBI agent on a leave of absence. Actually...fuck. I'm not sure what her sister's name is. Their father was FBI and he was compromised on an undercover job, and Kara and her sister were given new identities."

"If they're in witness protection plans it will be nearly impossible to get that information, even at the highest level where Royce has connections. Why is this important?"

"Kara is here, trying to find her sister. She seems to think she's one of the kidnapped women. I'll need to get back to you on the sister's name. Just get me everything you can on Kara and make sure no one but Kyle has been digging around in her file."

"You mean Royce digging around. If Kyle got you information on Kara, he got it from Royce. And Royce is going to be pissed when he finds out Kyle lied about why to protect you, because we both know he didn't tell him Kara tracked back to you hunting Alvarez."

"He was just doing as ordered."

Luke was silent a long moment before he said, "I'm not even going to bother asking the ten questions on my mind right now."

"Thank you for that little piece of heaven," Blake replied in mock relief.

"Royce—"

"Will turn heaven to hell. Believe me, I know."

Luke changed the subject. "Is Kara one of the women you're protecting?"

"I thought you weren't asking the ten questions."

"This is the eleventh."

Blake's lips thinned. "Yes."

He snorted. "Does she know you're protecting her? Because I'm pretty sure she's trained to protect herself and others for that matter."

"No," he confessed. "But she's about to."

Luke whistled. "The shit's about to hit the fan. She's going to bust your chops."

"You don't even know her."

"I know enough. She's FBI and her father was FBI. That enough to assume her to be tough and independent. To top that all off, she's gone undercover inside the cartel to save her sister. That takes a pair of balls."

"Alone," Blake said. "She went into this alone, which is a death wish."

"Sounds familiar," Luke replied dryly. "Like my brother who just went MIA."

"Screw you, Luke."

"I'm just speaking facts. And you better be prepared for what's coming when you try to shut down Kara. This is not a woman you send to her room and promise cookies or candy-coated orgasms, Blake. I assume that's your plan, right?"

"Seriously, Luke. Screw you."

Luke chuckled. "Yeah yeah, I love you too, bro. I'll let you know what I find out about your poor, helpless FBI agent." He hung up.

Blake growled under his breath and returned his phone to his belt, but he didn't move. He just sat there, thinking about Kara, and he didn't give a damn if she was FBI. She wasn't going back inside the cartel, even if that meant he had to tie her to a bed and keep her there. Of course, he wouldn't be in that bed. Not anymore. Not until Alvarez was dead. The distraction was too dangerous. He and Kara were not doing candy-coated anything.

Shoving to his feet, he entered the apartment, locked the door, and charged up the stairs, his adrenaline pumping in anticipation of a confrontation.

CHAPTER
EIGHTEEN

Blake rounded the corner of the stairs and found Kara standing by the couch, her long, dark hair in sexy disarray, her hand firmly holding a gun on him. He wasn't the least bit rattled or dissuaded, charging right on ahead toward her with long, determined steps.

Her eyes went wide at his continued approach and she backed into the couch. "Stop or I'll—"

Blake stepped in front of her and snatched the gun from her hand. "Did you really think I didn't expect this?" Flipping the safety into place, he slid the gun inside the back of his jeans, and then trapped her soft, too-feminine, too-tempting body between him and the couch.

"You only took that from me because I let you," she declared, her chin lifting defiantly.

"I couldn't agree more. We both knew you weren't going to shoot me."

"If you knew I was going to pull a gun, why leave me alone?"

"Trust, sweetheart," he drawled. "I want you to have it, so I have to give it in return."

"That's why you asked one of your men to check up on me? Because you trust me?"

"You wouldn't respect me in the morning if I didn't check on your story, any more than I'd respect you if you hadn't listened at the window." His gaze lowered, lingering on her full kissable lips he wanted pressed to his, before lifting. "Find out anything interesting?"

"Whoever you called wasn't Mendez."

"You would have chased me out the door with the gun if you'd have thought I was calling Mendez."

"Maybe."

"Maybe," he repeated, his lips twitching.

She shoved him. "Must you always crowd me?"

"Yes."

She glared. "I didn't shoot you this time, Blake, but if you try to shut me out of the cover I've worked long and hard to develop, I will."

Damn, she was hot when she was pissed. "Is that right?"

"Try me."

Blake stared down at her, the fire licking at his limbs at her challenge, telling himself not to act, not to do what he burned to do, before he cursed, and did it anyway. Tunneling his fingers into her hair, he dragged her mouth to his and said, "I will," before he kissed her, slanting his mouth over hers, with a hot, demanding slide of his tongue that demanded her response and told her who was in control. And it wasn't her. It was impossible for him to keep his hands off of her.

Kara moaned into his mouth, her body softening against his, her arms wrapping around his neck. Her submission should have been enough. But it wasn't enough. It was never enough with this woman, which was exactly why this had to be it. This last taste of pleasure, before he got her the hell away from him, where she couldn't distract him from killing Alvarez.

One of his hands slid from her face to her breast, caressing her, teasing her nipple. She arched into his touch and tugged at his shirt, trying to press her fingers beneath it. Blake shackled her wrists and pushed her hands to the couch behind her. "Keep them there," he ordered.

She glared up at him, her lashes heavy; her lips swollen from his kisses. "Not a chance in hell that's happening. You want to touch me, I'm damn sure touching you."

His cock thickened, his anger magnified. He leaned in and nipped her lip. "This isn't a negotiation."

"You're right," she assured him. "It's not. You want a woman you can control, and she's not me. Not in bed or out."

"We'll see about that." He turned her to face the couch, forcing her to press her hands to the cushions.

"Blake—" She moaned as he palmed her breasts, his thick erection nestling against her delectable little backside.

He leaned in near her ear, drawing her sweet floral scent into his nostrils, and pinching one of her nipples as he whispered, "We're doing this my way."

"You can't just claim me like property," she hissed, her hand covering his, molding it closer when he knew she meant to push it away.

"I can and I will until I know you're safe."

"I'm FBI. It's my job to never be safe."

He wasn't going to think beyond this mission and the cartel, or he might go insane. He nipped her ear roughly, making her yelp. "My way, Kara. That's how this works. And the FBI wouldn't put you in the danger you're in now."

She laughed bitterly. "You don't know my boss."

"I'm your boss now." He shoved his hands under her shirt and pushed her bra down, covering her bare breasts with his hands. "I own you until I say otherwise."

"Making me moan means you have skills, not authority. And using it against me means you're an asshole. It means you're a momentary escape, not the answer I'd hoped you were."

Blake went completely still, and something dark, something he refused to let take shape, started to burn in his mind. He tugged his hands free of her shirt and gripped the sides of the couch. "If anyone is using sex against the other, it's you, sweetheart."

"Me?" She shoved back against him and then laid a hard elbow in his ribs.

Blake grunted and lifted his body enough so that she twisted around, grabbed his shirt, and lifted her knee to his groin without making contact. "You're lucky I don't really want to hurt you, Blake."

He laughed and pulled her leg round his hip, fitting his cock into the V of her body. "That's more like it. And I was trying to fuck you, sweetheart, not hold you captive, but I guess I should have remembered—you like to strike when my pants are down or headed that way."

She flinched. "That's unfair. I thought you were part of the cartel when I drugged you."

"Life isn't fair and I don't know what answer you're looking for to your problems, but, like it or not, I'm the only one you have."

"Then be one, Blake. Help me. I can read between the lines. You want me out of the cartel and that's not happening. Don't treat me like I really am a helpless secretary. I'm not."

"I told you I'd get your sister back—and if it's possible, I will."

"And I'm supposed to just walk away and trust you to do it?"

"You don't have a choice."

"I'm not walking away, Blake."

"You walk away or I'll force you to walk away."

She drew back, shock in her face. "Are you threatening what I think you're threatening? Because if you are…"

His cell phone rang with an AC/DC tune. "Hold that promise to cut my balls off. That's my ringtone for my man escorting the women to safety." He hit the "answer" button to Kyle's incoming call. "Talk to me."

"The girls were followed. Does Kara have a way to call either of them?"

Blake glanced at Kara. "Do you have a way to call one of the girls and tell them I'm here to help?"

"Yes. We exchanged cell phone numbers."

"Yeah," he told Kyle. "We can call them."

"Give them the code word 'Midnight'."

"Copy that," Blake said. "We're on it."

"Great," Kyle said. "That solves one problem. I can get the women in the hotel and convince them I'm their Prince Charming, but the chance whoever is following the girls saw you and Kara is big. You need to shut them down and come up with a story to cover your asses."

"Where are you?"

"A few blocks from the hotel. When we get there, I'll make sure the girls get inside and try to get you a plate number. The perps are in a black Chrysler sedan."

"We're on our way." Blake ended the call and stepped away

from Kara. "Grab that extra gun and come on. We might need it."

"Why? What's happening?"

"I'll explain on the road, but let's just say you might not have to cut my balls off if we don't take action. Mendez might do it while you watch."

***

Kara settled into the truck next to Blake. She ended the call with Tami, the waitress from the restaurant, having given her the code word and instructions to let Kyle help them. "Done," she said, placing her purse, now weighted with two guns inside, between them. "The girls expect Kyle. They were about to pull into the hotel. I'm sure you heard, but I told them to park close to the door and stay close to as many people as possible."

"I heard," Blake said, pulling onto the road, out from under a streetlight illuminating her apartment building. "But then I expected nothing less from an FBI agent."

She studied his profile, the dark shadows of the late night masking his expression. "What do you know about FBI agents?" she asked, thinking about his claim she knew less about him than he did about her.

"My brother's ex-FBI." He cut her a sideways look. "Translation: Royce isn't on a leave of absence like you are."

"You really just can't stop yourself from being a smart-ass, can you?" she asked.

"It's a gift," he assured her.

"Well, you sure don't waste it," she assured him. "I assume your brother is how you managed to find out who I am."

"It pays to know people."

Pays. Blake was supposed to be all about money, but it didn't add up. "Is that who you called outside my apartment? Your brother?"

"I called Luke. He's the middle brother. Royce is the eldest."

"And you're the baby of the bunch," she laughed, unable to stop herself. It was hard to imagine him the baby of anything.

"Glad you're amused."

"It's just…you know. You're so…impossibly…"

"Impossibly what?"

Hard to resist. "You. You're you, Blake." She just wished she knew exactly what that meant. "Is Luke FBI?"

"You know I'm going to make you finish that sentence later, don't you?"

Please, make me. "You can try."

He ran a yellow light right as it turned red. "If I'm a smart-ass, you must be a gambler, because you like to push your luck."

She leaned against the door to face him. "I think that's what you like about me."

"It's why I want to tie you to a bed and keep you there, and yes"—he cut her a look—"there are many ways you could take that, and I mean that in all those ways. And so you don't start over-analyzing that and asking questions, no, to your prior question. Kyle is ex-FBI. Luke's an ex-Navy SEAL."

"And you? What are you, Blake?"

"Ex-ATF," he said—and with his reply, he confirmed what Kara had known from the start. There was more to him than met the eye.

"ATF," she repeated. "You're undercover."

"Ex, Kara. I'm not ATF anymore."

This was where she could think he was dirty, but she didn't.

She didn't believe that for a moment. "You investigated Alvarez when you were with the ATF." It wasn't a question. She knew it had to be true.

"Yes."

She went with her gut and didn't push for more, at least, not directly. "You and your brothers are an interesting mix of skills. Why did you all leave your prior careers?"

"We opened a private security company. It started with an airport consulting contract that grew into more."

She didn't point out that he wasn't exactly working on an airport job. She pointed out what was important to her, what her instincts had told her from the beginning with Blake. "You're not a criminal."

"Not yet."

"What does that mean?"

He didn't look at her. "I'm going to kill Alvarez and I don't care what the consequences are."

His bitterness poured over her and into her, adding to the same tainted emotions she already felt, enhancing them. Kara didn't ask him why he wanted to kill Alvarez. She knew now that Alvarez had burned some deep ache into his soul. She saw the pain bleed from his eyes every time she looked at him. Alvarez had taken her sister, too. And other people's sisters and daughters. Even after her parents had been killed by a man like Alvarez, she'd lived to please her father, to support the law, the system. Not anymore. Men like Alvarez always got by the system.

"Good," she whispered, letting her head fall back against the window. She didn't say more. He didn't say more. Silence carried them to the other side of the Bay Bridge.

CHAPTER NINETEEN

B lake parked his truck several rows back from the black sedan sitting in the exact spot Kyle had told him it would be in. "That's them?" Kara asked.

Blake checked the plate against the license Kyle had managed to text him and nodded. "That's them." He keyed in Kyle's cell.

Kyle answered on the first ring. "You're here?"

"With eyes on our target," Blake confirmed. "Get the girls out of here while we distract the jerk offs."

"Will do," Kyle agreed. "Luke set up rooms at the Oakland Marriott, so we're headed there. He and Royce already have a team headed to the airport. They'll be here in a few hours."

The muscles in Blake's shoulders bunched just thinking about Luke and Royce showing up. "Then what are you talking to me for? Get the hell over there."

"Right. Reading beneath your assholeness, I'm stressed about them showing up too. You better stay alive tonight. Your brothers want to kill you themselves." He hung up.

Blake ground his teeth and settled his phone back onto his belt.

"We need a plan," Kara said instantly. "If they saw us helping the girls—"

"We have to assume they did. And we have a plan. You stay here and I go confront them."

"I'm not staying here." Stubborn determination laced the words.

Blake turned to her. "You're supposed to be a secretary, Kara. The idea is that we convince them that's exactly what you are."

"You aren't going out there alone. We don't know how many of them there are."

"You're staying."

"I'll just follow you, Blake. This is what I do. I'm an agent. I'm—"

"Sweet Jesus, woman, I swear I want to beat your ass way too often. Fine, you can back me up. Keep your hand on your gun and fire the damn thing if you have to." She was already getting out of the truck and Blake cursed. He couldn't function at one hundred percent when he was afraid he'd get more than himself killed. When he was afraid he'd get her killed.

Blake exited the truck, meeting Kara at the hood, scanning the deserted parking lot at the same time. "You take the passenger side of their car," he ordered Kara, his hand sliding under his leather jacket to feel the cold steel comfort of his weapon.

"Copy that," Kara said, and Blake noted that her purse was strapped cross-body to free her hands, one of which was inside it, no doubt, closed over her weapon as well. She knew what she was doing. He wanted that to be comforting. Instead, it told him that getting her out of this wasn't going to be as easy as he'd wanted it to be.

Blake started walking briskly and he assumed with Kara's

skills, she'd automatically keep pace. She did, cutting over on the opposite side of the cars from him so that she was aligned with her target. Once the sedan was in view, Blake and Kara exchanged a look, pulled their weapons, and charged forward, both aiming at the front window and slowly moving to the side windows.

"Roll it down or I'll shoot it out," Blake shouted.

The window came down and Eduardo, the manager of the restaurant they had just been to, was revealed. "What's this about?" he demanded.

Blake quickly assessed the car to find only one other man he didn't recognize inside. "Other window down," he ordered, not about to let Kara stand outside, unable to see what the guy was doing.

The man didn't move. Blake held the gun between Eduardo's eyes and Eduardo grunted and said, "Roll it down, Juan."

Blake kept the gun on Eduardo's head, aware of Kara shoving her weapon into Juan's face. "And here I thought you only knew how to grill burgers," Blake observed. "Seems your job duties are much more vast."

"Ignacio is going to kill you for interfering. You and the bitch over here who ran off with two of our women."

"One of them was wired from the feds," Kara hissed. "I saved your piece of shit ass by getting them away from you."

Blake was impressed with her big fat white lie and ran with it. "In other words, she saved you from bringing the heat on the rest of the operation over some sideline profit gig you're running on Mendez's clock."

"He knows you, pinche white boy."

"Now, that doesn't sound nice," Blake said. "I might have to wash your mouth out with soap, but first I'll call Mendez and chat first. He might not think it's worth cleaning up." Blake reached for his phone, wondering why the hell Mendez wouldn't tell him about a sideline operation, not overly surprised when the man answered on the first ring.

"This better be important," Mendez growled, his tone as biting as Blake's gun in Eduardo's forehead.

"Are you running some sort of slave trade operation on the side you didn't tell me about?"

"Why is this important?"

That would be a "yes". Mendez knew about the women and just didn't tell him. He'd analyze why that felt so off later. "It's important," Blake replied, "because one of the girls told Kara she'd been contacted by the feds and that she was wearing a wire tonight. You all but got taken down. She saved everyone's asses."

"Kara," he said flatly. "My secretary."

"That's right. The same one holding a gun to one of your men's heads right now for being a pinche Mexican who almost destroyed you. We need to talk, Mendez. I'm going to deal with the problem this woman was about to cause and make her go away. Saving you from complete annihilation covers my contract. I won't operate with half the facts. We re-negotiate or I'm done."

Silence. "We should talk in person."

Blake ground his teeth. "Let me think about that while I save your ass. I'll get back to you." Blake hung up, but didn't drop his gun. "Mendez might know what you're doing, but he has no patience for stupidity like what happened with these two women. I'm handling them. You go think about how you're going to convince Mendez you should stay alive." He let his gun drop and stepped back from the car. The windows of both sides of the car rolled up a moment before it pulled away.

Blake joined Kara to walk side by side toward the truck. "The son of a bitch knew about the women and didn't tell me. He wants me to find out who's skimming drugs from him by playing head of security and he tells me half the story."

"I gathered that," she said, "but we have another problem."

"Of course we do." They stopped at the hood of the truck.

"Juan works in the finance department at the corporate office. He'd have the means to doctor the reports Mendez gets on product moving in and out of the restaurants."

"But you caught discrepancies. Wouldn't he stop that from happening?"

"I intercepted the reports before they went to finance. My guess is I caught what he hadn't had time to fix."

"And you know what?" Blake asked. "The only reason this matters to me is that it means you're a target. I couldn't give a rat's ass who's stealing from the cartel unless it helps us find the women they kidnapped, and Alvarez. When my brothers get here, we'll have resources we don't have now."

"Then why aren't they already involved?"

"Yeah, well, there's only one problem with my brothers. They really are the good guys." Blake left that piece of good news hanging in the air, walked to the truck, and climbed in.

Kara joined him and shut her door. "If they're the good guys, what are we?"

"Not 'we', sweetheart. Me. Just me, and I'm Alvarez's worst nightmare. I'm the guy who doesn't give a damn if he dies as long as I take him with me." He started the truck and pulled onto the road. Neither of them spoke but the air was suddenly thick, the tension in the small space thicker.

Several minutes passed before Kara said, "I care."

"What?"

"If you've already decided you're going to die, you will and I care. I don't want you to die."

"Don't. Don't care."

"Too late."

"Kara—"

"When are you going to get it into your thick head that you can't control me, and that includes what I feel? You can't stop me from caring, and if you think I'm going to sit back and watch you go on a death mission, you're the one who's sadly mistaken."

Blake felt like he'd been punched in the chest. He didn't want her caring, and her fighting for him, to matter anymore than he wanted to care for her. But at least she'd solidified his decision. He had to get her out of this city, and his life, before he dragged her to hell with him and they burned together.

***

"She actually told them one of the women was wired?" Kyle asked, scrubbing his light blond bearded jaw. "That was freaking genius. It made her a hero, not a traitor."

Blake glanced at the adjoining hotel doorway where he could hear Kara talking with the women, trying to comfort them and convince them that despite leaving all they knew as their life behind, everything was going to be fine. Pride swelled in Blake over how Kara handled herself. And Kyle was right. Her actions tonight had been genius. "Yes, well, smart as it was, it won't matter. I'm getting her out of this."

"Good luck on that one," he said. "Not only is her sister missing, but that woman is so sharp she managed to drug you and get away with it. She has fire in her eyes. She's not going anywhere without a fight."

"Kyle."

Blake glanced up from the small round table he sat at to find Kara standing in the doorway. And damn if his groin didn't tighten instantly at the sight of her long, dark hair looking rumpled and sexy, in a "just been fucked" kind of way he only wished were true.

Kyle twisted around in his chair. "What's up, darlin'?"

"Well, bubba, the girls want you to play poker with them again. They can't sleep."

"Bubba?" Blake laughed.

"Yeah," Kyle said, standing up. "What's with the bubba?"

"If I'm 'darlin', then you're 'bubba'. That's how it works. Since you're ex-FBI, you know the rules."

Kyle snorted and looked at Blake. "Like I said. Good luck holding this one back." He ran a hand through his short blond hair and headed toward the other room. "Never let it be said I failed a woman in need of entertainment."

He passed Kara, who stood inside the door and didn't move. "What does 'sweetheart' get me?" Blake asked.

She shut the door and locked it, then leaned against the wall. "Why don't you come find out?"

And there it was. She threw out another challenge. He wanted to take it. Every damn time he wanted to take it, take her. And it was a mistake. Over and over, a mistake, one leading her to a place she didn't belong. Right in the middle of his quest for vengeance. Blake thought of her words from the truck and they replayed in his mind. *You can't stop me from caring, and if you think I'm going to sit back and watch you go on a death mission, you're the one who's sadly mistaken.* Damn, he wanted her to care and it was selfish. It was wrong. He had to end this now. He had to lay down the law. For her own good.

CHAPTER
TWENTY

Blake stood up and stalked toward Kara, pressing his hands to the wall above her head, careful not to touch her. "We need to talk, Kara."

"Later," she whispered, and before he could stop her, she wrapped her arms around his neck, molding her body to his. "For once I want to kiss you knowing you aren't the enemy." She pressed her mouth to his.

For several seconds, Blake managed not to move, but when Kara's soft little tongue pressed into his mouth, he moaned, and settled one hand in the center of her back, the other at the side of her face. Slanting his mouth over hers, he claimed her in a hot, hungry, damning kiss, a kiss that screamed of how dangerously lost he was in this woman. She made a soft sound of pleasure and his cock thickened to the point of pain. He needed her. Needed. The word jolted him and Blake tore his mouth from hers, pushing her against the wall, but she clung to him.

"Blake?" she asked, sounding breathless, confused.

"I can't do this, Kara. I can't think when I'm inside you. Someone else, yes. Not you."

Her eyes went wide. "Did you really just say that? Did you say..." She let go of him and ducked under his arm and he reached for her but she was gone. She whirled on him. "You want to fuck someone else? There's the door. Go find a good 'fuck' escape. That's what you do, right? Fuck everything that moves to try to forget whatever it is that's eating you alive?"

"Kara, sweetheart…"

"Blake, go to hell, and stop calling me that. I'm not your sweetheart and I'm not your fuck buddy either. Damn, you've made me hate that word more than I already did."

"You took what I said wrong."

"I took it wrong? How am I supposed to take it?" She crossed her arms in front of her body. "It's fine, Blake. Just go."

Oh, shit. He knew enough about women to know the word "fine" was not a good thing. "I…damn it, Kara, it came out wrong."

"You owe me nothing, Blake. Not an explanation. Nothing. We hardly know each other."

"That's the problem, woman," he half growled in complete, utter frustration. "I can't just fuck you and forget you. And you were right. That's what I do. I walk away and if I never knew the woman's name, all the better. That's what I swore would be how I operated for the rest of my life."

She looked appalled. "What made you like this? What happened?"

Blake's skin started to twitch; the shadows swirling around in the back of his mind were threatening to take shape. He walked to the bed and sank down onto it. He dropped his face to his hands. "I can't do this, Kara." The shadows began to part, the bloody images started to take shape.

The bed shifted and Kara's fingers gently stroked his hair. "Blake…"

Her touch was both soothing balm and liquid fire. He grabbed her hand, trying to control what he felt, trying not to feel at all, and it was impossible. Steeling himself for her probing stare, he forced his gaze to lift. "Kara." His voice was hoarse, laden with emotions he couldn't seem to control. "You…you make me…"

Feel. He didn't put another name to it. He couldn't. He didn't want to. He didn't want to feel anything, and yet he did. He felt way too much.

Her expression softened instantly. "You make me…too. Blake, I know what pain feels like. I'm here. If you need me—"

"I don't want to need you," he said vehemently, unable to hold back.

"I know. Believe me, I know. I get it. I get you. I have from that first night we met in Denver." She reached up and touched his temple, letting her fingers trail down his cheek, and Blake felt her touch chase fire through his blood—but even more, it stirred a hot burn in his chest that had nothing to do with desire, and everything to do with emotion. Like it or not, and he didn't, he was feeling again and it was heaven and hell. It had to stop.

His lips tightened and he moved her hand to her leg. "I can't focus on what I have to do and worry about you." He started to get up.

She wrapped her arm with his. "Oh no. You were right. We need to talk. I'm FBI, Blake. I don't need you to worry about me."

"Believe me, Kara. I'm crystal clear on what your job is."

"Are you? Because all this talk about protecting me says you're not."

"I am. And it's part of why—" He stopped himself before he

said too much. "You think because you're FBI you know how to stay alive. You don't. Not with Alvarez. So I'll do it for you. You're out, Kara." His gut clenched, waiting for the impact of what came next. This was where her hating him came into the picture. "You either get out on your own or I'll blow your cover and force you out."

"What?" she gasped, shoving off the bed to whirl on him, her pale cheeks flushed red with anger. "I trusted you and you're threatening to expose me?"

"I'm doing what I have to. I'm keeping you alive."

"Oh right. Mr. Death Wish himself wants to keep me alive? Well, two can play that game, Blake. You expose me and I'll damn sure expose you."

Smack. He should have seen that one coming. "You're getting out, Kara, and you won't get the chance to expose me."

"You underestimate me, Blake, or you wouldn't have ended up drugged and asleep in Denver. Who else will you underestimate and end up dead while Alvarez is still alive?"

Double smack. His fingers curled into his fist, adrenaline pumping through his veins. She'd hit ten nerves, all of which had been raw since the night Whitney had died. "You're right. I underestimated you and you aren't the first." He'd underestimated too many people, or Whitney would be alive today. "I won't take the risk and I won't do it again. You're getting out."

"Not without my sister, and not until I make sure you don't go and get yourself killed. I might be furious with you right now, Blake, but I know you are trying to be a hero. I'm not a damsel in distress. I'm an FBI agent. You have my back. I have your back. That's how this works. That's how it is."

She hit the big nerve, the raw, throbbing, aching one he wished he could just bury in the hell of his past, and Blake snapped. He grabbed her and took her down on the bed, covering her body with his, fighting a memory that was sure to shred him to pieces. "Don't say that to me again," he growled. "Not ever again. Do you understand me?"

Pain sliced through her eyes. "Right," she said, her voice quavering. "Translation. You want a fuck buddy and nothing more. No partner. No…whatever else. Just a fuck buddy who goes away when you want her to go away. Check. Check. Get off me."

Her hurt cut through the adrenaline and pain eating away at him, and then it punched in the chest. He didn't want to get off of her. He didn't want to hurt her. He didn't want her to go away. "I'm sorry," he breathed out. "Kara…I'm sorry." He lowered his forehead to hers. "I am getting this all wrong. I'm just trying to keep you alive."

Her fingers curled on his cheek. "I'd rather have you by my side, helping me. I'd rather not be alone in this anymore, Blake. Don't make me be that again."

Alone. He felt the ache in that word when she said it. Her family was dead. Her sister was missing. He wanted to make it better for her. He would. He'd get her sister back, no matter what that meant. "I'm the wrong person to count on."

"Because you expect to die."

"Because I'm willing."

"I'm willing. There's a difference between being willing to die and wishing you were dead."

He inhaled sharply and lifted his head to look at her. She saw too much and he saw no point in denying the truth. "And that's why you're a problem, Kara. You make me want to live again and damn it, that's dangerous." Too dangerous. He had to find his control again. He had to do it now.

His mouth came down on hers, his tongue tasting her deeply, drawing in her sweet honey flavor. There was a desperation to his kiss, a need to get to that familiar place where there was only pleasure and escape. Blake skimmed a path up her slender waist, over her high, full breasts, and she rewarded him with a sexy half moan, half pant, that thickened his cock and set his blood on fire. Burning up, urgently wanting to be inside her, Blake shoved off the bed, shackled her legs and dragged her to the edge.

Wasting no time, giving her no chance to argue or challenge him, he undressed her. The sooner she was naked, the sooner he could feel pleasure and escape, not pain and the other things she stirred inside him that he refused to name. And still, with every touch, with every brush of their eyes, more than sex stirred in the air, in his body. In his chest.

He undressed, and disposed of his gun on the nightstand, and while it could protect them from enemies, he wasn't sure who would protect him from Kara. She'd seduced him into every emotion he'd never wanted to feel again and he was desperate to gain back the control she'd stolen. His knees hit the mattress and he lay down, pulling her to her side, her back to his front, his body cradling hers. He didn't want to look into her eyes, determined to make this just sex, two people surviving a small piece of hell. He nipped her ear. "Are you ready for me?" he asked, sliding fingers in the wet heat of her sex that told him her arousal matched his.

She made a soft sound of pleasure, and then challenged him.

"I'm ready, Blake. The question is, are you?"

His cock thickened with her response, and he pressed against her, inside the tightness of her sex, his hand flattening on her stomach, angling her body as he buried himself deep inside her. "Do I feel ready?"

"Just know this," she whispered, arching into him. "Wherever you're trying to escape to, Blake, I'm here. I'm with you."

He stilled with her words, their content shaking him to the core. Blake buried his head in her neck. She was with him. He wanted her with him. He shouldn't. He couldn't. He did. He was falling for this woman, and he could almost feel her carving away at his anger and pain, could almost feel the raw, aching parts of himself being exposed. Could almost imagine Alvarez using those weaknesses to slaughter him, and everyone he cared about, including Kara. "You're going to get us both killed."

"I'm going to keep you alive."

This wasn't working. He had to get away from this woman before he couldn't. Blake pulled out of her and turned her to face him. She instantly pressed her mouth to his, her soft, tempting tongue teasing its way past his lips, to caress and seduce. To hell with it. He stopped fighting what he was feeling, stopped denying this was more than sex with Kara, and with a low growl, he pulled her close again, sinking into the kiss, and guiding his shaft back between her legs, pushing back into the tight, warm center of her sex. He was falling in love with this woman and she was right. Denver had been the beginning of what was inescapable today.

For the first time in years, he didn't think about who was in control. He thought about who he was with, and he saw Kara as more than a body, more than a way to suppress the flashbacks. He was lost, but not in the sensations of edgy need and pleasure. In this woman.

Blake savored Kara. He kissed her, touched her, tasted her, made love to her. Every touch of her hand was waking up a new part of him. Every brush of her hair on his skin like an electric charge. Every collision of their eyes a touch of his soul to hers. When they melted into satisfaction together, sated and exhausted, and he pulled her to his side, her head resting on his chest, he was alive again and he wasn't sure what to do about it. How did a man, on what he knew was most likely a suicide mission, embrace life? How did he not, with Kara in that life and in his arms?

Blake stared at the ceiling, listening to Kara's breathing slow, feeling her body relax against his into slumber, his mind racing. Kara had been hurt by Alvarez as well, and as much as he wanted to bring her sister back to her, he knew, and he knew she knew, that it was a long shot. That bitter truth only made his mission more important. This wasn't just about vengeance, though he didn't deny he wanted it. Too many people had died directly and indirectly because of Alvarez. It had to end. Blake had to kill him no matter what the consequence.

***

Kara woke with a gasp as the hotel door burst open, instinctively clutching the blanket to her naked body as she sat up. Heart in her throat, she blinked a new day's sunlight—and the huge man with long dark hair now standing at the foot of the bed—into view.

"What the hell were you thinking, Blake?" the man demanded.

Beside her, Blake, undaunted by his nakedness, threw off the covers and stood up to grab his pants. "In case you didn't notice, Royce," he said irritably to the bigger, crankier version of himself, "I'm not alone."

Royce, Kara thought, processing the name with relief. Blake's brother.

Royce snorted. "When are you ever alone?"

Irritation and embarrassment prickled at Kara, and she scanned desperately for her missing clothes. "Kara," Blake said. "He's an ass. Ignore him. Way to be a gentleman, Royce. Thanks a fucking lot."

"I suppose 'thanks a fucking lot' makes you a gentleman?"

"This wasn't the way to announce our arrival, Royce," another man grumbled, appearing in the doorway and clearly of the same genetics but with his hair cut to his nape. The Navy SEAL, she assumed.

Blake glowered at the newcomer, tugging his pants, sans underwear, over his hips. "How about some warning, Luke?"

The instant Blake glanced at Luke, like a predator waiting for an opening, Royce stalked forward, heading straight for Blake—and good gosh, the man really was huge. He stopped in Blake's face, but Blake was seemingly unfazed, clearly used to Royce's attempts at intimidation, standing toe to toe with him. "Back off, Royce," he warned in a low, tight voice.

"Killing Alvarez isn't going to do anything but put you behind bars or in a grave."

Kara watched the muscles in Blake's body bunch, his fingers curling into his palms as he leaned forward, right in his brother's face. "And if Lauren had been killed? Would you sit back and let her murderer live the high life?"

Luke stepped beside them and shoved them apart. "Enough. This isn't solving anything."

If Lauren had been killed. Lauren must be Royce's woman. Kara's stomach knotted with realization. Blake's woman had been killed by Alvarez.

"Enough, I said," Luke barked again. "Not now. Not here."

Tension curled in the air, the two men glaring at each other, and Kara knew, despite Royce's gruff approach—perhaps because of it—that he was terrified of losing Blake. Her chest burned and her soul ached. Royce was afraid of losing his brother, like she was her sister.

Finally, in unison, as if they'd come to a silent agreement, Blake and Royce took several steps backwards, both crossing their arms in front of their chests. Royce glanced at Kara and then back at Blake. "You do know that to get these women proper protection and identities that will carry them a lifetime, we have to call the feds." It wasn't a question.

Kara's heart lurched. No. No this was not happening. They were not going to call the feds. The implications to her sister were devastating, and the hard steel and determination of Royce's expression, told her he was set on doing this. This was his way of saving his brother. He wasn't going to back down.

Adrenaline rushed through Kara and her gaze went to the gun on Blake's nightstand where he'd left it. Training and instinct kicked in and she dove for it, and somehow she managed to keep the sheet at her chest in the process. The cold steel was relief in her hand. It was her control among all these men, and she aimed it at Royce. "No one is calling the feds."

She felt the room's attention shift to her a moment before Blake growled, "Are you crazy, Kara? Put the damn gun down."

"Not a chance." The mattress shifted with his weight but she didn't dare look his direction. "Don't even think about taking the gun, Blake. I'll drop the sheet and fight you for it. I don't care who's watching." She lifted her chin at Royce, praying she'd successfully held Blake at bay. "We aren't calling the feds, Royce. You and I both know they will take over the operation and my sister will be a fatality of a bigger investigation. I can't let that happen."

Royce snorted. "You're naked and half my size and you're telling me what's going to happen?"

"Law enforcement 101. My bullet trumps your size. And yes. I am. I get that you're desperate to save Blake from his death wish."

"Hey," Blake barked.

"You do have a death wish, Blake," she said, and continued talking to Royce. "And I get you'll do anything to protect him, but remember that this is my sister we're talking about here. I feel the same about her. She isn't trained like we are. She doesn't have a chance inside the cartel and I will do anything to protect her. If that means tying your big ass up and feeding you three meals a day like a baby in a chair to control you, until she's safe, that's what I'll do."

"Kara," Blake said softly this time, the mattress shifting again with his approach.

"I told you, Blake," she warned, "I'll fight you for the gun."

"Royce is an overbearing ass," he replied. "But he's one of the good guys. He won't leave your sister to be a statistic any more than I will."

"I won't," Royce agreed. "You have my word."

"And mine," Luke added.

"And mine," Kyle said, appearing in the doorway.

"We'll talk it through, Kara," Royce added. "We'll come up with a way to save her. We won't let her be sacrificed."

Kara didn't have to study their faces to believe them. She had this overwhelming sense of commitment from these men, commitment like she'd not even felt from her own FBI unit, a sense of family coming together. A sense she hadn't felt in a very long time and, unbidden, her eyes started to burn. "Thank you," she whispered, and damn—the burn was getting worse and it seemed to have spread from her eyes to her chest. "And, for the record, I'm not going to let Blake sacrifice himself either."

Blake moved in front of her, his back to his brothers, his eyes meeting hers. He took the gun from her and set it on the bed. "Kara," he whispered softly, wiping away a tear that had slid down her cheek. "We're going to save her." There was shuffling behind them and a murmur before Kara heard the door shut and knew they were alone.

She never cried, but she felt a waterfall coming and the last thing she needed was Blake thinking she was weak. He'd use any excuse to keep her out of this thing with Alvarez, and she wasn't letting that happen.

Kara cut her gaze from his. "I need to shower and put my clothes on." She started to scoot off the bed. "There are too many men running around here." Darting toward the bathroom, she didn't look back, thankful Blake actually let her escape. The minute she was inside, she shut the door and turned on the shower, impatiently waiting for it to heat. She wanted under the water where her tears would be hidden. Where, for just a few minutes, she could let go.

Stepping under the hot water, emotions erupted and she sobbed. Body-shaking, intense sobs she couldn't control. Her sister was all she had. She couldn't lose her. She couldn't lose her. But she knew the chances of getting her back were small. So very small. It hurt. It hurt so much and she fought against the memories of losing her family. She didn't think about it. She didn't go there.

Abruptly, the shower curtain ripped backwards and Blake, now naked again, stepped inside and pulled her against him. "Kara—"

"You can't die," she croaked in a sob, her fists balling on his chest. "You made me care about you when I haven't let myself care about anyone but my sister. You made me care, and damn it, you're begging to die. And don't say you aren't. You are. You feel guilty about something. You want to die and feel like you did it making some assumed wrong right."

He stroked wet hair from her face. "I'm here."

"For how long? How long, Blake?"

He studied, and then softly prodded, "How old were you?"

She didn't have to ask what he meant. The tears burned in her eyes again. "Seventeen. Myla was fifteen."

"Myla's your sister?"

"Yes. We lived in North Carolina and we woke to the roar of motorcycles. My parents hid us in a small hole in the basement wall. We barely fit. They wouldn't fit, Blake. I heard the gunshots. I heard them and I knew...I knew they were dead, but I was strong for Myla. I kept her quiet. I kept her from..." She dropped her head to his chest and the damn sobs just wouldn't let go. "I can't lose her."

His hand slid to the back of her head. "If there's a way to get her back. I will," he promised.

If there's a way. Kara sucked in a breath and looked at him. "Thank you for being honest, for not saying you'll get her back no matter what. We both know the chances. They aren't good, but I have to try."

"And we will. With every resource and piece of energy we have, we will."

She believed him. She wasn't alone in this anymore. At least for now...at least until Blake left, too.

CHAPTER
TWENTY-ONE

An hour after Kara had her meltdown in the shower, she and Blake walked into the hotel restaurant and headed toward the table, where Royce and Luke were waiting on them. The idea was that they would calmly talk through how to deal with their "situation", as Royce had called it. Kara was pretty sure she'd bump heads with big brother again, and she'd done her best with her bag of makeup to hide the effects of her tears and feel pulled together. Not that anyone would notice her face. The t-shirt she'd borrowed from Tami was way too low cut for her taste, though it seemed Blake's "Navy SEALs" t-shirt was getting the attention of several women at a table they were passing. Or maybe it was just Blake who had their attention. He certainly had hers.

Both Luke and Royce stood up when Kara and Blake arrived at the table and, with a murmur of greetings, Kara settled into the seat next to Blake, directly across from Royce. Somehow she thought having Blake and Royce sitting across from each other— a head-on confrontation waiting to happen—didn't work. At least, not for her and Luke.

The waitress stopped to fill their coffee cups and take their orders, and Blake's hand settled possessively, warmly, on her leg.

The brothers exchanged a few comments, more manly jokes than anything, and Kara covered Blake's hand with hers. There was a new intimacy between them, a sense of being together, not just wanting to strip each other naked. For the first time in her adult life, she'd let a man slip inside her life. No. Inside her heart. It felt both wonderful and terrifying. She and Blake were bonded in pain, she thought, and she couldn't help but wonder if that was a good or bad thing.

Kara sipped her coffee and glanced around the table, a smile sliding onto her lips. The Walker brothers were a sight to behold—genetics at their best. "There's enough testosterone at this table to shatter all the windows," she teased them all and, focusing on Luke and Royce added, "Why do I know you're all just as difficult as Blake and I'm about to be ganged up on?"

"You seem to like Blake's flavor of difficult," Luke commented, his lips curving in a charming smile. "So we'll take that as a compliment."

"Let's talk about our plan," Royce said, getting right to the point.

"Okay," Kara said. Apparently there was no small talk for this big guy. "As long as it doesn't include calling in the feds."

"Just because we bring them in—"

"No," Kara said, cutting off Royce. "I know why you're pushing this. I know it's to put the brakes on Blake. What you fail to see in your concern for your brother is that we're both inside the operation in a way the feds only dream of being inside. We not only have a chance to find my sister, and the other women that have been kidnapped, but to bring Alvarez down completely."

"You're both too personally involved," Royce said. "You

know that. I know you do."

"I've had time over the last two years to remove myself from the situation," Blake said.

Kara turned on him. "This is removed?"

He grimaced. "You aren't helping our case here, Kara."

"I just think we should be honest about where we all stand. We are both too personally involved." She glanced around the table. "Maybe that's what it takes to break into something this big. We're more inside the cartel than the task force working on this for years. The one insider close to Alvarez the feds had went missing three months ago."

"You don't think the feds will see the value in that?" Luke asked.

"I went off the radar," Kara said. "I'll be considered a risk."

"She's right," Royce said. "The feds will be concerned. I'm not sure that means they'll shut her down, but they might."

"I can't take that risk," Kara said. "Not with my sister on the line."

"The FBI and the ATF will both be all over this," Royce said. "They won't throw away an opportunity to take down Alvarez."

"That's the point," Kara said. "They will get involved and they'll red-tape everything. My sister won't live long enough to go through the crossed T's and dotted I's. I need her out of this thing, and then I'll hand over everything I've discovered."

Royce gave Blake a pointed look. "It won't matter if Alvarez is already dead and my brother is either dead or behind bars from killing him."

"If he's dead," Blake said tightly, "then we won't need to waste taxpayer money on a trial, now will we? And give me a little credit for protecting my own ass."

"I haven't seen you act like it's worth protecting in two years," Royce bit out.

"Stop pushing me, Royce," Blake said softly. "You and I both know it won't take us to good places."

They glared at each other and Kara cast Luke a pleading stare. He sighed and scrubbed his clean-shaven jaw. "We have a team of men and two scared women upstairs waiting for us to tell them what happens next," Luke stated. "What do we know about the kidnapped women?"

"How they profile and who's working this end of the operation," Kara said, eager to get everyone talking again. "We don't know who the buyer—or buyers—are, or where the girls are being taken."

"Human trafficking is second only to drugs as far as profit goes," Royce said. "It doesn't surprise me the cartel is into this."

"Yeah, well," Blake inserted, "funny thing about that. Mendez hired me to find out who is stealing drugs from him, but he left this part out. Something about that smells fishy to me." He glanced at Kara. "And you're too exposed to work this from the front line, Kara."

"Don't start, Blake," Kara warned. "You know I'm staying in this."

"Hear me out," he argued. "I'm not suggesting you get out. I'm suggesting you work with our team and let me handle the up-close-and-personal with Mendez and his crew."

"I have access to documents that Mendez might not give you."

"He is suspicious of you being more than a secretary. Add to that we came face to face with someone from accounting tonight, who is also working with Eduardo in the trafficking operation. They're going to worry that you'll put the pieces together and know who has been doctoring the reports Mendez gets. You're not only a target, you're female, and a perfect candidate to get sold off like the other women. It's too risky."

"He's got a point," Royce said. "All good agents know there's a time when you pull out of a cover. We have a team of ten men here. We're going to find out where the women are being taken. You can be right here with us, making that happen."

Blake's cell phone rang and he pulled it from his belt. "Mendez," he reported, and then answered the line. Kara would have tried to read the conversation but it lasted all of thirty seconds. Blake set the phone on the table. "Mendez wants me and Kara in his office in an hour."

"Did he say why?" Kara asked.

"Just to be there," Blake said.

Luke shook his head. "I don't like it. We don't have anything in place yet."

"Kyle has surveillance set up on the main headquarters for Mendez's cover-up operation, which is where we're going," Blake informed them.

"He does?" Kara asked. "How?"

"He's a tech genius," Luke said. "And so is Blake."

This was news to her. It seemed there was a lot she didn't know about Blake. She'd confessed her heartache to him, and he'd confessed absolutely nothing. He'd promised nothing, not even a desire to stay alive. He was the wrong man to count on, he'd told her. He was certainly the wrong man to fall in love with. And yet, she had.

***

Blake pulled the truck into a space near Mendez's offices, and while he wasn't happy about taking Kara with him to this meeting, he took comfort in it being a work day and mid-morning with plenty of people around. He texted Kyle and confirmed they had several men nearby and glanced at Kara. "We're officially on the Walker clan's radar."

Her brows furrowed. "Walker clan?" She shook her head. "Never mind. I get it. Blake Wright is a cover. Blake Walker is the real you. I guess it's time to go face the firing squad."

"Mendez is going to question your ability to handle a gun."

"My fisherman father would be proud of how well I defended myself. I'm sure Mendez will agree."

Her father. Damn, just thinking about her being a young girl forced to hide while her parents were gunned down ripped a new hole in his heart. He shoved away the thought and focused on their cover stories. "You're fucking me."

She gaped and laughed. "Now?"

"I'm serious here, Kara. It's part of you keeping your cover. You're now my woman. I want him to know that. There's a certain level of respect for a man's woman with these people. It makes you less of a target for the trafficking operation."

Her eyes met his. "If you want me to act like your woman, Blake, I'll act like your woman."

A hot, possessive fire lit in him and it took all that he was not to drag her against him, declare she was his woman, and kiss her. He'd known standing in that shower with her this morning that he wanted her to be his. They stared at each other and he sensed she wanted him to say something, to put meaning to their relationship. He just wasn't ready. It wasn't fair to her. He didn't deserve her yet. He had to get the past behind him and see this mission through. For Whitney. For closure. To be a better man for Kara.

"Let's go get this over with," Kara said, cutting her gaze sharply and reaching for her door.

Blake fought the urge to reach for her again, feeling her hurt, knowing she expected something he hadn't given her. But he would, damn it, and soon. He caught up with her at the front of the truck and when she wouldn't look at him, he couldn't take the idea of causing her more pain than she'd already felt this morning. He grabbed her and pulled her close, planting a kiss on her mouth. "One day not so long from now, I'm going to make you my woman, Kara, even if I have to tie you up again until you agree."

A slow smile slid onto her lips and warmed his heart. "I love this soft, romantic side of you," she teased.

He laughed and set her away from him when he really just wanted to hold her for the rest of his life. "There's plenty more where that came from, I promise." He motioned to the door and they fell into step together, their laughter fading, tension crackling in the air as they headed into what could be a trap.

A few minutes later, they exited the elevator into the lobby of Mendez's offices. Kara greeted the receptionist with a wave and they headed straight past her desk and down the hall towards Mendez's office. "Wait!" the woman said. "I'm supposed to buzz Mr. Mendez when you arrive."

Blake curled his fingers on Kara's elbow. "Just keep walking."

"I planned on it," she assured him.

Once they cleared the hall and found Kara's desk, there was yet another roadblock. A twenty-something brunette was sitting behind Kara's desk, her spine stiff, her expression puckered and high and mighty. "Hello, Kara," she said, a snide bite to her voice.

"Hello, Evelyn," Kara replied. "I guess they pulled you from payroll to cover my desk?"

"Something like that," she said, and the inference was that she'd replaced Kara. "I'll let Mr. Mendez know you're here." She picked up the phone and dialed.

Blake didn't like the feel of this, and a shared look with Kara told him she didn't either.

"You can go in," Evelyn said, waving a hand at the door.

Blake motioned Kara forward, reaching around her to open the door, intentionally wrapping her body in his, silently telling her they were in this together, before he pulled it open. Kara walked into the office and Blake followed, shutting the door behind him again.

Mendez sat at his desk, elbows on top, fingers steepled. He gave Kara an up-and-down, lingering on her cleavage in a way that made Blake want to rip his eyeballs out. "I see Mr. Wright's sense of style has rubbed off on you, Kara," Mendez commented. "Apparently his skill with a gun has as well." He motioned to the chairs in front of his desk. "Both of you. Sit down."

"My father taught me to shoot when I was a young girl," Kara explained as they moved forward and she settled into a chair. "He believed a woman is supposed to look like a lady but be capable of biting like a shark. He was a fisherman."

"I read that in your file," Mendez commented, glancing up at Blake, clearly noticing he hadn't sat down.

Mendez arched a brow. "Problem, Mr. Wright?"

Hiking his hip on Mendez's desk, Blake crossed his arms in front of his chest. "Yeah. I tend to get testy when people send me out to the sharks to get eaten. If the same people you suspect of stealing drugs from you are running your trafficking operation, you don't think that it's important to tell me?"

"I hired you to find out who is skimming drugs from me. Have you?"

"Funny thing about that," Blake commented dryly. "The same people I suspect of stealing your drugs almost got you put behind bars last night for trafficking. They're greedy with your drugs and careless with your business. This shit is way deeper than the pig hole I thought I was wading in. I need facts to continue forward, and I need more money."

"You do have a profound way with words, Mr. Wright," Mendez observed, disdain in his voice.

"So I've been told," Blake commented and the only disdain he had was for this man and his cronies. "More money and more information, or I'm out."

"What did you do with the women?" Mendez asked, shifting the conversation.

"I sent them far away and told them that everyone they ever knew or might know in the future would be slaughtered if they ever said a word about what happened to them."

"And why not kill them?" he queried.

"I don't do bloodbaths. Dead bodies come with complications I don't need."

Mendez pursed his lips. "I want them dead."

"Find them and kill them. And good luck. I'm damn good at hiding what I don't want to be found. Almost as good as I am at finding what others don't want discovered."

His eyes bored into Blake's for several seconds before his attention turned sharply to Kara. "You aren't offended by the females being sold off by our organization?"

"It's not my job to judge," Kara replied coolly. "It's my job to protect the organization."

"And why would you be that loyal?" he questioned.

Impressively, Kara didn't so much as blink. "Because I'm tired of being poor and struggling. I want more."

Mendez leaned back in his chair, his expression unreadable. Seconds ticked by, which Blake used to envision slamming the man's head against the desk. He couldn't help it. He believed dreams could come true if you visualized them often enough.

Finally Mendez spoke. "You've caught the attention of my boss, Mr. Wright. He'd like you to meet with him this evening, and since Kara has proven so effective by your side, she's to attend as well. You're to be at the docks at nine o'clock. A boat will be there to pick you up. The location, as you can imagine, will be undisclosed. Please dress appropriately. My boss is a very powerful man. He deserves to be treated as such."

By the time Mendez shut his big yap, Blake had enough adrenaline pumping through him to fuel a jet liner. He was a hair from Alvarez, so close he could taste him, but he had to play this cool. "My time is money," Blake said. "Why would I attend this meeting? What's in it for me?"

"More money and more opportunity than you ever dreamed possible, Mr. Wright." His phone buzzed and Evelyn said, "Your lunch appointment is here."

"Send her in," Mendez replied, pushing to his feet, and addressing Blake and Kara again. "Nine o'clock. Be there." The door opened. "And now, if you'll please be on your way. I have another meeting."

Blake pushed off the desk. "Maybe your boss will shoot straight with me."

Mendez's lips twitched. "He definitely shoots straight, Mr. Wright."

Unease slid through Blake at the subtle threat beneath the words he couldn't let go. "I guess that's why he's had a long and prosperous life." Blake turned away from Mendez, ending the conversation, following Kara toward the door. A twenty-something blonde in a red dress, with deep cleavage, entered before they could depart, sashaying toward them, a "come and get me" look in her eyes. Apparently Mendez's lunch didn't involve food.

Blake and Kara exited the office and headed toward the lobby. When they entered the elevator neither of them spoke. Blake stood there, thinking of how close he was to killing Alvarez and he expected the hunger for vengeance to expand and grow inside him, but it didn't. This meeting with Alvarez that should be a long desired victory was a bittersweet triumph for one reason and one reason only. Kara. Everything he'd been living for the past two years, everything he'd thought he wanted, had transformed. Those things had become her. He wouldn't lose her to Alvarez. He couldn't let her go to this meeting.

Once they were inside the truck, Blake knew he had one shot to get her to agree to stay behind. Staring straight ahead, unable to look at Kara and control the emotions the past created, he said, "Her name was Whitney. We were on a task force together targeting Alvarez. Word came that Alvarez wanted a trilingual translator and there were only a handful of agents that met the criteria, and only one of those was available."

"Whitney," she whispered.

"Yes." He forced himself to look at her. "She was a new agent and scared, but brave. So damn brave. She'd seen the horror that was Alvarez and she wanted him to go down." He leaned against the door. "Once she was inside the cartel, Alvarez was taken with her, too much so, and…I try not to think about what she might have done to stay alive." He glanced up at the ceiling, thinking about how many times he'd lain awake wondering if Whitney was in Alvarez's bed. "She traveled everywhere with him." He drew a deep breath and leveled his gaze back on Kara to find tears streaming down her face. She knew what was coming. Of course she knew. "About six months into her cover, Whitney was sure she had something big that would take Alvarez down. I was meeting her to pick up the data, but we got word her cover was blown before I got here. I tried to call her and get her to run but she didn't answer. I arrived at the hotel where we were meeting at and…and her throat was sliced and she was bleeding out. She…" He squeezed his eyes shut. "She died in my arms."

"Oh God. I…" She moved across the seat and cradled his face in her hands. "I don't know what to say. I know sorry doesn't make it better. I know that so damn well."

"Say you won't go to this meeting. Say you'll stay behind and you'll let me handle this."

"No," she whispered. "No." She shook her head. "I can't do that, Blake. Remember. I have your back and you have mine."

Emotion burned in his chest. "I didn't have her back, Kara. I let her die. I let her live the hell of having her throat sliced open, and drowning in her own blood. I let that happen."

"You didn't let her die. She did her job. And you're right. She was brave. And damn it, we'll take down Alvarez. We will. We'll let her rest in peace. But we have to do it together. We need each other."

She was right. He needed her. That's why this time, he really was going to make her hate him because he was going to do whatever it took to keep her off that boat.

CHAPTER
TWENTY-TWO

With only an hour until they headed to the docks, Kara paced the new hotel room she and Blake had rented close to her apartment, waiting for his return. After seeing the girls off to the Oakland airport and New York, where Walker headquarters was, they'd both agreed they didn't dare risk going back to her place, or his hotel—even for clothes. By the time they'd returned to San Francisco and shopped, it had been six o'clock, three hours until they were to meet at the docks. Blake had gone to meet Kyle and his brothers to show them certain surveillance points. She'd called him twice and he assured her he was headed back soon, but she was getting nervous. He'd been withdrawn ever since she'd insisted she had to go with him tonight. Had he left without her? Surely he knew she'd show up at nine at the docks on her own.

The door to the room jiggled and Kara rushed forward as Blake walked in, and she let out a breath of relief. He was still in jeans and a leather jacket. He hadn't left without her. Kyle followed him in and her relief faded inside the crackling tension in the air.

"What's wrong?" Kara asked.

Blake settled his hands on her arms. "Kyle's going to stay

with you while I go to the meeting."

"What? No. I'm going."

"No, Kara—you aren't." His hands came down on her shoulders, his brown eyes hard, determined.

She wet her lips, knowing two big men weren't a battle she could fight. At least, not head on. A good agent—and she was a good agent—used smarts. "If you do this—"

"You'll hate me," he said. "I'd rather you hate me alive than bury you like I did Whitney."

Like Whitney. A part of her softened. He cared about her. He was worried about her. But she cared about him too, and neither of them could survive his guilt and fear. He had to overcome it. She had to make him. She removed his hands from her shoulders. "Do what you have to do, Blake."

His eyes narrowed. "That was easy."

She glanced around him to Kyle, who had rubber cuffs in his hands. "I know when I'm beat. And I don't need to be cuffed. I'll stay." Kara leaned in and kissed Blake. "And you stay alive, damn it."

He molded her closer and kissed her deeply, passionately, and she tasted the bitterness of his guilt and his fear. "I will," he promised. "For you, I will." He turned and left and Kara stared after him.

"I guess that leaves you and me, darlin'," Kyle teased.

"I guess it does, bubba," she said thinking how bad she was going to feel in a couple of minutes. She liked Kyle and he was a good friend to Blake.

He grinned and sauntered into the room, sinking down into the desk chair and grabbing a room service menu. "I'm starving. You hungry?"

"Yes. I am." Kara sat down on the bed and kicked off one shoe and then carefully removed the second where she'd hidden the secret weapon she'd gotten from an FBI lab. The same weapon she'd used to put Blake to sleep in Denver. "Anything good on the menu, or should we order pizza?"

He glanced down and she pulled off the sticker that exposed the sleeping drug, careful not to touch her own skin. "Looks good to me," he said. "You want to take a look?"

"Sure, I..." She started to get up and feigned a cramp. She needed to get him to the bed so he didn't fall over and hit his head when she knocked him out. "Oh, ah. Stupid Charley horse." She rubbed her foot several seconds, making a pained face. "Okay. Ouch. That hurt. I can't walk. Can you bring me the menu?"

"You must be dehydrated," Kyle said, pushing to his feet. "I used to get those when I played football." He handed her the menu.

Kara looked up at him. "I'm sorry, Kyle. I really am." She grabbed his arm and pressed the drug against his skin.

His brows furrowed. "Sorry for what?" And then his eyes rolled back in his head.

Kara jumped to her feet and somehow turned his big body so that it fell back on the mattress. She didn't give herself time for guilt. She quickly put her shoes back on, grabbed her purse, and headed for the door.

CHAPTER
TWENTY-THREE

Where's your innocent little secretary who isn't a secretary at all—or she wouldn't handle a gun so well?" Ignacio demanded.

Standing on the dock, the cold night wind whipping around him, Blake wanted to do some whipping of his own. On Ignacio. But since the asshole was his ticket to Alvarez right now, he'd refrain until a later date. "That's like saying a lawyer can't bake a cake," Blake observed. "But then your brain seems to operate like a mud pie."

Ignacio's face reddened under the too-dim lighting along the wooden walkway to their right. "Where is she, asshole?"

"Kara's…tied up," he replied. "She couldn't make it."

"My uncle specifically said I was to transport you both. I'll have to call him."

Blake yanked his phone from his belt. "I'll do it for you."

"I'm here!"

Blake froze at the sound of Kara's voice, every muscle in his body turning to ice and then heating with anger. How the *fuck* was she here, and why hadn't he tied her up? And while he wasn't on mic with his brothers, he was sure they were nearby and cursing, too. They all knew how dangerous this meeting could get and Kara had no business being involved. He'd flipping warned Kyle she was skilled and she'd proven it, clearly outsmarting him.

At the sound of Kara's heels clattering over the wooden dock, Blake turned to stare at her, watching her hair and the red silk of her dress flutter around her. She looked sexy and feminine and a ripe target for a human-trafficking operation. What part of that didn't she understand? Blake ground his teeth at the sight of two goons stepping behind her and stopping to guard the walkway, their weapons glinting in their shoulder holsters like shined silver despite the barely there light. There was no way he could get her out of this trip. She was here. It wouldn't be easy, but he was damn sure going to try.

"I made it after all." She stopped between him and Ignacio and shivered, hugging herself. "I forgot my jacket. I'm freezing."

Blake almost laughed at her obvious attempt at playing the innocent little secretary after she'd clearly just outwitted one of the best damn men Walker Security had on their team. Innocent, and held a gun at one of the cartel member's heads only hours before.

"Where exactly were you?" Ignacio demanded.

Blake grimaced and before Kara could reply, answered for her. "What the hell business is it of yours?"

Ignacio cut him a hard look, his gaze flicking over Blake's jeans and leather jacket, before raking an obscene path down Kara's body and back up. "She's late, but at least she's dressed for a meeting with Alvarez."

Blake curled his fingers into his palms and told himself not to punch the living crap out of the man. He'd had a lot of urges to pummel people since meeting Kara, it seemed. Pulling her to his side and under his arm, he would keep her close. He didn't give a damn how tough she thought she was—she didn't belong here. If there was any way he could get her out of here, he would. He lifted his chin at Ignacio. "Just get us to Alvarez."

"Gladly." Ignacio's lips twisted. "I'm going to enjoy how much he won't like you and how much he *will* like her." He glanced at Kara. "Give me your purse."

Kara didn't hesitate, handing it over to him. Of course, she was prepared. She'd been prepared for Kyle. She'd be prepared for Ignacio. "Ignore the lipstick," Blake said dryly. "It's not your shade."

Ignacio grimaced. "I wouldn't be surprised if it was yours."

"It is," he said, unable to stop himself from staking his claim on Kara every chance he could find. "Every time I kiss it off her lips."

Ignacio did a search and handed Kara back her purse. "Hold your hands to your sides."

Blake pulled her tighter against him. "If you so much as think about touching her, that lipstick will be up your ass."

"Better her lipstick than Alvarez's foot. She has to be searched."

"We'll see about that." Blake grabbed his phone and punched in Mendez's number. It started to ring.

"What the fuck are you doing?" Ignacio demanded.

"Calling your uncle."

"Wait," Ignacio bit out. "Hang up."

Blake let the phone ring. "Why?"

"There's a metal detector at the destination. We'll use it."

"You better be on your way to meet Alvarez," Mendez barked into the phone, answering the call.

Blake eyed Ignacio. "Since your nephew and I just worked out our travel arrangements, we're headed to see him."

"Make sure you are," Mendez spat, and the line went dead.

"Now what?" Blake asked, shoving his phone back onto his belt. He'd bet one of his balls, and he was as attached to both of them as he was to breathing, Kara had used that same drug she'd zapped him with on Kyle. He hoped like hell that she had some of it with her now. What he'd packed himself wasn't going to make it through the detector.

Ignacio motioned toward the boat. "All aboard."

Blake turned Kara toward the boat, keeping her so close her hip was pressed to his. "If you had any idea what I was thinking right now..." he murmured.

"If you had any idea what I'm thinking right now..." she countered.

"Where's Kyle?"

"Asleep."

Blake grunted. "Well, at least I won't get shit from him about you pulling that crap on me anymore."

She laughed; a soft, delicate sound that reminded him how female and how breakable she really could be. How much she didn't belong here. "He gave you a hard time?"

"You have no idea," Blake assured her as they stopped at the edge of the boat and he glanced behind him to find Ignacio talking to the goons. He eyed yet another goon on the deck and all but growled at Kara. "I should throw you in the water and make you swim for it."

"If I go, you're going with me."

"Only because I'd be afraid you'd drown."

She turned into him, pressing to her toes, her soft curves

molded to his, her lips teasing his ear. "I won't drown. I promise."

His chest tightened at a promise that had nothing to do with his promise to throw her overboard. He wrapped an arm around her and buried his face in her neck. "Don't make promises you can't keep." Ignacio's heavy steps warned of his approach. "And neither will I." If they survived this, he'd be damn sure to tie her up and keep her safe, and that was a promise she could bank on.

He pulled back and motioned her forward. She glared at him, obviously reading between the lines, but Ignacio, with his men behind him, successfully ended their banter, stopping beside them. Kara stepped onto the boat, where another goon waited for them.

Blake followed Kara on board with Ignacio on his heels and things went downhill from there. "You two go into the cabin below," Ignacio ordered, stepping to Blake's side.

"Not a chance," Blake said, all kinds of alarm bells going off.

Blake could feel movement behind him, more people joining them on the boat. Ignacio crossed his arms in front of his chest. "You won't be allowed to see your destination, plain and simple."

Going below deck with Ignacio above was beyond foolish. "We'll ride on top."

He flicked a look at Kara. "She's freezing and topside isn't an option."

Blake was all about giving Kara his coat, but it was huge and heavy and he wasn't so sure he wasn't going to have her running here in a minute. "I'm claustrophobic," she offered. "I'd rather be cold and topside."

"We have a schedule," Ignacio said, his tone clipped. "Inside the cabin, both of you."

"Then Kara isn't going," Blake said, no compromise in his voice.

Kara opened her mouth to insert what was sure to be an objection, but was silenced by the sound of several guns being cocked from behind them. A gun pressed to the back of Blake's head. "She stays," Ignacio said, evil satisfaction in his eyes. "And while I'd hate to have to deliver you to Alvarez bleeding from a leg or shoulder, don't think I won't."

Blake ground his teeth. Beneath the deck, they were blind. They wouldn't know if they'd traveled a mile up the bay or headed out to sea, and the tracking device in his boot was short range at best.

"I'd like you to make my day special," Ignacio added. "Stay where you are for another sixty seconds and give me a reason to put a bullet in you."

Blake accepted the inevitable. He was going into that cabin and, damn it to hell, so was Kara.

CHAPTER
TWENTY-FOUR

Talk about being locked up with a tiger who considered you prey. That was exactly how Kara felt with Blake on her heels as she headed down the stairs and into the small cabin. Instinctively she scanned the windowless space, taking in the mini kitchen, a couch attached to the wall, and a door to a bathroom before she whirled around to face her wild beast. And Blake was definitely a wild beast.

He stalked down the stairs toward her, anger etched in his handsome face. Unsurprisingly, the door slammed and locked behind him. They were officially caged, prisoners who could very well be headed to their death. Right now, though, Blake was headed for her. He didn't stop until he stood toe to toe with her, but she didn't back away. Not that there was anywhere to go.

His hands came down on her shoulders, the touch solid, the impact sending spirals of heat through her body. "You and I are going to have a talk."

"Oh yes," she assured him, biting back what she really wanted to say, all too aware they were likely being recorded, maybe even videotaped. "We will."

"What you're going to do is exactly what the fuck I tell you to do." He eased closer, whispering in her ear. "They cannot know you matter to me." He leaned back and glared at her. "You're here to do paperwork and fuck me. Nothing more. Understand?"

She knew his crudeness was an act. She knew he was trying to send a message to whoever was listening that he owned her that she wasn't emotionally important, but she couldn't completely keep it from cutting. "You know I do," she bit out.

His gaze pierced hers for several more seconds, his handsome faced etched in anger, strands of dark hair falling loose from the tie at his nape, before he dropped his hands away from her. He turned away and Kara hugged herself, watching him shrug out of his jacket, forcing herself to inhale, trying to catch her breath. Why did this man always steal her breath?

Tossing the jacket onto the couch, he sank down on a cushion and patted the one on his other side. "Come sit. It won't matter if we're going a mile up the way or ten, they'll make this a long ride to keep us disoriented."

Kara told herself to do as he said, to play her role, but her feet didn't seem to move. The truth was, she wanted to smack him for talking to her like she was his property. She shouldn't, though—not when they were undercover—but beneath the facade of his being master and her his damnable puppy dog slave, was true anger. Both his and hers. He'd tried to shut her down tonight, to leave her behind when her sister was in trouble. He was pissed it didn't work. She was pissed he'd pull such a thing.

"Kara," he said softly, his tone a low command, a warning telling her to stay professional.

He wanted her to come to him. Fine. She'd be right there. Kara stalked toward him as he had her, and took pleasure in the flash of surprise in his face at her determined approach. She halted in front of him, this time *her hands* settled on *his shoulders*, and did her best to ignore the instant zip of heat through her body when she did.

Leaning closer, she pressed her lips to his ear, the spicy male scent of him teasing her nostrils and stirring a cluster of butterflies in her stomach. "You'll survive this night because I won't let anyone hurt you but me. That's my privilege."

His fingers laced into her hair and he gently, but insistently, tugged—forcing her to look at him. "And this is mine," he declared a moment before his mouth covered hers, his tongue pressing past her lips, hot with demand, and he tasted hunger, passion, and possession. He was claiming her, and it wasn't for the camera. She could feel the raw need in him, the near desperation in each lush stroke of his tongue. Kara had no clue if that need was really for her or for an escape from the emotions this trip to meet Alvarez had stirred in him. It didn't seem to matter. A mix of desire and attachment to this man rushed over her, through her. Whatever he needed, she wanted to give it to him.

Kara sank into the kiss, clinging to him, holding him close, silently telling him she wanted him, she needed him, and in that moment she admitted to herself what that truly meant. Needing him reached beyond this kiss, this trip. In such a short window of time, he'd climbed into her soul and become a part of her. She couldn't lose him *and* her sister. She couldn't lose either of them.

Kara shoved at his chest, tearing her mouth away from his, her chest heaving. "Damn you, Blake." Again, her lips found his ear, a firestorm of emotions balling in her chest. "You made me feel what I'm feeling right now, and damn it, you aren't quitting on me. Damn it, you will stay alive. For me. I need you to do it for me."

"What are you feeling, Kara?" he whispered, his voice barely audible.

"Like I can't lose you."

He stiffened, not moving, not responding, and then, suddenly, his arms wrapped around her and he buried his face in her neck. "I promise to stay alive on one condition."

Relief washed over her with his response, at the possibility he might actually try to survive what she knew he saw as a death mission. Moving to look up at him, she searched his face, looking for a sign he needed her, too. "What? What is it?"

Several heavy seconds thick with tension ticked by, his expression unreadable until a slow smile transformed his features. "You have to *let* me spank you."

She barely contained a flinch at the unexpected question. She'd been hoping for an emotional connection, and he'd dodged it completely. His warning that he wasn't the guy for her to count on replayed in her mind. Kara shoved away from him and when he let her, a chill raced down her spine and spread to her heart. He didn't plan on staying around. She didn't mean to him what he did to her. Damn it, why had she picked Blake to finally let her guard down with? Why?

Snatching up his jacket, she leaned against the wall at the end of the couch, and pulled her knees under the heavy weight of the leather. Physically distancing herself from Blake, as he'd emotionally distanced himself from her. Trying to survive herself now, when everything inside her felt like metal shards and broken glass.

Now in profile, Blake just sat there. She sat there. Seconds became minutes before he sank lower into the cushion, stretching his legs in front of him. Kara let her lashes lower, feeling the tension between them like a thick, icy blanket that only chilled her further. Helplessness filled her. All she could do now was sit and wonder if they would both share a destiny, if not a life, and end up as Blake had suggested—sinking in the bay in concrete blocks.

***

For an hour, Blake didn't look or talk to Kara. He *couldn't* look at her. If he did, he'd want to touch her and if he touched her, he'd make promises he couldn't keep. Okay, he still wanted to touch her, but at least he wasn't spilling out things he'd regret later. He wasn't promising her either of them would survive this night. He wasn't sure they would. All he could promise was his willingness to die to protect her. But promise to be there for her tomorrow? He couldn't do it. Not this night. But for the first time in years, he did want to survive. He wanted to survive with Kara.

Slumped down on the couch of the godforsaken deathtrap of a boat cabin, with the soft, sweet scent of her teasing his nostrils, his fear for her safety was shredding his insides. It didn't help that he'd created at least one hundred ways the rest of this evening could go wrong, and he could come up with a counter-move for only about twenty-five of them.

Abruptly, the doors to the cabin opened, and Blake cut Kara a quick look, taking in her long brown hair, her pale skin, her delicate features. Fear punched him in the chest. Damn it, she couldn't die. "Don't move or speak unless you have to," he ordered her.

"And you don't get killed or kill anyone before it's time."

Blake opened his mouth to reply, but footsteps sounded, forcing Blake's gaze to the door where Ignacio tromped down the stairs with about as much grace as an elephant on a stepladder. Ignacio stopped in the center of the cabin, glancing between Blake and Kara, a crude glint in his eyes. "Am I interrupting anything?"

"We managed to control ourselves," Blake assured him dryly, stretching lazily as he sat up, maintaining a facade of boredom. "We know how delicate your sensibilities are and all. Are we done joyriding?"

"Yes, Mr. Wright, you are."

Blake's gaze jerked to the man walking down the stairs, and the hair on his nape lifted at the sight of the tall, forty-something Latin man in a fitted gray suit who joined them in the cabin. Adrenaline rushed through Blake's body and acid spilled over his taste buds. For several beats, Blake could barely process what was happening. Alvarez. Alvarez was fucking here, so close he could smell the evil wafting from him. A flash of Whitney's lifeless face, the blood pouring from her throat, shook him to the core. Anger burned in his chest and he grappled for control. The ease at which he could jump Alvarez and kill him had him struggling to remember what the downside would be. Hatred bled through his body and he could feel it darkening his mind, reddening his anger. He wanted this man dead, and there was no guilt in him at the idea to hold it back.

Suddenly a hand was on his arm, spreading warmth through him, jerking him back with a familiar, calming quality. Kara. Kara was here. *Don't go get killed or kill anyone before it's time.*

Her words replayed in his mind, pulling him back to reality, to a place where more than hate filled his heart, where she did. He couldn't kill Alvarez. Not yet. He had to protect Kara and find her sister.

Blake blinked himself back into control, and not a moment too soon. Alvarez halted directly in front of him and the game was back on. Blake flicked a look up and down the kingpin. "Am I to assume the expensive monkey suit means you're the boss?"

Amusement flashed over the arrogant asshole's finely carved features. "I'm the boss no matter what I'm wearing, Mr. Wright."

"Right," Blake said flatly. "Had I known you were dressing up for me, I would have worn my new boots."

"Seems Ignacio was right about you being a smartass," Alvarez commented, his gaze shifting to Kara, his eyes drifting over her, and lingering on her hemline. "He also said Kara was quite beautiful." Blake curled his fingers on his knees and decided Alvarez had three seconds before his eyeballs got ripped out. On the three count, the kingpin shifted his gaze away from Kara and added, "No wonder you keep her close." He spoke of her, not *to* her. She, like all women, was subservient to this man. No better than a cold beer to be sold off during happy hour.

"She's here because you requested she be here," Blake commented. "What's this about?"

"Business," he replied. "What else is there?"

"Money," Blake said. "That's what I'm about." He glanced around. "And comfort. This isn't what I call comfort."

"I never invite anyone into my kingdom without my personal assessment—and I must say, I found your performance during the boat ride uneventful, boring, and downright Oscar-worthy." He lifted his chin at Ignacio. "Leave us."

Ignacio headed for the doorway, unknowingly leaving Blake alone with the man he hated the most in this world and a woman he was pretty damn sure was becoming his world. Not the most stable of situations for any of them.

"So, Mr. Wright," Alvarez said the instant the door shut, "back to your Oscar-winning performance. Your complete silence this past hour allowed me little opportunity to assess you or your relationship with Kara. While frustrating, it was also quite brilliant. You have my attention."

"If that's supposed to give me a hard-on, it doesn't." Killing him was another story.

Surprise and a flash of irritation registered on Alvarez's face. "You do know who I am, I assume?" There was an arrogant bite to his tone.

"We've covered this. I get it. You run the show, but I'm not part of the show. I'm contract. Free as a bird in a blue sky, and I plan to keep it that way."

"I have no problem with you being 'as free as a bird in a blue sky' as long as it's my blue sky."

"That's not happening."

"You like money. I'll make you a rich man."

"Why do you want to make me anything?" Blake asked.

"Because I have a puzzle missing a piece. I think you're that piece."

"The only puzzle I fit is my own."

"Your Oscar-winning performance we just discussed says you fit wherever you want to fit. I need people who know how to stay off the radar. You do. I also need people who know how to problem solve." His gaze shifted abruptly to Kara, his dark eyes narrowing on her. "I understand you saved us from a potential disaster with the feds." It wasn't a question.

"I did what I had to do," Kara replied, her tone as steady as if she were talking to a grocery store attendant, not the worst, most deadly kingpin.

"Au contraire," Alvarez disagreed. "You didn't have to do anything but run."

"I'm smart enough to know that anything that happens while I'm working for you, and perhaps even after, will come back on me. Protecting you means protecting me."

"You could have helped the feds," he observed.

"If you're on their radar, so am I," Kara answered coolly. "And besides, the government isn't paying my bills. You are."

He studied her, and each second felt like nails on a chalkboard grating on Blake's nerves before Alvarez replied, "Indeed," and then looked at Blake. "Find out who is stealing from me in the next two weeks and there's half a million in it for you. Since Kara seems to work well with you, her compensation is in your hands. If you succeed, then we'll talk about a bigger paycheck and bigger role in my operation."

"I'm contract and I plan to stay that way. If you can't live with that, then you might as well find someone else now."

"I can be highly persuasive."

"Aren't we just two peas in a pod, then? Because so can I. How do I reach you when I have a list of your thieves?"

"Mendez."

"And if he's part of the problem?"

Alvarez considered Blake for several lingering moments, before he said, "I'll contact you." His eyes moved back to Kara and narrowed slightly, before he announced, "You remind me of someone." And then he turned away and started to walk.

The air in Blake's lungs lodged at what had to be a reference to Kara looking like her sister. Warning bells went off in his head. Ignacio had mentioned metal detectors, which they'd never encountered, which meant Ignacio had expected them to go on to Alvarez's home. Blake had to assume the worst, that Alvarez had recognized Kara, and had ended this night early. In other words, they were as good as dead.

The kingpin headed up the steps and Blake reached for his boot, ready to yank out a blade he'd hidden inside a leather flap. Suddenly, Kara was squatting at his feet, her hand covering his. "No," she ordered in a hissed whisper. "This isn't the end game."

Blake tried to get up but Kara used her body to block him. The door slammed shut and Blake cursed, picking Kara up and moving her out of his way, and then charging for the door. It was locked and he tried to kick it open. He had to get them out of here. For all he knew, they were the only ones left on a boat about to be blown to pieces.

Abruptly, the cabin door burst open and Ignacio shoved a gun in Blake's face—and for once, Blake was damn glad to see Ignacio. They were not alone and the boat was not about to be blown up. "What the hell are you doing pounding on the door?" Ignacio barked.

"Kara wants a Diet Sprite," Blake explained dryly. "You didn't answer when we knocked nicely."

"A Diet Sprite?" Ignacio asked.

"It's called Sprite Zero," Kara commented from behind Blake. "But anything diet works. The boat movement is making me sick."

Ignacio grimaced. "I don't know what you two are trying to

prove, but you aren't funny, either of you. So either sit down and shut up or I'll have you tied up." He backed away and slammed the door shut. Blake turned to Kara and their eyes locked, fury radiating from the depths of hers. Yeah, well, he'd show her fury when they got off this boat. Now that he believed they were going to make it out of this alive, he was downright pissed about her drugging Kyle and showing up here tonight.

Blake moved to the couch and sat down. When Kara just stood there glaring at him, he shackled her wrist and pulled her to stand in front of him. "Save it for later, sweetheart," he warned.

The glint in her green eyes said she didn't want to do any such thing. She was furious that he'd wanted to kill Alvarez before they had her sister back. What she didn't understand was that he'd save her at all costs, even his own life. Regardless of his reasons, of logic that had made sense, seeing the contempt in her eyes didn't sit well. In fact, it pretty much sucker-punched him right in the face.

His gaze lowered to where his hand circled her wrist, and he realized right then that he didn't want to let her go. Not now or ever. Just touching her did funny things to his chest, and this left him with a decision to make. He had to put distance between the two of them before things got complicated, or he had to hold her close and never let go. Who was he kidding? The decision was made the day he met her. This woman had woken him up from the dead. He wasn't letting her go.

Blake pulled her to sit next to him and he could almost feel her wrestling for control. She was downright furious with him and the one thing he knew for certain was that she was only going to get more so. She was out of this mission, end of conversation. She wasn't risking her life again and he'd make sure of it, no matter what that meant. The boat might be secure, but an explosion between him and Kara was imminent.

CHAPTER
TWENTY-FIVE

The sickening sway of the boat, mixed with the tension between her and Blake, had stretched nearly an hour according to Kara's cell phone clock, but it felt like an eternity. Each second passing should have given her the peace of mind they'd survive this trip, but it didn't, and she had Blake to thank for that. His willingness to kill Alvarez, the only person she could be certain could deliver her sister back to her, cut deeply. She'd opened up to Blake. She'd told him her torment over losing her family and her need to save her only sister, and he'd dismissed it in a blink of an eye. And for what? Vengeance. He'd lost someone and didn't care if she did, too.

She glanced at his profile, cursing the flutter in her stomach created in her by just looking at him. Once again she wondered why, of all the men she'd encountered in her life, her work, that it had to be a man with a death wish that got to her. But then, maybe she understood. What did she have left without her sister? Him? No. She didn't have him. Not for more than sex and a spanking if she wanted one. He could hold his breath forever. There would be no spanking. There would be no more anything for them. After what he'd pulled tonight, that should feel like the right choice.

Why didn't it?

Suddenly, the door to the cabin opened and Kara jumped to her feet, aware of Blake doing the same beside her. Ignacio appeared and didn't make even one wise remark, which struck her as unusual. Ignacio didn't seem likely to miss a chance to prove he was "boss" to everyone, especially Blake.

Whatever the reason, Ignacio was quick to tell them they were back in San Francisco. In fact, he seemed like he couldn't get them off the boat fast enough.

"Ignacio sure was eager to get rid of us," Blake muttered as they stepped onto the dock, a deep scowl on his face.

"There was something he didn't want us to see," Kara agreed, putting her anger at Blake aside and letting the agent in her take over. "Either drugs or girls, I assume."

"Something was off with him," he said as they tracked a fast pace down the dock toward the parking lot.

"Like your priorities tonight," she commented. Okay, so maybe she didn't put her anger aside.

He didn't comment. He didn't even look at her. That only ticked her off more. In order to work with him, she had to know she could trust him—and right now, she didn't. His betrayal bit so hard that she was only remotely aware of the cold wind crashing over them, lifting her dark hair from her shoulders and piercing the thin layer of her silk dress.

Beside her, Blake shrugged out of his jacket and draped it over her shoulders. The tender protectiveness of the act, so unfamiliar to her, punched at her heart, and for a moment—just a moment—her anger wavered. Coat or no coat, he'd tried to hold her hostage tonight and followed that up by trying to kill the one man certain to have answers about her sister.

"Keep walking," Blake ordered as they approached his truck in the parking lot. "No way in hell are we getting into a truck that could have been tampered with."

So much for her assumption that they'd had a surveillance team in place. Apparently the truck hadn't been a priority—but then, she wouldn't know. It wasn't like she'd been included in the plans for tonight, and even if she wanted to ask him what had been, Blake was already punching a button on his cell phone. "Tell me you tracked us and whatever boat met up with ours," he said into the phone. He cursed. "It was Alvarez. He met us on the boat and pretty much said he was testing us to take us deeper into his operation." He paused and listened. "No, I didn't kill him. And don't ask questions I don't have time to answer. Yeah. I know. We'll meet you at the hotel. I left the truck at the dock. I wasn't taking any chances it was wired. Yeah. Good. Hurry." He listened again and glanced at her. "It was a drug she got from an FBI lab. He'll be okay in the morning."

Kara looked away and scanned the side street they took, lined with residential buildings, looking for trouble. She felt guilty over Kyle, but he'd be fine, she reminded herself. Her sister might not be, though. If it were Kyle's sister, she was willing to bet he'd have done the same thing she had. And Blake too, damn it.

Blake ended the call. "Luke has eyes on us. He's got a car coming to pick us up."

"Did they get a trace on our boat?" she asked anxiously.

He gave a disgusted shake of his head. "We went too far out of range. The tracking device I have on me wasn't powerful enough."

The implications stabbed at her heart. "That's not the answer

I wanted." They were no closer to finding her sister.

"You and me both, sweetheart," Blake assured her. "They're working on better technology and some off-the-record Coast Guard support."

Kara stopped walking. "But—"

"A friend of one of our men. He'll keep things off the feds' radar, and we need water support."

"You're sure you can trust him?"

"I'm positive."

He sounded confident. He looked confident. And while she felt uncertain about much about Blake and his brothers, after tonight, she was crystal clear on his mindset. "Since you want Alvarez's blood too much to risk the feds or the ATF slowing things down, I'll trust you on this one." She started to turn away but Blake had other ideas. Before Kara knew his intent, he'd maneuvered her into a small alcove between buildings, out of the wind. Suddenly, she had a concrete wall at her back and his hard body pressed to her front. Heat rushed over her at his nearness, desire burning in her belly.

Frustrated that she wanted a man who'd betrayed her, Kara shoved his chest. "Stop manhandling me, Blake, because I swear to you, I have nothing to hide anymore. I'm going to start fighting back."

"Do you fucking look like your sister, Kara?" he demanded, a beam of moonlight stroking the angry lines of his face.

"No," she hissed, and—no longer forced by an audience to fight the hurt and anger he'd created in her—she let it fly. "My sister's taller, prettier, *and missing*. Obviously you didn't remember that fact when you tried to kill the man who can give her back to me." Her lips tightened. "Or maybe you just didn't care."

He ignored her accusations and focused on his own. "Alvarez sure as hell thought you looked familiar."

"Alvarez was just playing a power game. Getting inside his close circle is my way to my sister, and you knew that. You knew and still you were going to kill him."

"To keep him from finding out who you are and killing you."

She jabbed her finger in his chest. "Don't use me as an excuse to carry out your grand plan. I know the risks and it's my decision to take them."

"My 'grand plan', as you call it, is to keep you alive. I didn't forget your sister. You have to be alive to welcome her home, Kara." He leaned in, his hands on the wall beside her head, a familiar pose she'd come to expect from him. His way of caging her, controlling her. "You ask me to stay alive for you, and then you tempt fate with your own life. What the hell am I supposed to do with that?"

He hit a raw nerve. She wanted to be more to him than a temporary escape until he killed Alvarez. She wanted him to feel what she did, but now she knew he didn't. Not after tonight. "I asked you to stay alive for me and what did you reply? I have to let you spank me."

"That was my way of saying I was with you in that moment."

The moment they were having sex. It was all sex and escape to him. "That was you avoiding commitment." The words were out of her mouth before she could stop them and she instantly felt like a deer in the headlights. Kara tried to duck under his arm. He tightened his legs around hers, holding her in place.

Her fingers curled on his chest. "Let me out of here, Blake. I need out."

"Not until we're done talking."

"We're done. I'm done."

"I'm not," he said, but the sound of a car pulling up behind him sent him whirling around, and Kara didn't miss the way he sheltered her with his body, ready to take a bullet for her, before he relaxed and turned back. "It's our ride, and yes, we're leaving—but be clear, Kara. We're far from done with this."

"You're such an arrogant, bossy asshole."

"If protecting you makes me an asshole, then I'll happily be the biggest asshole of your life, sweetheart." He grabbed her hand and pulled her out of the alcove and toward the black sedan waiting on them, like she was his property. She wasn't his damn property and he had her fuming.

Blake opened the back door for her and she wanted inside, she wanted a private room where she could blast him, once and for all, but just as he was about to slide in, he grabbed the lapels of his coat she was wearing and pulled her hard against him. "Just remember, Kara. I'm the asshole who'd die to protect you."

He leaned in to kiss her and she nipped his bottom lip just hard enough to let him know he wasn't in charge. His lips quirked, wicked heat and amusement dancing in his eyes. "You can take you anger out on me in bed tonight."

"Who says I'm going to be in your bed?"

"Me, sweetheart. You can count on it. And me, Kara."

"Yes," she whispered, and she didn't have it in her to hold back. "I can always count on you to fuck me, Blake, but that's all you ever promise. I need more." More than she believed he could give her after tonight.

"Blake, man," the driver called out, a voice Kara didn't recognize. "Come the hell on."

Kara shoved out of Blake's arms and he let her, and a silent part of her cried out in protest. He'd said nothing about her desire for "more". Feeling like a wounded puppy, she slid inside the car and as far away from Blake as possible, shrugging out of his jacket and setting it between them.

Blake settled into the seat and shut the door. "Kara, meet our driver, Jesse. He works for Walker Security."

Jesse lifted a hand. "For the record, I'm smarter than Kyle and Blake. I won't get drugged. No toilet hugging for me."

"Funny man," Blake grumbled. "Just drive the car."

Kara cringed. Obviously everyone knew about Kyle now. Of course they did. She'd have a bucket load of cranky men to face soon.

Jesse pulled the car away from the curb and Blake moved the jacket, scooting closer to Kara and pulling her tight against his side, his leg molding hers, his hand possessively on her knee. Tingling sensations raced up her thigh to her sex, and guilt twisted in Kara's gut. How could she want a man who didn't care if her sister lived or died?

Kara reached for Blake's hand, intending to move it from her leg, only to have his fingers flex on her knee and her hand rest over his. The contact triggered a flashback of him telling her about Whitney's death. She remembered the torment she'd seen in his eyes at least a hundred times, and she knew why. Guilt. He blamed himself for not saving Whitney. Kara squeezed her eyes shut, recognizing that her emotional pain over her sister had made her blind to his pain over Whitney tonight. Killing Alvarez was all Blake had lived for these past two years, and thinking back to the boat, he'd had plenty of chances to make that fantasy reality. But he hadn't, and if he'd really intended to, he would have. God, she was such a fool. He'd contained that desperate need, for her.

Kara turned to face him. He seemed to have turned at the same moment, and his hands slid into her hair, framing her face. "I'm sorry," she whispered, her hands covering his. "I'm just...my sister and—"

"Make sure you can handle what 'more' means before you ask for it, Kara." His mouth came down on hers, his tongue parting her lips, delving deep, and she tasted more than desire on his lips. She tasted absolute need in him, and that need was for her. And for just a few moments, she wanted to block out the world and lose herself in Blake. But the world didn't like that idea.

Jesse cleared his throat. "Hate to break up the back seat loving, you two," he said. "But we have company."

CHAPTER
TWENTY-SIX

I t had taken them an hour to outsmart whoever was following them. Finally, Kara entered the elevator of the hotel they'd rented a room in earlier in the day. Blake followed her inside. Kara leaned against the wall, taking off her shoes, while Blake punched in their floor and leaned against the opposite wall. Their eyes locked and held, and suddenly, the elevator shrank, and the kiss in the car, the unspoken words and mixed emotions between them that they'd let simmer while running from the cartel, flamed back to life. But neither of them spoke, and she wondered if he was as afraid as she was that they'd end up fighting over the next step in the investigation. And they would. They both knew they would. Before that happened, she wanted to make sure he knew she regretted her reactions tonight.

The elevator dinged and they made their way to their room, and still they didn't speak. Blake swiped the key and pushed open the door and Kara bit her bottom lip, hesitating with the sudden realization that Kyle was probably still here. They weren't going to be alone at all, and a fight was definitely about to ensue. She glanced at Blake and he nodded. "Yes. He's still here."

She inhaled and let it out. Blake arched a brow when she still didn't move. "Afraid to face the music?" he asked.

"That about sums it up."

"Once it's over, it's over," he reminded her.

"Right," Kara said. "And getting it over with sounds good."
She headed into the room and dropped her shoes by the door. A
few more steps inside and she just about swallowed her tongue at
the sight of Royce sitting at the hotel desk, his big, burly body
making it look like it was meant for a toddler. Luke lounged at a
small round wooden table, his MacBook open on top. This was
so *not* good. She needed to be her best to fight this much
Walker-bred testosterone, and she wasn't.

Kara stopped beside the nightstand, not sure what to say or
do. Blake stepped to her side, shrugged out of his jacket, and
tossed it on the bed. "Where's Kyle?" he asked.

"Next door," Royce said, abandoning a surveillance setup
Kara assumed to be of the hotel, and rolled his chair around to
face her, motioning to the open adjoining room.

Luke snorted. "He prefers privacy while heaving up his guts."

Kara cringed. "I guess he's pretty sick?"

Luke surprised her by looking amused rather than angry.
"Let's just say that he won't live this down anytime soon, but
he'll live."

"Interestingly enough," Royce said, fixing a hard stare on
Blake, "so did Alvarez."

Blake leaned a shoulder against the wall, looking as cool as if
they were talking about the weather, not the man who had his
fiancée slaughtered. "Unfortunately, he not only survived, he
thought Kara looked familiar."

Royce narrowed his eyes on Kara. And man, what a stare that
man had. "And why is that?" he asked, making her feel like a

school kid reprimanded by the principle.

Kara opened her mouth to defend herself but Blake didn't give her a chance. "She looks like her sister," he said flatly, as if he knew for certain. Kara whirled on him, and anticipating her move, he pushed off the wall and faced off with her, and once again beat her to the punch. "He recognized you, Kara."

"I told you I don't look like my sister," she rebutted, barely keeping her voice down, a sign she really didn't have control right now. No. He did. He had the control. These men she didn't even know were taking her life by storm.

"Alvarez sure thought you did, sweetheart."

"You don't know that."

"I know," Blake ground out. "And so do you. Your cover's blown."

"If my cover's blown, Blake, then by association, yours is, too."

"I inherited you from Mendez as far as the cartel is concerned."

Kara grimaced. "Oh, please. You've made sure they all know I'm in your bed."

"Fucking you and caring about you are two different things."

The crass words hit her like a blow and Kara stepped backwards. Clearly her romance fantasies were just that. Fantasies. "Right. Thanks for putting it into perspective."

"Kara," he said softly. "You took that wrong. I wasn't talking about reality."

"No? It seems pretty realistic to me."

"You know—"

"Don't," she bit out. "Not now. Not here."

Luke cleared his throat. "As much as I hate throwing myself

into the obvious war zone, I'm with Blake, Kara. Your cover's blown."

Kara threw her hands in the air and turned to Luke. "Do all Walker men think they know it all? You just got here and you weren't with us on the boat. How can you possibly say my cover is blown?"

Luke turned his computer screen around and Kara sucked in a breath at a large picture of her sister filling the screen. Her heart ached just seeing Myla's face, and her fist balled over the ache. Blake grabbed her hand and pulled her hard against him, her hands settling on his chest. "You don't look like her?" he demanded.

She glared at him, all too aware of the similarities between her and Myla. "It was a risk I had to take—and don't tell me you wouldn't have done it, too."

"A risk you won't be taking again."

The command in his voice splintered along her nerve endings and she wasn't letting an audience silence her tongue. "Like you said, Blake, *sweetheart,* fucking me is not caring about me. It also doesn't give you ownership over me, no matter how much you seem to think it does. And for the last time, stop manhandling me and let me go—or I swear to you, Blake, I will give you a knee that will make sure you don't fuck anyone anytime soon."

Luke barked out laughter and Blake's eyes sharpened on hers, burning hot with anger. "We'll finish this when we're alone."

"No," Kara snapped. "We're just finished, Blake. The end." She couldn't fight for her sister while on this rollercoaster of emotions he kept her riding.

"We aren't even close to finished."

"Kara!"

Kara jerked around at the roar of her name to find Kyle slumped in the doorway, his blond hair standing on end, his skin a kind of bluish color. "What the hell did you do to me?" he demanded before he gagged and disappeared back into the other room.

Male laugher followed him, but Kara didn't think it was funny at all. She'd done what she had to tonight, for both her sister, and for Blake—but Kyle had paid the price. She tried to push away from Blake and go after Kyle, but Blake captured her arms, forcing her to look at him. "He's pretty furious right now, Kara," he warned.

"I can handle furious, especially when it's deserved. And if you're afraid I'm going to run out of the other door, I'm not. I know you'd come after me."

"Yes," he said softly, his eyes simmering with heat and promise. "I would and I'd catch you. Don't forget that."

He let go of her and Kara all but ran away, needing out of this Walker-filled room to get a grip on herself, but Royce didn't let her. He stood up and stepped in front of her. "You're a good agent, Kara," he said, towering over her by about a mile. "You know when it's time to let go of a cover."

"If it were your brother—"

"I'd stay alive to keep fighting for him."

Air rushed from her lungs. "I'm not giving up on my sister."

"Neither are we."

"Help us find her from behind the scenes," Luke suggested. "You'll know everything that's happening."

"We're in this all the way," Royce promised. "We would be no matter what, but you're with Blake. That makes you family."

A rush of unfamiliar emotions all but doubled Kara over. She wasn't sure what impacted her more. Her doubt about being with Blake after tonight's events or the use of the word *family*. She had no family. She wasn't sure she had Blake. She wasn't sure she had Myla.

A loud moan coming from the other room was the escape Kara claimed. "I need to go check on Kyle." It was lame but it was all she had.

Royce stared at her another few seconds and then stepped aside. Kara wasted no time darting away, and damn it, her eyes were burning. She didn't even know what she was feeling, just that it was powerful and she couldn't control it any more than anything else lately, it seemed. What was it about Walker men that did this to her?

Inside the next room, Kyle was nowhere in sight and she kept moving toward the bathroom, needing to do something, anything, to keep from crumbling. Rounding the doorway, she found Kyle sitting against the wall between the toilet and the sink, head against the wall, eyes shut, knees lifted.

"Go away," he groaned without opening his eyes.

Kara went to the tub and sat down. "You were screaming for me a few minutes ago."

His lashes lifted and he fixed her in a bloodshot stare. "I fluctuate between capable of throttling you one minute to fantasizing about it while hanging over the toilet."

"At least you have something to occupy your mind," she said mildly, reaching for a soda on the sink and squatting down in front of him. "Drink. It'll help."

"You did hear the part about me wanting to throttle you, right?"

"Yes, but you're less intimidating than three Walker brothers in one room, so I'll take my chances. Drink."

His brow furrowed. "I'm not sure how to take that, but I think you just insulted me." He reached for the drink and gulped down several swallows before setting the can on the floor beside him. "You drugged me and now you come in and play nursemaid. Feeling guilty?"

"Yes," she admitted. "But someone had to save Blake from himself." And suddenly it occurred to Kara to be angry at Kyle and Blake's brothers for letting him go after Alvarez. "Nobody else was doing it. You all just let him chase his death wish." She started to get up but Kyle captured her arm and she grimaced. "What is it with you men manhandling me?"

"You think I'd let him go in there if I thought he was going to do something stupid?"

"You did let him."

"He has himself in check. If I didn't think so, I would have tied him down myself rather than let him go. Do you know about Whitney?"

"Yes."

"Do you care about Blake?"

"Yes," she said, and her chest tightened with the words, with her fear that Blake would go after Alvarez and end up dead. "Yes, very much."

"Then recognize that if you're with Blake, you're with his past. It's a part of who he is. Think about what Alvarez killing you would do to him. You shouldn't have gone tonight."

"You don't seem to get it, Kyle. If I hadn't have gone, he would have killed Alvarez and himself in the process."

"Before he met you, yes. Now, no. I'm not buying that.

Protecting you and finding your sister gave him a reason to live."

"You weren't there."

"Did he kill Alvarez?"

"No, but—"

"Did he have the chance?"

"Yes, but—"

"Then I'm right. He's in check. Before meeting you, Alvarez would have been dead the instant Blake set eyes on him."

"He wanted to. He almost did."

"But he didn't. You shouldn't have been there. You're too close to this. You saved him, Kara. You brought him back to us, which is exactly why none of us are going to let you destroy him again." He paled and let go of her arm to lean over the toilet. "Go. Get out of here."

Destroy him? How and why would she destroy him? Kara backed away from Kyle and sat back down on the edge of the tub, waiting to ask those questions. When he sank back against the wall she handed him a towel. "You okay?"

He glanced at her and snatched the towel. "Can't a guy throw up in peace? Why are you still here?"

"I wouldn't hurt Blake."

"Then don't get killed. You die, you'll take him with you."

"I'm a federal agent, Kyle. I'm going to be in danger."

"Believe me, I'm aware of that and so is he."

Her hands went to the tub, steadying herself. "You think I'm bad for him."

"I think you're the best thing that could have happened to him."

Baffled, she shook her head. "I don't understand."

"He's going to struggle with your job, but he'll get through it—if you help him. But damn, woman, wake up. Alvarez killed Whitney. How do you think the idea of Alvarez killing you affects him? If you die, he'll die with you. We'll find your sister. I'll find her. You have my word. I will not stop until I do."

Kara blinked at the vehement declaration. This man whom she barely knew was vowing to save her sister. So were Blake's brothers. And she believed them. She wasn't alone. She didn't have to take insane risks with no backup. Because of Blake. Kara pushed to her feet, realizing there was actually one big risk she had to take.

Without another word to Kyle, Kara rushed out of the bathroom and tracked a path to the other room, ready to tell Luke and Royce to get lost, only to find them gone. Blake sat on the edge of the mattress, fixing her with a tormented look that tore at her heart. She pulled the door shut behind her and rushed toward him, falling on her knees in front of him. She took a deep breath and then made her confession. "Blake, I…"

CHAPTER
TWENTY-SEVEN

I love you, and I've never said that to anyone. If you don't—"
Blake slid his hands into Kara's hair, pulling her lips to
his, his tongue sweeping into her mouth, and she tasted like the
love she'd proclaimed, like sweet surrender and a chance at
happiness he never thought he'd know again. But no matter how
much he wanted happiness to be as easy as a confession, it
wasn't.

He tore his mouth from hers, staring down at her, this
woman who'd pulled him from a certain grave. She loved him
and it was heaven, but it was also a hell he couldn't escape. *They*
couldn't escape. His thumb stroked her cheek. "I love you, too,
Kara, but you *need* to know what 'more' means with me."

He watched relief wash over her expression, her body
softening into his, as if she'd been on edge, as if she actually
doubted his feelings. "Whatever you are, Blake," she vowed,
"whatever you have been or will be, I'm here. Like I've never
been with anyone in my life."

He wanted nothing more than those words, and to kiss her
again, to make love to her and show her how much she meant to
him, but it wasn't that simple. He knew how messed up he was
over Whitney and how deep that damage ran. How it had

impacted not only who he was, but who he and Kara, would be together. He owed it to her to make sure she did, too.

Blake moved off the bed to join Kara on the floor. He moved behind her, his knees straddling her knees, so that she faced the bed, her back to his chest. He inhaled on regret, hating that for a few minutes, he was about to make her feel uncomfortable, but he had to do this. Without any preamble, no soft words, no seductive caresses, he tugged her dress up her body, over her head, and then tossed it away. Before her arms were even down, he reached for her bra and unhooked it, shoving it forward down her arms so she'd get rid of it. He wasn't gentle. He wasn't tender. He didn't kiss her or caress her. He was what he'd been before her, what the hell of his life had made him. What she needed to fully understand.

Blake's gaze skimmed a path over her body, his cock throbbing with the sight of her slender, perfect curves before settling on the thin strip of lace between the cheeks of her gorgeous backside. He reached for the delicate lace and he ripped it away. Kara gasped and he leaned forward, her hands gripping the sheets in front of her. His hands down beside hers, his mouth finding her ear. "I'm going to spank you, Kara."

"What?" She gasped, trying to jerk around, but he had her pinned, pressed fully between him and the mattress.

"That's right," he said. "I'm going to spank you."

"No," she said, sounding urgent, almost panicked. "No. You aren't."

"Do you trust me, Kara?" he asked, resisting the urge to nibble on the delicate spot behind her ear. This wasn't the time to be gentle. This wasn't the time to show her how much he loved her. Not yet, but soon.

"Yes," she whispered. "Yes, Blake, but—"

"There is no 'but'. There is only trust or no trust." The feel of her body pressed to his was driving him crazy and he curled his fingers around the sheets, forcing himself not to touch her. He couldn't touch her. Not like this. Not until she understood what he was trying to tell her.

"I don't understand why this is important."

He didn't miss the tremble of her voice, the shiver of her body against his. "It is," he told her. "And I need you to say yes, Kara."

Her head fell forward, the soft strands of her silky hair draping her face, and it took everything in him not to lean forward and inhale the sweet scent, to taste the salty sweetness of her skin. And he *would* taste her. Hell, he was going to lick every damn inch of her before this night was over. Just not right now. Right now he held his breath for her answer, the seconds ticking by like hours, until finally she whispered, "Yes. For you. Yes."

He squeezed his eyes shut, letting the relief flow through him, absorbing the impact of how much trust she'd just given to him, promising himself he would never take that for granted. "Lean forward on the bed and flatten your arms and hands on the mattress."

She shook her head. "No. I can't do that. I need some control. I need to stay upright."

Yes. She needed control. That was part of his message, part of why he needed her to understand where he was at inside, and what he'd become. He covered her hands with his on the bed. "Then promise to keep your hands right here. No matter what, don't move them."

"Yes. Okay. I promise."

He began to pull away but she grabbed his wrists, pulling him forward. "Wait. Will it hurt?"

This time he let himself be gentle, nuzzling her neck, trying to calm the panic in her voice. "I would never hurt you."

"I know that." But still she held onto his arms.

"Then let go, Kara."

"Let go," she repeated, as if the words weren't quite making it to her brain. "Okay." Slowly, her grip loosened and she released him.

Blake's hands settled on her slender waist and traveled downward to cup her backside. She stiffened instantly and he began a gentle caress of her cheeks. He could almost feel her holding her breath, almost taste her anticipation. He leaned in, pressing his face to her face, drawing in the sweet floral scent of her, and demanding, "What are you thinking? Exactly what is in your head right this moment? Say it. Say it now."

"Blake," she protested.

He squeezed her cheeks. "Now, Kara, or I'll spank you this instant."

"Nothing," she panted. "Everything. I don't know what is about to happen. I don't know what to expect. I can't believe I'm doing this or you're doing this, and—"

Blake turned her around to face him, her back against the end of the bed, his legs caging her. "That's what I was after," he said, his hands resting on her shoulders.

"What?" she asked, looking confused. "What you were after? I don't understand."

"I'm not going to spank you. I was never going to spank you. I just needed you to feel what you just felt. I wanted you to experience that moment when you could think of nothing but what came next. That moment when nothing else could find its way into your head. That's the kind of escape I've used to get through these past two years. It's the only way I survived and I got it however I could get it. I lived on the edge and I pushed every limit I could push. Kara, I need you to know that's how far gone I was over Whitney, because that's how just the idea of losing you makes me. Your job is going to make me insane and I'm going to be overbearing and impossibly protective. I'll try not to be, but I'll fail sometimes. I might fail more than I don't. We'll fight. We'll probably fight a lot."

"I can handle it." Her hands went to his face. "We'll get through it. I promise, though, you didn't have to do the whole spanking thing. I'm going to pay you back for that."

"Kara—"

"I can handle it, Blake."

He covered her hands with his and pulled them down between them. "Can you? Because, Kara, I can't let you go back undercover with Alvarez. I won't let you."

"I'm okay with that. My cover is blown, and—"

Blake kissed her, swallowing the rest of her words, drinking them in, claiming them as he wanted to claim her, as he *would* claim her. She was his and he had no intention of ever letting her go. No intention of anyone taking her from him. His hands caressed her back, over her ribcage to skim her breasts, and her soft whimper drove him crazy.

He cupped her breasts, pushing them together to lean down and lick one nipple and then the next. Her fingers tunneled into his hair. "What do I have to do to get you naked?" she whispered. "Please tell me now."

Blake's lips curved and he glanced up at her, suckling one of the stiff peaks and then twirling his tongue around it. Her lashes fluttered. "Blake…" she panted, and then moaned.

He laced his fingers into her hair, hungrily kissing her one last time before pushing away from her to stand up to undress. Kara moved off of the floor, sitting on the edge of the mattress, her breasts high, her nipples tight little buds. His cock pulsed at the sight she made, urgency driving him to shove down his pants and boxers. And Kara seemed to sense his need, mercilessly egging him on, her beautiful green eyes sliding over his body, settling boldly on the thick pulse of his erection, and Blake groaned with the impact.

Blake closed the distance between them and went down on the mattress on top of her, laughing with a flashback of Denver. "What's so funny?" she asked, her fingers lacing together at the back of his neck, and biting her lip as he settled thickly between her thighs.

"You drugged me," he said incredulously. "How did I fall in love with the woman who drugged me?"

"I got your attention, didn't I?" she asked, smiling, her voice thick with desire and sexy as hell.

He slid his cock along the seam of her sex, back and forth, until she was panting. "Do I have your attention?" he murmured, nipping her ear.

"Yes," she whispered. "You most definitely have my attention."

Blake rolled to his back and molded her on top of him. "You let me take your control a few minutes ago. I'll give it to you now."

Surprise slid over her face and she pressed on his shoulders, lifting herself so that her eyes met his. "No," she said, suddenly serious. "I gave it to you." She slid off of him, curling herself at his side, her fingers stroking his cheek. "I don't need it. I just need you."

Blake pressed her to her back, settling on top of her, staring down at her in wonder. He knew what a control freak she was. He knew how much she valued control. And he knew this was her way of telling him she could handle what was before them. That she was with him all the way and, if it was possible, he'd just fallen more in love with her. "We'll share it," he promised her. "We'll share it, Kara."

Her mouth curved playfully. "I'd like that very much. Can I tie you up and have my way with you?"

"Only if I can tie you up and have my wicked way with you."

"You already did that. It's my turn next."

"Let me give you some incentive to give me an extra turn," he suggested, stroking his cock along her sex. Teasing them both, and then driving into her, burying himself inside her, where he planned to spend a hell of a lot of the rest of his life. "How is that for incentive?"

"It's a good start," she teased.

"This is *just a start*, Kara," he promised, and then he kissed her, silently vowing to make this the first night the first of forever. She was his. He wasn't letting her go.

***

Kara's day started with the wonderful feeling of being wrapped in Blake's arms, and she had been amazed it was nearly noon when she'd looked at the hotel clock. Any guilt at the late hour that might have driven her out of bed faded when Blake gave her a reason—or two or three—to stay a little longer.

Now, at nearly two o'clock in the afternoon, freshly showered and dressed in dark jeans, a turquoise silk blouse, and black lace-up boots, Kara exited the bathroom, expecting to find only Blake. Instead, she was once again submerged in testosterone overload, with Blake, Royce, Luke, and Kyle all present, all eating hamburgers from a takeout joint.

"There has to be a fire code about this many men in one room," Kara said, as Blake, who was sitting on the bed, wrapped his arm around her hip and pulled her close.

"Hungry?" he asked, glancing up at her, his long, dark hair damp and loose, framing brown eyes that said he wasn't talking about food.

"Starving, actually," she replied, barely containing a smile sure to make their flirtation more obvious.

"Kyle isn't," Luke said with a bark of laughter. "First time I've ever seen him miss a meal."

Kara cast Kyle a closer inspection to realize he actually wasn't eating. He was slumped over in a chair, his blond hair mussed, though he wasn't quite as bluish. "You any better?"

"I'm sitting in a room without a toilet," he said. "That's an improvement, but I hear you've decided to be smart about Alvarez. I won't throttle you." He winked.

Kara laughed and Blake's fingers flexed at her hip. "Something I need to know about you two?"

Kara grinned. "Don't worry. I drugged you first. You're my number one."

"Kara," Royce said, drawing her attention to where he'd claimed the desk as his own again. "We were just talking about how to get you out of the cartel without blowing Blake's cover."

"Yes, well," she said, "I was thinking about that. Before we pull me out—"

"Kara," Blake growled, turning her to face him.

"Relax," she said, her hands settling on his shoulders. "I'm not suggesting I stay in."

"You just said—"

"I didn't say anything. You cut me off. I was going to say that I have access to Mendez's office. It's Saturday. We should go in and dig up everything we can before Monday morning."

"I don't want you anywhere near Mendez."

"The offices are closed, Blake. I know my way around. You and I can go in, and if we're caught we say we're auditing the books to find the thief who's stealing drugs from the operation." Kara glanced around the room. "You all know it makes sense." No one said anything and she grimaced. "Come on, someone say something." Still nothing. Crickets. In fact, the big, brawny, overbearing Walker brothers, and Kyle along with them, looked like deer in the headlights. Kara refocused on Blake. "They know I'm right. They're afraid of you."

"If only you were," he complained.

She ignored that comment. "Once I'm out, I'm out. This might be our last chance to get to certain information. We have to do this, Blake."

Blake's jaw flexed. "I don't like this, Kara."

"I know. But you'll be with me. Nothing is going to go wrong."

CHAPTER
TWENTY-EIGHT

"Any luck?"

Kara glanced up from the desk she was sitting at to find Blake, dressed in black jeans and a black t-shirt that stretched deliciously over his impressive chest, standing in the doorway of the human resources manager's office she'd been searching for the past hour. She shook her head. "Nothing. I took pictures of the files for female employees who seemed like obvious targets for the trafficking operation, though." Thankfully Kyle had hacked the computers, but pictures reinforced the evidence trail.

"Mendez's office is clean," he said, scrubbing his jaw, and while he was every bit the tall and dark, and gorgeous man she'd fallen in lust, and then love with, he practically radiated edginess. Her being here after Alvarez recognized her was making him crazy.

"I've only got a few more files and I'll be done," she promised. "We need to hit accounting before we go."

"Great," Blake said, looking relieved. "I'm headed to the lobby to dig through messages and then we're out of here. Five minutes, Kara, and then we go to accounting. We've already been here too long in my book." He disappeared and she quickly finished with two more files before she stood up.

Her cell phone rang and a chill ran down her spine. No one but Blake and the rest of his team had this number, and she was on mic and camera. They wouldn't call her. She dug it from purse and glanced at the "unknown" number on her screen.

Swallowing hard, Kara answered the call and immediately heard, "Kara."

Oh God. "Myla?" She started walking toward the door.

"Stop," Myla said, sounding panicked. "Don't leave the office. If you say anything to anyone right now Alvarez told them to kill me. And they said to tell you Blake's at the reception desk and they have a gun pointed at him. They'll kill him too, Kara."

No. No. This wasn't happening. "Are you okay?"

"Yes," a male voice said. "She's fine but she won't be if you aren't downstairs at the back door sixty seconds after we hang up. And Kara—we have a camera on you, too. We'll know if you dial, text, or call out. We'll kill Blake first. That way you see the bloody results of your failure." The line went dead.

Kara squeezed her eyes shut, and for the sake of Blake and Myla, she willed herself into "calm agent" mode, her mind racing. If she used the mic, Blake would hear and come to help, which would be sure to get him killed. She had to count on Kyle realizing something was off once she'd hit the stairwell, but she couldn't let him know there was a problem any sooner. She had to get out of the building before they killed Blake. And what if they killed him anyway? She couldn't think of that or she'd panic.

Somehow, she calmly walked out of the office and went to the exit door. Once she was inside the stairwell, she took off running. She had a tracking device in her boot, one that Kyle had assured Blake was about ten times better than the one he'd used on the boat. They'd find her. She'd be okay and she'd bring Myla home with her.

At the bottom of the stairwell, driven by her deadline of one minute, Kara burst out of the doorway and ran for the back exit, punching the red button and the glass. The instant she stepped outside, she was aware of the dumpster to her left—a moment before a man grabbed her. Another man was in front of her as she kicked, but they were too big, and the cloth one of them held found her mouth, fumes penetrating her senses. And just like that, everything went black.

***

"Meet me at the back exit now. Kara's gone. Go now and I'll meet you at the door."

Blake went completely still at Kyle's words for all of two seconds, before he took off running. "Do you have her on camera?"

"She took off down the stairwell and exited the back door, and—"

Blake was already in the stairwell, headed down the steps, and his heart felt like it was going to explode out of his chest. "And what? What happened?"

"Blake—"

What the fuck happened, Kyle?" he growled, jumping four steps to get to the next flight.

"Two guys grabbed her and a car pulled up and"—a pause—"she's gone, Blake."

Every nightmare he could possibly have came to life in that

moment. His world spun. His stomach rolled and his muscles ached as he pushed harder down the stairs. Everything was a blur until he burst out of the back door of the building. The van his team was using waited with an open door. Blake was inside and it was moving before Luke shut the door behind him.

"Tell me you're tracking her," Blake said to Kyle, who was sitting at a computer panel. Kyle pointed out the beeping dot on a large screen mounted on the wall. "That's her. They've got a lead on us but we're gaining."

"Royce and the rest of the team are falling in behind us now," Jesse called from the driver's seat.

Blake cut Kyle a damning look. "I thought we had the exterior of the building covered. How did someone get to her?"

"They came out from behind a dumpster," Kyle explained. "We never caught them on camera before that."

Blood rushed in his ears and he flexed his fingers, fighting the urge to shake Kyle for letting this happen. "How the fuck did we not see them? And why did she leave in the first place?"

"You want to see this," Kyle said, punching a keyboard. Another smaller screen lit up with an image of Kara. Blake squatted by Kyle, watching Kara take a call, and he saw the panic in her face, the calculation and fear in her eyes.

"Whatever they said to her, she felt like she couldn't communicate with us," Luke said.

"Thanks for pointing out the goddamn fucking obvious," Blake spat. "Why don't you point out how fucking stupid I was to let her come here today too, while you're at it?"

"Blake—"

"Shut up, Luke. Just shut the fuck up." Blake ran a hand through his hair and held it there. His scalp was splintering with pain. His chest was tight. Kara couldn't die. Why the hell had he let her come today? Why? Why? Why? He was coming unglued at the seams. He leaned on the wall, fighting the adrenaline of fear and failing. He punched the wall and welcome pain radiated up his arm. Luke shouted something at him but he tuned it out. He was already throwing another fist. His knuckles hit steel and there was more pain, but it wasn't enough to stop the image of Whitney bleeding out from the throat, or how her faced morphed into Kara's. *Kara*. He was going to lose Kara, too. He reared back to hit the wall again and Luke grabbed his arm. Blake whirled on him and shoved him but Luke grabbed handfuls of his shirt.

"Blake, damn it," Luke ground out. "Stop. Stop now."

"If it were your wife, would you stop? Would you fucking stop, Luke?"

"You can't save her if your hand is broken and you're climbing out of your own skin. Get a grip, Blake. Get a fucking grip now."

Blake sucked in a deep breath and let it out, and he suddenly became aware of his shaking. Jesus. He was shaking all over. He *was* out of control. He inhaled, and slowly, somehow, pulled himself back from the edge. Luke seemed to realize it, loosening his hold on Blake's shirt and letting it fall away.

Blake turned away from his brother and lifted the lid to a locker sitting beside the tech setup, pulling out a shoulder holster and two Glocks. The cold steel didn't come close to matching the ice in his veins. He should have killed Alvarez when he had the chance. He was taking Kara back and making sure that bastard never took another breath.

***

Kara blinked awake to the sound of soft music playing and intense throbbing in her head. For a moment, she couldn't remember what had happened, but a rush of memories filled her mind. She sat up and blinked and then blinked again. She had to be dreaming, because not only did she appear to be in a sitting area of an office with a fireplace crackling in a full orange glow to her right, but her sister was sitting across from her. And, impossibly, Myla didn't look bruised and beaten. She looked perfectly fine. She was also sitting next to Alvarez, smiling up at him, her hand resting on his leg.

"Myla?" Kara whispered.

Myla turned, her green eyes lighting with excitement. "You're awake." She jumped up from her seat and rushed past the shiny mahogany coffee table separating them to throw her arms around Kara's neck. "I've missed you."

Kara hugged her sister and whispered, "What's going on?"

Myla leaned back, her green eyes aglow, her long, silky brunette hair groomed to perfection. "I found out you were looking for me and I wanted you to know I'm okay. Kara, I'm in love. I'm the happiest I've ever been in my life."

"In love? With who? Ignacio?"

Myla laughed, and Kara noted the dress her sister had on was a clearly very expensive silver sheath no waitress could afford. "Ignacio?" Myla asked. "Oh God, no." She motioned to Alvarez.

Kara looked at Alvarez and gaped. He arched a brow. "Is there a problem, Kara?"

"Yes," Kara said. "Yes, there is." She turned to Myla. "We need to talk alone."

"Michael is with me, Kara. I'm with him."

"Michael?" Kara asked. "You call him by his first name?"

Myla took Kara's hand. "I want you to come back with me. Spend some time with me and Michael and see what life can be like for us."

"Back with you? Back where?"

"She can't tell you that," Alvarez said. "Not until we know you're with us."

"I'm not with you. I'll never be with you." Kara's hands went to her sister's face. "Listen to me. Whatever he threatened you with—"

"I love him, Kara. I'm the happiest I've ever been."

Kara shook her head. "No." Myla's words didn't ring true. Not in her tone. Not from her sister. Myla hated crime. She hated everything associated with its poison. "No, I don't believe you. Our parents—"

"Michael would kill anyone who tried to hurt us."

There was a coldness to her tone that Kara barely recognized from her sister. "Do you know who and what he is?"

"You don't know all there is to know about him." She took Kara's hand again. "I need you in my life."

"I can't be in your life if you're with him. I won't."

Tears suddenly pooled in Myla's eyes. "I don't want to say goodbye to you." She wrapped her arms around Kara, holding her as if she was clinging for life.

"Please don't stay with him,' Kara whispered.

"I have to," Myla whispered. "You have to see that."

Was there torment in her words? Kara leaned back to try to read her sister, but Myla pushed away and stood up. "Goodbye, Kara," she said, and the tears were gone.

Alvarez stepped beside Myla, taking her hand in his. "You will be escorted back to your hotel, Kara."

Hotel? He'd said hotel, not apartment. He knew where she'd been staying? The door to the office opened and a man with a well-equipped shoulder holster stepped inside. Myla and Alvarez turned away and Kara's heart lurched. "Myla, wait!"

Myla turned. "You'll come?"

"No. Don't go."

"I have to go." She walked toward the man with the gun and he held the door open.

Kara took a step forward, but the man stepped in front of Myla and Alvarez and placed his hand on his weapon. Law Enforcement 101 replayed in her mind. Bullets didn't believe in second chances. All Kara could do was watch the door shut and feel helpless.

Seconds turned into minutes and she didn't move. She just stood there, staring at the man with the gun, him staring back at her. Suddenly, a roaring sound filled the room, radiating through the ceiling. A helicopter. Myla was leaving on a helicopter. Panic rushed over Kara. She could never track Myla if she left by sky. Her mind raced, seeking a solution, but before she could come up with one, the door behind her burst open. The man guarding her whirled around and pulled his gun. A second later he was on the ground and Blake was holding the gun that had put him there.

"Myla!" Kara screamed, running towards him. "The chopper!"

Blake handed her a gun and Kara gladly accepted it, and in the process he grabbed her and kissed her. "Don't ever fucking scare me like this again."

"I'll try," she promised. "My sister, Blake. She's with Alvarez on that chopper." She took off for the hallway of what appeared to be an office building, with Blake on her heels.

"Here!" he shouted, pointing at a stairwell entry.

The charge up the four flights of steps was eternal, and they cleared the door and made their way to the roof too late. The chopper was lifting off. Kara slumped in defeat. "No. No. No." She turned to Blake and shouted. "Alvarez is with her. He has her. He—" A blast sounded and Kara and Blake both turned to watch the chopper go up in flames.

Shock surged through Kara and the gun fell from her hand. She began to shake, and she couldn't catch her breath. "No. No. Nonononono." And then her knees gave way and she was falling. Blake caught her to him and she grabbed his shirt, tears streaming down her cheeks, a waterfall she couldn't control. "Save her. Please. I…Please. Help her, Blake. You have to help her."

He pulled her tight against him and hugged her, and she clung to him, the only strength she had left. "I'm here, Kara. I'm here."

But Myla was gone.

CHAPTER
TWENTY-NINE

After hours of officials swarming the secluded office building off the San Francisco shoreline, feeling hollow and stunned, Kara sat in the back seat of a van. Blake was beside her, practically attached to her side, acting like he'd never let her go again. And she needed that. She needed him. Without Blake, she wouldn't even be sitting upright, trying to survive.

"Send it to my phone," Kyle said and ended a call, punching a button on his cell and watching something on the screen.

"You okay?" Blake asked.

Kara teased a strand of his hair, wishing she could wash the torment from his eyes. It had killed him to think she might be dead. Like losing Myla was killing her. "Yes," she whispered. "Because of you."

"You need to see something," Kyle said, moving to squat in front of them.

"When you say that it's never good," Blake said grumpily. "Not now."

"This time it's good," Kyle insisted.

"Nothing can be good right now, Kyle," Kara said, and when she thought she was done crying, her eyes burned all over again.

"Watch this," Kyle insisted, shoving his phone at her and

Blake.

"Kyle…" Blake started.

"Just watch," Kyle repeated.

Blake grimaced and punched the "play" button. An image of Alvarez climbing into a car had Kara sitting up straighter, her heart racing as Myla appeared behind him and paused to glance up at the flame-filled sky. She whispered something Kara couldn't make out and disappeared into the car. "Oh my God," Kara murmured as the screen went blank, her gaze lifting to Kyle's. "She's alive? Myla's alive?"

"She's alive," Kyle assured her. "The explosion was a setup to make us think she and Alvarez were dead."

"How'd you get this?" Kara asked.

"As soon as we arrived," he explained, "I set up surveillance and one of the cameras wouldn't download. Luke just got it to roll."

Kara looked at Blake, a new kind of pain filling her. "What is it?" he asked, stroking her cheek. "What's wrong?"

"She's not a prisoner." It hurt her heart to say it out loud. "Myla's with Alvarez by choice. She told me she loves him. She's alive, but I've still lost her."

"No," he said. "He's brainwashed her. We'll get her back." He slid a hand to her neck and rested his forehead against hers. "You and me, sweetheart. We'll find a way."

***

The ringing of a cell phone pierced the silence of the dark hotel room and beside her, Blake groaned and reached for it on the nightstand. Two days had passed since she last saw Myla, and every clue to finding her again had come up empty. It was as if her sister and Alvarez had really died in that crash.

Kara sat up as Blake murmured, "Yeah," into the phone and climbed out of bed. Now that she was awake, the image of the helicopter blowing up played in her mind again, as it had a million times over. It didn't matter that Myla hadn't been in the explosion. Kara kept reliving the moment she thought she was, the moment she was sure her sister was dead.

In nothing but Blake's shirt, Kara stepped onto the chilly balcony and rested her hands on the rail, staring out at the twinkling lights of the Golden Gate Bridge without really seeing them. How could Myla put her through so much hell? Did her sister really love Alvarez that much and her so little?

The door opened behind her and Blake slipped a robe over her shoulders. "You're going to freeze. What are you doing out here?"

Kara slipped her arms into the giant terry garment and turned to let him tie it, noting he'd thrown on nothing but a t-shirt with his boxers. "You're going to freeze, too."

"I'm not worried about me," he said, wrapping her in his arms. "I'm worried about you. Are you okay?"

"I'm fine. Who called at whatever ungodly hour this is?"

"Two o'clock," he supplied, "and it was Royce. The Coast Guard picked up Ignacio off the coast of Mexico on a boat full of drugged women. He's singing like a bird. The feds are raiding Mendez's operation tomorrow and closing down the entire restaurant chain."

"And Alvarez won't be anywhere near here when it happens." Which meant neither would her sister. "I don't know how I'm going to find Myla, and do I keep trying? She doesn't want to be saved."

"You save her anyway. That's what siblings are for. They look out for you, when you don't look out for yourself. And I would know, since mine live in the same building with me and never let me forget it."

"You live in the same building as your brothers?"

"Separate units, but the same building. Walker Security is on the bottom floor." He stroked a hand down her hair. "Kara, I want you to come to New York with me and consider working for Walker Security."

"Work for you?"

"Work *with* me. Live with me." His eyes softened. "Marry me."

Her eyes widened with surprise. "Marry you?"

"I know we haven't known each other long, but I know all I need to know about you, Kara. But if you need time, you have it. I'll ask you every day until you say yes, starting with today." He went down on one knee. "Marry me, Kara."

She smiled. "That sounded like an order."

He smiled, a devastatingly sexy smile, and stood up, pulling her hard against him. "To hell with asking. I'm going to make you my wife."

Kara wrapped her arms around his neck. "You know I don't take orders well."

"Take this one, Kara." His voice was husky, roughened with emotion.

And once again a Walker brother made her eyes burn. "Yes," she whispered. "Yes, I'll—" He kissed her and Kara melted into this man who'd changed her life. This man who would never let her be alone again. This man who would be her husband.

***

Kyle had promised Kara he'd find her sister, and he'd meant it. Now, after two days of trying to decipher the audio on Myla's video, he'd given up and called on his buddy, Jason, a twenty-seven-year-old tech genius who worked at the FBI lab, for help. Now, only a few hours after he'd handed over the tape to Jason, he was standing in Jason's Virginia apartment, waiting for the playback.

"I've got visual and audio," Jason explained. "I zoomed in on the woman's face so you can get a better look at her eyes when she says the words. You know, the eyes are the windows to the soul."

"Just punch the damn button," Kyle ordered.

Jason hit a button and Myla's image appeared on screen, zoomed in on her face, as promised. There was a look of complete anguish Kyle hadn't been able to make out on the fuzzy video before this any more than he could her words. But this time he not only saw the pain in her face, he heard her words as she whispered, *I'm so sorry, Kara.*

"I'll be damned," Kyle muttered, scrubbing the light blond stubble he'd let sprout on his jaw. Could Myla be protecting Kara from Alvarez? Was she a victim in survival mode? Was this how she'd kept from being one of the women sold off to the highest bidder?

He glanced at Jason. "Replay it." He watched it again. And again. After a half dozen views, with the tape in hand, he headed to his rental car. Once he was inside, he sat behind the wheel and stared ahead before he turned on the engine. "Hang in there, Myla. I'm coming for you."

THE END

The Tall, Dark and Deadly series
Book 1: Hot Secrets (Royce's story)
Book 2: Dangerous Secrets (Luke's story)
Book 3: Beneath the Secrets (Blake's story)

And coming April 7, 2016
A Tall, Dark and Deadly spinoff series:
WALKER SECURITY
Book 1: Deep Under (Kyle's story)

Want more BLAKE WALKER? Read the INSIDE OUT series in which he is a very prominent character and his brothers make an appearance too!

And now a sneak peek into IF I WERE YOU, book one in the New York Times bestselling INSIDE OUT series by Lisa Renee Jones

The INSIDE OUT series is now in development for television with producer Suzanne Todd (Alice in Wonderland, Must Love Dogs, Austin Powers, The Boiler Room, and more)

Stay tuned to Lisa's website for updates on the TV show!
www.lisareneejones.com

Excerpt from
IF I WERE YOU

We begin our walk, faster this time, and the cold wind has nothing on the chill between us. Conversation is non-existent, and I have no clue how to break the silence, or if I should even try. I dare a peek at his profile several times, fighting the wind blowing hair over my eyes, but he doesn't acknowledge me. Why won't he look at me? Several times, I open my mouth to speak but words simply won't leave my lips.

We are almost to the gallery, and a knot has formed in my stomach at the prospect of an awkward goodbye, when he suddenly grabs me and pulls me into a small enclave of a deserted office rental. Before I can fully grasp what is happening, I am against the wall, hidden from the street and he is in front of me, enclosing me in the tiny space. I blink up into his burning stare and I think I might combust. His scent, his warmth, his hard body, is all around me, but he is not touching me. I want him to touch me.

He presses his hand to the concrete wall above my head when I want it on my body. "You don't belong here, Sara."

The words are unexpected, a hard punch in the chest. "What? I don't understand."

"This job is wrong for you."

I shake my head. I don't belong? Coming from Chris, an established artist, I feel inferior, rejected. "You asked me why I wasn't following my heart. Why I wasn't pursuing what I love. I am. That's what I'm doing."

"I didn't think you'd do it in this place."

This place. I don't know what he's telling me. Does he mean this gallery? This city? Has he judged me not worthy of his inner circle?

"Look, Sara." He hesitates, and lifts his head to the sky, seeming to struggle for words before fixing me with a turbulent look. "I'm trying to protect you here. This world you've strayed into is filled with dark, messed up, arrogant assholes who will play with your mind and use you until there is nothing else left for you to recognize in yourself."

"Are you one of those dark, messed up, arrogant assholes?"

He stares down at me, and I barely recognize the hard lines of his face, the glint in his eyes, as belonging to the man I've just had lunch with. His gaze sweeps my lips, lingers, and the swell of response and longing in me is instant, overwhelming. He reaches up and strokes his thumb over my bottom lip. Every nerve ending in my body responds and it's all I can do not to touch him, to grab his hand, but something holds me back. I am lost in this man, in his stare, in some spellbinding, dark whirlwind of...what? Lust, desire, torment? Seconds tick eternally and so does the silence. I want to hold him, to stop whatever I sense is coming but I cannot.

"I'm worse." He pushes off the wall, and is gone. He is gone. I am alone against the wall, aching with a fire that has nothing to do with the meal we shared. My lashes flutter, my fingers touch my lip where he touched me. He has warned me away from Mark, from the gallery, from him, and he has failed. I cannot turn away. I am here and I am going nowhere.

IF I WERE YOU is available on all platforms. For more information, buy links and the INSIDE OUT reading order visit: www.lisareneejones.com

Also by Lisa Renee Jones

The Inside Out Series
If I Were You
Being Me
Revealing Us
*His Secrets**
Rebecca's Lost Journals
*The Master Undone**
*My Hunger**
No In Between
*My Control**
I Belong to You
*All of Me**

The Secret Life of Amy Bensen
Escaping Reality
Infinite Possibilities
Forsaken
*Unbroken**

Careless Whispers
Denial
Demand (May 2016)
Surrender (December 2016)

Dirty Money
Hard Rules (August 2016)
More information coming soon…

**eBook only*

About the Author

New York Times and USA Today bestselling author Lisa Renee Jones is the author of the highly acclaimed INSIDE OUT series, which is now in development for a television show to be produced by Suzanne Todd of Team Todd (Alice in Wonderland). Suzanne Todd on the INSIDE OUT series: *Lisa has created a beautiful, complicated, and sensual world that is filled with intrigue and suspense. Sara's character is strong, flawed, complex, and sexy – a modern girl we all can identify with. I'm thrilled to develop a television show that will tell Sara's whole story – her life, her work, her friends, and her sexuality.*

In addition to the success of Lisa's INSIDE OUT series, she has published many successful titles. The TALL, DARK AND DEADLY series and THE SECRET LIFE OF AMY BENSEN series, both spent several months on a combination of the *New York Times* and USA Today bestselling lists. Lisa is presently working on a dark, edgy new series, Dirty Money, for St. Martin's Press.

Prior to publishing Lisa owned multi-state staffing agency that was recognized many times by The Austin Business Journal and also praised by the Dallas Women's Magazine. In 1998 Lisa was listed as the #7 growing women owned business in Entrepreneur Magazine.

Lisa loves to hear from her readers. You can reach her at www.lisareneejones.com and she is active on Twitter and Facebook daily.

CPSIA information can be obtained
at www.ICGtesting.com
Printed in the USA
BVHW03s0902160318
510774BV00001B/45/P

9 780985 817015